DARK LEGACY

Julie Ellis

This first world edition published in Great Britain 2005 by
SEVERN HOUSE PUBLISHERS LTD of
9–15 High Street, Sutton, Surrey SM1 1DF.
This first world edition published in the USA 2005 by
SEVERN HOUSE PUBLISHERS INC of
595 Madison Avenue, New York, N.Y. 10022.

British Library Cataloguing in Publication Data

Ellis, Julie, 1933-
    Dark legacy
    1.   Family owned business enterprises - Fiction
    2.   Widows - Fiction
    3.   Illegitimate children - Fiction
    4.   Romantic suspense novels
    I.   Title
    813.5'4 [F]

    ISBN 0-7278-6257-X

Except where actual historical events and characters are being
described for the storyline of this novel, all situations in this
publication are fictitious and any resemblance to living persons
is purely coincidental.

Typeset by Palimpsest Book Production Ltd.,
Polmont, Stirlingshire, Scotland.
Printed and bound in Great Britain by
MPG Books Ltd., Bodmin, Cornwall.

For Norman and Lila Paul

Prologue

Andrea Winston—sitting at the desk in her large but unpretentious office at Winston Mail Order Inc. in upstate Woodhaven, New York—appeared to be listening intently to young Paul Cameron, her "second in command." Her eyes—a dramatic blue that sometimes seemed to mesmerize new employees—clung to Paul. In truth, her mind dwelt on that horrendous evening thirty-seven years ago today—when she had arrived home from a PTA meeting to find David—her husband of fourteen years—lying dead in the circular driveway before their house.

The police were convinced David had jumped to his death from the small balcony off the master bedroom. The balcony he'd had built so they might view special summer sunsets over the pond below. The police had rejected her insistence that David would never kill himself. *"There's no evidence pointing to murder."* David had been alone in the house except for their three children asleep in their rooms. *"Nobody reported seeing a stranger in the neighborhood. I'm sorry, Mrs. Winston. This is a case of suicide."* The detective hesitated, trying to soften this conclusion. *"Unless he suffered a dizzy spell, fell from the balcony."*

She'd never accepted their disposal of the case. David had been murdered. Why? By whom? The questions were etched on her mind. Never ceased to trouble her.

"I know we shouldn't panic," Paul's voice intruded on Andrea's thoughts. "So we're seeing a delay on shipments from Singapore—that doesn't mean we're in deep trouble. But if there's a new SARS outbreak, we could face some serious problems. Factories could close down. We need to—"

"We'll watch the situation," Andrea broke in. "So far we've managed." Through the years she'd encountered problems and

1

dealt with them. Warehouse mismanagement, billing headaches, transportation tie-ups, training programs that required updating. But she'd always dealt. She was proud of that. "We're no competition for Sears," she conceded with a faint smile, "but Winston Mail Order has kept rolling for forty-seven years." David had fought hard to hang on during those first rough years. By the time he'd died, the company was well established—though neither of them had envisioned the extent to which it would grow.

"I'd like us to check into possible Latin American and Mexican suppliers—" Paul seemed guarded, as though he might seem presumptuous. *He realizes he was hired—at an impressive salary—because his grandmother was my closest friend before she was hit by Alzheimer's. When he came back home to care for her after his father and mother died in that plane crash, he needed a job. It was a good deal for the company. He's so sharp. He's proved himself invaluable.* "I mean, in case our current suppliers have to close down."

"Look into it," she agreed, almost brusque. Today she was upset by Leon's hints that perhaps—with her seventy-fourth birthday only weeks away—it was time for her to retire. *How can I retire? Who'll take over the company? Not Leon. Not Carol. Not Celeste. They have no interest in running Winston Mail Order. The company is a monument to David. I want it to live on.* "Show me some figures, Paul."

"Right." He appeared relieved.

Andrea glanced at her watch. "I have to get out of here." Unfailingly—on the next-to-the-last Friday evening of each month—Leon and his wife, Carol and her husband, and Celeste—when she was available—came to the house for dinner. The three grandchildren sometimes accompanied them. All three spoiled rotten, she thought in distaste. Because that was the easy way. She brought herself back into the present. "You know my next-to-the-last-Friday-in-the-month sched-ule—"

Paul grinned. "How did they settle on that particular Friday?"

Andrea chuckled. "I never quite figured it out."

She left the office, headed for the parking area. Face it, she taunted herself, she wasn't looking forward to this evening's dinner. Leon would start harping again on her retirement, bring the girls in to support him. *I'll know when it's time for me to retire.*

David would be proud of how she'd built up the business. She ought to feel herself on top of the world. But who would take over when she decided to step down? And God willing, that was ten years away.

She longed to know that when she left this earth, she'd leave someone behind who reflected David and herself. Neither Leon nor Carol nor Celeste bore any resemblance—mentally or physically—to David or her. They were throwbacks to an earlier generation. But enough of this, she rebuked herself as she approached the car.

She'd felt self-conscious when she bought the white Mercedes eight years ago—fearful of appearing ostentatious. God knows, she could afford a fleet of Mercedes.

David had loved cars. He'd talked of one day owning a white Mercedes. For David she'd bought it. All these years later—especially on the anniversary of his death—it plagued her that his murder had never been solved. *Whoever killed David walks the streets a free man—or free woman.*

Driving home, she remembered Leon's protests that she still drove herself. It was as though he feared people would consider him an uncaring son: "Mother, it's time to take better care of yourself. You can afford to have a chauffeur." Or did Leon feel their status demanded this? Carol, too, scolded her for driving.

She frowned as the traffic light—one of three in town—turned red. She was running late—she liked to be home before the kids arrived. Her smile wry as she considered this. So Leon was forty-nine, Carol forty-seven, and Celeste forty—and lying away ten years to strangers. In her mind and in her heart they were still "the kids."

Why should I stop driving because I'm almost seventy-four? My health is good. My vision's good. I'm not falling apart. Damn, I'm a better driver than any of them. I'll know when it's time to stop.

Why should she retire? People looked at the calendar and said, "Enough, it's retirement time." So much talent going to waste. She'd backed Leon in half a dozen ventures through the years. Each one had bombed. He hadn't inherited his father's business instincts—nor hers. Along with a lot of others, he'd taken a bath in the last one—the Internet venture. Or rather, she had.

She grimaced, remembering the item she'd read in the *New York Times* about the prestigious publishing company that was offering early retirement to everybody over fifty. When Alan Greenspan was accepting a second term as Federal Reserve Chairman at seventy-seven.

Leon was "between projects" now. He was making inquiries into buying some franchise. She would go along with that— with the flagging hope that he could achieve some success. He kept trying—give him credit for that.

She'd set Carol's husband up in his own business, and—to her satisfaction—he was doing well. There'd never been a thought of Carol coming into the business. She married at twenty, was only interested in her social position in this town. And Celeste—God help her—roamed from one escapade to another. With two divorces behind her she was involved now with a man fifteen years her junior.

Her face softened. Celeste had given her the one grand-child—secret though she must be—who seemed a young replica of herself. Pregnant at seventeen and terrified of having an abortion, Celeste had been sent away to have her baby— then insisted the baby be put up for adoption when she'd hoped by some device to pretend to have adopted "a late friend's grandchild."

By the time Emily was born, Celeste was eighteen—of legal age, able to make her own decisions. There was nothing she could do to stop the adoption. Celeste knew her weak threats would never be carried out. To Celeste, it was as though she'd never given birth.

The adoption records were sealed—but she had not been without means to follow this precious grandchild's path. During the first year private investigators had provided weekly reports. After that—through the years—monthly reports were delivered to her. With relief she'd realized that Joan and Robert Mitchell were devoted, loving parents. Emily—that was her name—had a fine family.

She smiled in tender recall of her cache of secret snapshots, hidden in a drawer in the night table beside her bed. Most of them taken at a distance. So many nights through the years she sat up in bed and pored over those photographs. She felt a passionate love for this grandchild she'd seen only once, when she was a few hours old. She felt pride in her academic achievements, her approach to life.

Emily was teaching school in a small town barely a hundred miles from here. This summer—after her first year at the school—she'd organized a project to provide a summer day camp for a group of underprivileged students. She was involved full-time, had coaxed a group of fellow teachers to provide two weeks each of their own time.

A thought that was becoming obsessive darted across her mind again. She'd become convinced that Emily could be trained to run the business. Emily possessed all the talents lacking in her uncle, aunt, and mother. *Emily has my blood. David's blood. Our skills. She could carry on the business—that would be a kind of immortality.*

The children—especially Celeste—will be furious if I bring her into the family. Celeste will throw tantrums, run off, make threats. But Celeste has a native shrewdness—she won't cut ties to her financial support.

Would Emily be willing to come here—for a year? That's all I'd ask. That she spend a year living in the house and working in the company—at a far higher salary than she's earning as a teacher. And in turn—even if she wants no part of the company at the end of that year—she'll inherit a grandchild's share of Winston Mail Order. An inheritance worth millions.

She was approaching the house now. She turned into the circular driveway of the white brick colonial that David had loved and which—through the growingly prosperous years—she'd enlarged as he had hoped they could do one day. She pulled to a stop, sat immobile behind the wheel. Her mind darting back through the years.

This date each year—the anniversary of David's death—was always painful. Always she was frustrated that his murderer had never been brought to justice. David would never have committed suicide. He loved life. He loved his family.

Oh, how he would have loved Emily! From the bits of

5

information private investigators had produced over twenty-three years, she knew this precious—secret—grandchild reflected themselves.

If Emily learns the truth, will she come to me? Do I dare intervene in her life?

One

The Mitchells' small, gray ranch house—trimmed in sunlight yellow and flanked on each side by tall birch trees—sat on a well-cared-for quarter-acre in Evanston, New York. Rose bushes soared to impressive heights across the front of the house. Lush coleus lined the walk to the entrance with an air of majesty. This was the only house Emily Mitchell had known in her twenty-three years.

On this sultry Friday evening of the Labor Day weekend—with dinner over and the dishes stacked in the dishwasher—Emily sat with her parents—Joan and Bob Mitchell—in the living room. A neat, charming room without the new slipcovers her mother had planned because the economy was shaky and her father's business was suffering.

She listened in shock—disbelief—while Joan Mitchell stumbled over a confession that had just turned her world upside down. *I was adopted at birth? I'm having a nightmare—this isn't real! Who am I?*

"This woman—Andrea Winston—wrote me a letter, then phoned me two days ago and introduced herself. I was astonished. She's head of a big mail order company—you've heard of it, Emily."

"Yes—" Emily's voice barely audible. *This isn't happening.*

"I told myself it was some crank letter. Somebody pretending to be her. But then she called. She knew all the details of your adoption—" Her mother—her adoptive mother—paused for a deep breath, exchanged an anguished glance with her adoptive father. "The date, the hospital where you were born, your birth weight. The agency that handled the adoption. She was almost apologetic—but determined. So like you, my darling. She's your grandmother—I have no doubts about that."

7

"Even though all the records were sealed, she's contrived to follow the family through the years," her father picked up, his smile wry. "With money you can do that. She wanted to know that you were being well cared for."

"We'd tried for years to have a baby. It didn't happen. We looked into adoptions—but that wasn't easy. We were told we might have to wait years." Now her mother's face lighted. "We were so thrilled when we were called in and interviewed about adopting you. Perhaps we did wrong in not telling you," she agonized, "but we loved you so much—from the day we saw you in the hospital—that we wanted you to believe you had been conceived by us—"

"We knew when your birth mother was only five months pregnant that you would be ours," her father broke in, clearly distraught. "And you've brought us such happiness through the years. But now—with this chance for you to have a lifetime of very comfortable security—how could we not tell you the truth?"

"I'll never feel that you are anything but my real parents." Emily's voice was taut, defiant. "My—my birth mother was willing to give me up. Why should I feel anything for her now?"

"She was seventeen when she discovered she was pregnant—it was as though her whole life was about to be destroyed." Joan Mitchell struggled for poise. "And it's not she who wrote to us. It was your grandmother."

"Now—all these years later—she wants to know me? Why?" *My whole life has been a lie. But Mom and Dad are my real parents. Not this family lurking in the shadows!*

"Darling, nothing has truly changed about us," Joan insisted. "We don't love you any less—" She hesitated. "And I don't think you love Dad and me any less—"

"Oh Mom, I wish this—this person who calls herself my grandmother had never come forward this way. Why?" Emily demanded again.

"You've never been out of her thoughts," her father said with compassion. "And now she's had—had the courage to try to bring you into her life. She's getting on in years—"

"This wasn't supposed to happen." Her mother's face tightened. "We adopted you—you were ours. Your—other family—

8

was not supposed to approach you. The adoption papers were sealed," she reiterated.

"But right at the beginning Andrea Winston—your grandmother—contrived to learn our identity. She never intruded," her father pointed out. "She just wanted to know that you were well and happy."

"Read her letter, darling—" Her mother held out the two tightly typed pages. Read, Emily. And remember, she's offering you a fortune—"

Emily reached for the pages. Her mind in turmoil. A stream of questions hammering at her.

What are they like—this other family? My birth mother. My grandmother. Do I have aunts and uncles? A sister or brother? This is all so strange. Why is this happening?

Mom had been an only child. Dad's older brother died in Vietnam. It has always been just Mom and Dad and me. Did this grandmother I've never known mean what she said in the letter? That one day I'll share in her estate?

In time—if that happens—I can make life easier for Mom and Dad. Give them things they've never been able to afford. They've been so good to me—I know they took out a larger mortgage on the house to put me through college.

But to live in her house for a year? To work in her company—a big corporation? Can I do that?

She ordered herself to read impassionately. Her grandmother had wished to raise her. Her mother had rejected this. Even at seventeen, shouldn't her mother have felt love for her? What about her father? What did he have to say about this?

And then her grandmother explained that her birth mother refused to this day to say who had made her pregnant. *What about my father—what is he like?*

"You don't have to accept her offer," her mother acknowledged, but her eyes said she welcomed this promise of security.

Mom was such a realist, Emily thought tenderly. Dad always said Mom had her feet on the ground. She loved them both, yet her thinking was so different from theirs in some areas. In unwary moments they'd talked about the late sixties, how they'd met at a Peace Corps training camp in Hawaii. But somewhere along the road they became timid, scared, fighting for security. *Will I be like that at their age?*

Two years ago when she'd gone with Wendy to Genoa for a week, they'd both lied to their parents, said they were going to Rome—forever feeling guilty, yet exalted by the experience of being part of the G8 summit protest. They'd spent one day in Rome, sent postcards home, then moved on to Genoa.

Chain letters had reached them through the Internet—urging young people everywhere to be in Genoa on July 20th to protest the way multinational corporations were taking over the world. Governments were accepting orders from business tycoons. High offices were being bought by the Right.

To Wendy and her to go to the G8 summit protest had been a wistful dream. And then Mom and Dad had offered her a week in Europe as a college graduation present—and Wendy's parents had been persuaded to do the same.

They were fated to be there, they'd told themselves. But their parents would have been terrified if they'd known she and Wendy were at the protests in Genoa. They would have been so fearful of violence. What had happened to their youthful sense of "we must make a contribution to improving the world"?

For a moment Emily felt transported back to that opening day of the meeting in 2001. The leaders of the most powerful nations in the world were gathering for their annual summit. She and Wendy had been mesmerized by the scene. The atmosphere had been electric.

The harbor—under a blazing sun—had been surrounded by security fences, closed to all but those with official passes. The world leaders—including President Bush—were staying on a ship in the harbor. In the center of town the awesome Ducal Palace was guarded by hundreds of armed police. The flags of all attending nations were on display.

She and Wendy had gravitated to the other part of town, where the protesters were gathering. Word was that over 200,000 protesters were present. Many young like themselves. Security was unbelievable.

"It's like being part of a police state," Wendy had whispered.

A teenaged protester told them that 15,000 armed soldiers and police moved around the town. They'd seen the surface-to-air missile launchers at the Christopher Columbus Airport when they arrived—just hours before all planes and trains were canceled to keep out protesters.

They were told anti-terrorist scuba divers were at the harbor. The center of the city had been declared a "red zone"—open only to residents, journalists, and officials. Store windows were boarded up. People were being pulled off the streets and searched for no recognizable reason.

Internet chain letters had convinced them it was urgent to be there to protest. Elected officials—from the lowly to the very top—took their orders from corporate heads. Examples were rampant.

"Emily, you don't have to make an immediate decision." Her father gently punctured her introspection.

"Where does she live?" *Will I be able to come home to see Mom and Dad?* "Is it far away?"

"In Woodhaven," her mother said quickly. "Less than three hours away. You'll be able to drive home for visits."

"Why does she want me to work at the company?" She recoiled from the realization that her grandmother was head of a major corporation. *I hate huge corporations. And I'd be expected to be part of it. Ugh!* Bewildered, Emily turned from her mother to her father. "What can I do there?"

"Probably be involved in office procedure," her father assumed. He paused. "I suspect she has hopes that you'll be drawn to the business, be eager to carry on in her footsteps. I suspect," he continued, "that her children and other grand-children have no such interest."

"I've bought from their catalogues," her mother confessed, as though this was a guilty secret. "Several times."

"I wouldn't be able to go there right away." *I don't have to go. How can I be involved—for a whole year—in a large corporation? But if I do, the time will come when I can make life easier for Mom and Dad. They've always been so good to me. Oh, it's all so weird!* "I mean, school opens Thursday," Emily forced herself to continue. "They'll have to appoint a substitute teacher. For one year," she said, her voice uneven. "If I go, will the school hold the job open for me?"

Not that she wanted to spend the rest of her life as a teacher, she thought truantly. Already she was restless in that role. She loved kids, yes—yet part of her was searching for something else. She'd felt so alive at the Genoa protest—as though she was part of something important.

To Mom and Dad, teaching was like a trust fund. They'd been through tough financial times in their early years. They found much satisfaction in their current middle-class lifestyle. The mortgage on the house had only a few years to go. Dad's hardware store provided a comfortable living—so far. The state of the economy was scary.

Neither Mom nor Dad had forgotten the hard, early years. She should do whatever she could to make life easier for them. They'd always been so concerned about security. That's why Mom had urged her to go into teaching. *"Darling, think of all the benefits—the short working day, the holidays, the summer vacations. And there's the pension. Dad and I will know you'll always have an income."* To Mom that was so important.

"You'll talk to the Board of Ed," her father soothed. "I'm sure something can be worked out."

"This is so crazy!" Emily shook her head in fresh disbelief. Still, part of her was impatient to learn about the family she'd never known. *Who am I?*

"No fast decision," her father decreed. "Think about it over the weekend. Your grandmother has waited this long, she can wait a bit longer."

Two

A night silence pervaded the office floor of Winston Mail Order Inc. on this Tuesday evening after the Labor Day weekend. Andrea Winston lingered at her desk, steeling herself for the unexpected family dinner meeting Leon had called. Instinct told her it would be a frenzied effort by the children to persuade her to give serious consideration to retirement. On their last dinner she'd managed to shut them up on that subject before they were through the first course.

What was so urgent that it couldn't wait for their usual dinner? And she understood why Leon had chosen Tuesday evening. On Tuesday evenings Hannah—her longtime house-keeper—went to sleep over at her sister's house and remain the following day. Hannah would serve dinner, then take off. Leon wanted privacy. But tonight Hannah's sister and family were on vacation at Lake George.

Has Leon come up with a prospective buyer for the company? He's been fascinated by all the takeovers lately. But I'm not ready for retirement!

She had a surprise of her own for them, she thought with ironic amusement. She reached for the letter that lay on her desk—read and re-read since it arrived this morning. Emily— the granddaughter she hadn't seen since she was a few hours old—was coming to live with her for a year. She would arrive tomorrow morning.

Two days ago Emily's adoptive mother had called to confirm that Emily was accepting her invitation. "A letter is in the mail," she'd said.

"Dear Grandmother whom I've never known," Emily's letter began. *"I'm still trying to accept the fact that I was adopted at birth. I must be honest—I don't know how I will feel about all that is happening now. It's as though I'm moving*

into a strange world. But I need to know who I am. I'll arrive tomorrow morning at your house, as arranged with Mom. I love my adoptive parents dearly."

The large upward swinging signature, surprisingly like her own, brought fresh tears to Andrea's eyes. So many years squandered. But David would be pleased if he knew she was bringing this precious granddaughter into their lives.

Whatever the children had cooked up, she told herself, would be matched by her announcement of Emily's arrival. Her face softened. Hannah was almost as excited as she. What a fuss Hannah had made about preparing Emily's room.

She felt a recurrent touch of unease at the prospect of Celeste's reaction. Celeste would be furious. So she would take off again with her toy boy. But she'd be back. Her tastes were extravagant—and the trust fund was modest. Celeste, she thought with recurrent frustration, had not worked a day in her life. She'd been on a "temporary allowance" for over twenty years.

Aware of the passage of time, Andrea prepared to leave the office. She wasn't surprised to see a sliver of light beneath the door of Paul's office down the hall. Like herself, he was addicted to a long work week. She debated for an instant, then knocked on his door.

"Yes?" Slightly querulous, as though annoyed at this intrusion.

"It's me—" Andrea opened the door, took a few steps inside. "I'm knocking off for the day. What about you? Don't you allow yourself any social life?" Affection in her voice.

"I'm in love with my job. That's my social life." Like her, Andrea thought, he enjoyed their good-humored raillery. "But I'll be cutting out soon. I want to drop in on the 'Stop the Mall' meeting." His tone almost apologetic, as though he might be depriving the company in this. Actually, he'd founded the "Stop the Mall" group.

"You know I'm with you on that." Hadn't she encouraged him to hold on to his grandmother's farm that a New York City developer was trying to buy? The perfect acreage for a mall—if the zoning for that was changed. "We don't need that damn mall. We don't want to be a carbon copy of every other small town across the country." She grunted in distaste.

14

Paul nodded in agreement. "A line-up of fast food joints and discount stores—all paying little above minimum."

"Or chains like the Clifford Stores, thriving on part-time workers at seven bucks an hour and no benefits."

"Local people expect better than that."

"Not every employer is as generous as you," Paul said softly.

"It's good for business. I realized back in the early years—as David did—that in the long run paying decent wages keeps employees with the company. Avoids a constant turnover—which is destructive."

Paul approved of this approach. Leon insisted she "spoiled" her workers, that they didn't appreciate it. *Paul thinks like a child of David and me.*

"Tomorrow's the Big Day," he said tenderly.

"Yes." Her smile was dazzling. Only Paul—thus far—knew that Emily was coming into her life.

A rare sentimental thought flashed across her mind. Wouldn't it be wonderful if Paul and Emily were drawn to each other? Together they could carry on Winston Mail Order. David's monument.

Yet Paul had seemed so uneasy when she told him about Emily. He didn't put his feelings into words, but she suspected he feared that Emily meant only to use her. That Emily viewed this as a lucrative business deal.

But that's a gamble I'm willing to take.

The three—Leon, Carol, and Celeste—sat in the elegantly furnished living room of the spacious house that David Winston had built in a wildly extravagant moment after the birth of his first child. He and Andrea had struggled to make the mortgage payments until—at last—the business was on a sound footing and this was no hardship.

Leon paced about the room while his sisters sprawled on a green-velvet-upholstered sofa designed for comfort.

"Mother's late again," he complained. "Why must she always be late when we're here for dinner?"

"She's busy making money," Celeste drawled. "Which we all covet."

Carol grunted in distaste. "You just adore to say shocking things."

Leon abandoned pacing. "You two have to back me up," he warned. "It's time she listened to reason. She's admitted that business has fallen off. She—"

"Darling," Celeste drawled, "haven't you heard? Even the biggest companies are complaining about shitty profits."

Leon grunted impatiently. "Where's your head, Celeste? Don't you realize the company—our company—could go down the drain? She'd be devastated."

"We'd be devastated." Celeste shuddered at the implication.

"With the economy so bad you're sure you can make a deal?" Carol asked Leon. Clearly skeptical.

"I've been talking to people. People at the top," Leon emphasized. "Right now they're interested. But if she dawdles—" He grimaced as he considered this. "Like I said, the company could go down the drain."

"She's going to piss up a storm. But there's no way we can have her declared incompetent," Celeste flipped.

Leon winced in reproach. "Celeste, don't be absurd. But we've got to make her understand she'll run the company into the red in another year." *Damn Paul for encouraging her excesses.* "This could be the deal of her lifetime." *She's seventy-four years old—hasn't she had enough? She's talked for over a year about declining sales. It's time to get the hell out—with big figures.*

"Tom says the whole country—the world—is facing bad times," Carol recalled. "What makes you think you can pull off a big deal?"

"I've had several serious talks with the Clifford people," Leon reiterated. He felt a surge of triumph. He'd had bad luck in other deals. This would make up for all of them. "They're standing by to talk with her." He paused. She would balk when she heard the name, but this wasn't the time to be choosey. A company noted for its ruthless tactics—that was good business. She was too soft—all those unnecessary expenses. Pensions, health care, the day care center. "The three of us have to stand together." *Later, she'll be grateful that I pushed her into retirement. She'll realize how sharp I was.*

"It's not just her future that's at stake—it's our future, too." All at once Carol seemed anxious.

"That makes us sound like vultures," Celeste taunted. "You're mentally burying the old girl."

"We have to be practical," Carol shot back. "How can we let her throw away a fortune?"

"No way we can push her into retirement," Celeste warned. "You know how stubborn she can be."

"And Paul's always there, feeding her ego." Carol was contemptuous. "He wants her to hold on to the business. He figures when she goes, he'll take over."

"Over my dead body," Leon began and stopped dead as they heard a car pulling up before the house.

"She's here. We go through dinner without bringing up the subject," Leon ordered. "After dinner we talk."

They heard Hannah at the door, listened to the brief conversation between their mother and her housekeeper. Then Andrea appeared at the arch that led into the living room.

"I just want to change into something comfortable," she told the others. "Dinner on the table in ten minutes."

In the charming master bedroom she'd shared with David until his untimely death, Andrea changed from her workaday pantsuit into a Chinese caftan. She claimed that she left the business behind when she changed attire, but she acknowledged to herself that she never left business behind.

She glanced about the room—the original pseudo-traditional furniture replaced by elegant antiques. This was her retreat from the world—where in troubled moments she carried on a one-sided conversation with David. If Leon and his sisters knew, they would suspect she'd lost her mind. But it was a comfort she allowed herself.

Why had Leon called for this dinner meeting? What was so important, she asked herself again, that couldn't wait until their regular monthly dinner? And all three had stressed that they would be coming alone. Leon's wife, Carol's husband, Celeste's toy boy were otherwise occupied this evening. At their orders, she surmised.

Once, she recalled, they'd had a family dinner *every* Friday evening—with Leon's wife, Carol's husband and Celeste's husband of the moment present—and later the three grandchildren. But that had petered out through the years. Perhaps that happened in most families. Children developed lives of their own.

She was often exasperated by Raymond, Leon's fourteen-year-old, and Carol's twins—Elaine and Deirdre. The three of them sulked when they didn't get their way—and their parents did nothing to change this. Leon and Carol—and their spouses—too wrapped up in themselves to recognize their responsibilities to their kids.

She'd spoiled her three, too, she conceded—out of guilt at being so tied up with the business after David had died. Ever conscious that they were missing a father in their lives. But they'd been taught to recognize limits. She loved the grand-children, she analyzed—but she felt no pride in them. No joy in their presence. And that was sad.

Of course, she was aware of Leon's hints for the past several weeks that she consider retirement. *But what will happen to the company? Leon's made it clear he has no interest in taking over—nor would he be capable of that. He's made a mess of every project he's undertaken. Neither Carol nor Celeste would be interested—even if they had the capability to do this.*

Her face tightened. Be honest. The three of them were terrified of the current bad economy. They were afraid she was too old to run the company at a profitable level.

Paul doesn't feel that way. He respects my ability. He doesn't see me as an old crone losing her powers. He sees a fine future for the company with me at the helm. He's excited about building the business to even greater heights. If David was alive, he'd never consider abandoning the company.

She glanced at her reflection in her cheval mirror. As slim as she was at twenty, she thought in satisfaction—appearing years younger than her age. Her hair—white now for years—was worn short to require little attention. For David she'd worn her hair long. Men adored long hair.

Enough of this. Go down to dinner. Listen to the three of them. And make them understand I have no intention of retiring—nor going public nor accepting a takeover. It's my company. Let them remember that.

She recalled a remark a longtime employee had mentioned earlier in the day: "I'm disappointed in my children." Maybe parents expected too much of their children—as though to see their personal dreams reflected in their kids. Was she asking too much to have hoped Leon would show interest in carrying on the company?

He'd gone through a fortune in these grandiose schemes he was sure would make him a successful CEO. The patents he'd acquired—sure each would make him a fortune. Jane was terrified that one day he'd blow up the house with one of his experiments. *Does he feel in competition with me? Is that at the root of all of his would-be entrepreneurial efforts?*

Still debating about this, she left her bedroom, headed downstairs. She was conscious that conversation froze as the others heard her approach. All right, she was geared for battle. She made her own decisions.

They would exchange greetings and go into the dining room. Leon would make sure nothing was said about why he'd brought them together this evening until after dinner. He figured he'd rushed in precipitately at the last dinner—when she'd cut short his efforts to prod her into retirement.

She strode into the living room with a warm smile.

"I hope you're all starving because Hannah's probably been cooking up a storm all day. You know how she loves having you all here together." Hannah was like a member of the family.

They exchanged dutiful kisses, headed for the dining room. Andrea took her place at the head of the beautifully laid dining table. As he'd done—at his mother's direction since his father's death—Leon sat at the foot. She remembered now how solemn he'd been when she'd told him he was now the man of the house. Even at twelve he'd exuded a formidable charm.

She'd thought Celeste—her baby—was the brainy one. But brightness too often gave way to capriciousness. Carol had always fretted that she was neither the oldest nor the baby. What Paul's grandmother—before she descended into the darkness of Alzheimer's—labeled "the middle child syndrome."

Hannah served her delicious gazpacho—a recipe she admitted to having acquired from a famous resort chef years ago. A longtime favorite of Leon and Celeste. Carol was spare in her praise of anything. Carol was given to pouting—even at forty-seven. David had said she inherited that tendency from his mother. His parents had often been absent from his life, but he'd adored the grandmother who raised him.

Andrea allowed her children to carry on their usual inane conversation. Her own thoughts dwelt on Emily. Tomorrow morning Emily would arrive at the house. She must handle this first meeting with care. Mustn't rush her. She felt a surge of excitement, of love for this secret grandchild.

Hannah removed the soup plates. Celeste was into what Leon called her "hip chick" mode—making an effort to shock the others with reports of her lifestyle.

"What's the main course?" Leon asked, affecting a humorous attitude. "Some new health food delight Hannah's discovered?"

She knew Leon considered Hannah—a frustrated nutritionist—a "health-food nut." He'd prefer an artery-clogging two-inch-thick steak and vegetables floating in cream-rich sauce. His waistline reflected this, she thought impatiently. She'd given up on trying to persuade him to be more judicious in his eating, to indulge in exercise more stringent than climbing behind the wheel of his Lincoln Town Car.

"Be careful of the plates," Hannah warned as she came into the dining room with a laden tray. "They're very hot."

"No steaks?" Leon chided in a spurt of good-humor. "No rare roast beef?"

"Not when I'm cooking," Hannah shot back. "If you want to kill yourself when you eat at home, that's your business. Here you eat healthy."

Leon would be happier eating at a fast-food restaurant. But he seems in good spirits. When the devil is he going to spill their message for me? If it's what I think it is, he'll go home unhappy.

The main course was piquant chicken Marsala—whose recipe Hannah guarded with her life.

"Normal people use veal," Celeste chided.

"That's savage," Hannah reproached, in some way enjoying this sparring with Leon and Celeste. "You know how they raise those poor little animals." She'd been in this household since Leon was twelve, Carol ten and Celeste a cherubic three. She knew every family secret—including Celeste's pregnancy all those years ago.

Hannah's so excited about Emily's coming to stay with us. Look at the way she went out and bought fancy new sheets and towels for Emily's room, She took that special reading lamp from the den—so Emily can be comfortable reading in bed: "She'll be a bedtime reader like you."

Andrea ate dinner without tasting—impatient to be past the encounter ahead. She could feel the mounting tension in the others about the table. Then Hannah served dessert—bananas and pears poached in white wine with a touch of Grand Marnier liqueur—and she knew the moment had arrived.

"Mother, we're all concerned about the pace you keep. I mean—" He allowed himself an indulgent chuckle. "I mean at your age you deserve to relax, enjoy life. You've spent enough years in a grueling business. We—"

"Leon, I'm not retiring," she broke in. "I love running the company."

"Mother, be sensible." *Carol's been coached.* "It's time you learned to take care of yourself." She glanced for an instant at Leon, as though for approval. "It upsets us to see you working so hard—"

"The economy's in dreadful shape," Leon picked up. "It's—"

"We've survived bad economies in the past." Andrea was sharp. *They're blaming Paul for my refusing to retire. They resent my closeness to him.*

"This is an era of mergers. An era of bigness." *God, he sounds so pompous.* "That's the road to cutting back, combining services, instituting enormous savings. It restores—"

"Leon, I'm not firing people who've been with the company for years. I'm not trimming health insurance and pensions." She felt only contempt for such economies.

Leon contrived an indulgent smile. "Mother, everybody knows your philanthropic views. But these are dangerous times. Some of the biggest corporations are facing bankruptcy—"

"So profits are down—that's cyclical," Andrea shot back. "The company can handle it."

Leon pushed ahead. "I just happened to run into a multinational company that's interested—despite the rotten economy—in talking to you about a takeover. At top money," he pronounced. "Of course, I had to do a lot of fast talking. 'No way,' I told them, would my mother consider selling except for top dollar. She—"

"She's not selling." Andrea was grim. *He's furious at me but too disciplined to show it. Why can't he show that discipline in business? He does a great selling job, then unsells it.* "I'm not falling apart. So the company is feeling a drop in profits," she conceded. "Like most companies. We can handle the occasional bad year. Tell your friends that Winston Mail Order is not for sale." She took a deep breath. "Now I have an announcement of my own to make." Again, she paused. Steeling herself for the opposition of her children. *Celeste will blow her stack.* "I know this will come as a shock to you, Celeste. I've been in touch with your daughter." She saw Celeste turn white in disbelief. From Leon and Carol's expression she realized they'd been aware of Celeste's pregnancy all those years ago. *They didn't believe my story that Celeste was suffering from a touch of TB, had to be sent away to a sanitarium for a few months.*

"Why are you doing this?" Celeste screeched. "To punish me for what happened when I was fifteen?"

"Seventeen," Carol corrected, then focused on her mother. "Why?" Her expression indicated she considered this a personal catastrophe.

"Because this is my granddaughter. I pleaded to be allowed to raise her. But you were eighteen by the time she was born, Celeste—and I had no say in the matter."

"I don't believe you're doing this to me!" Celeste raged.

"How can you subject the family to that kind of disgrace?" Carol demanded. "Who's supposed to be the mother?" Her eyes glazed. "People could believe I had this illegitimate child!"

"I doubt that." But Leon was clearly unhappy.

"People will believe she's my daughter!" Celeste gaped in horror.

"She *is* your daughter," Andrea reminded. "And considering your escapades through the years, people won't gasp in shock. But she is, also, my granddaughter. I want to know her—" Andrea allowed herself an ironic smile, "in my late years. So prepare yourselves. Emily is arriving tomorrow—to live with me for a year. She's part of this family. My will has always reflected this," Andrea emphasized. *My estate will be equally divided between children and grandchildren.* "Don't either of you ever forget that."

Three

There was an unseasonable chill in the air this evening. A slanting rain pounded at the windows. The atmosphere in the Mitchell dining room was tense. Strained. Mom was chattering away, as she did when she was anxious, Emily realized. Dad managed a cheery expression, but his eyes were somber.

Emily dawdled over her strawberry shortcake—usually her favorite dessert. Her mind in turmoil. *Have I made an awful mistake in agreeing to go to live—for a year—in the house of the woman who says she's my grandmother? A stranger! But if one day I share in her estate, I can give Mom and Dad the security that's so important to them. I owe them that.*

"It'll be an adventure, Emily. You'll be living in a whole new world," her mother effervesced. "And you'll come home often—you can drive it in less than three hours."

"You're sure I should take the car?" Emily was uneasy. Dad needed one car for the business. She and Mom shared the second car.

"Darling, yes," her mother insisted. "I'll feel good that you have easy transportation to bring you home."

"We'll pick up another car," her father promised. "A little later—when the prices drop as new models come into the market."

"Mrs. Winston seems a very nice person," her mother pushed on. "I've read about how she took over the company when her husband died. How she built it far beyond what it was in the early days." She hesitated. "When I talked to her, she told me about her husband. Your grandfather. The police were sure he'd committed suicide. She's never believed that. She's convinced he was murdered—"

"Joan," Bob Mitchell scolded. "She probably couldn't

accept a verdict of suicide." He turned to Emily. "You know Mom and her suspense novels. She'll make a murder mystery out of anything."

"If it's—unpleasant, I don't have to stay." A touch of defiance in Emily's voice now. "The school promised they'd hold my job open for me for a year. Della Jackson's in my place on a substitute basis."

But it's going to be weird! I'll be meeting a whole, strange family. How do they feel about me coming into their lives? How can I feel kindly towards my birth mother, when she abandoned me? Mom says she was just a teenager when I was born—but I couldn't have given up my baby even at seventeen.

"The rain is supposed to stop somewhere around midnight." Her mother was determined to appear cheerful. "You'll have a pleasant drive in the morning."

"What about a game of chess after our coffee?" her father asked. "I know," he chuckled. "I haven't won a game since you were twelve."

"You taught me too well," Emily teased. "I learned all your little tricks."

"Take the chess set with you," her mother said impulsively.

"No." Emily was involuntarily sharp. "Dad and I will play when I come home to visit." *My grandmother won't complain if I come home a lot of weekends, will she? What am I letting myself in for? Maybe I'll hate all of them. My grandmother and birth mother, and the uncle and aunts Mom told me live there in Woodhaven. What about my father? Will I ever know who he is?*

They lingered over coffee—as though loath to end the evening.

"All right, you two go into the living room and play chess," Joan Mitchell ordered. "I'll load the dishwasher." Normally this was Emily's task. But this wasn't an ordinary night.

Earlier than usual they retired for the night—at her mother's insistence.

"You'll want an early start in the morning."

Mom's scared she'll break down. She dreads this separation as much as I do. Am I making a mistake?

*　　*　　*

24

Emily's right hand gripped the phone with unnecessary force as she spoke with Wendy about what Wendy called her "marvelous adventure." She leaned against the pillows, propped against the headboard of her bed while they talked.

"Emily, I know it's scary—but it'll be exciting, too."

"It's crazy—to discover Mom and Dad are not my birth parents. It's like I don't know who I am—"

"You haven't changed," Wendy protested. "You've just found new relatives. Yeah, your birth mother sounds like a creep—but Andrea Winston is your grandmother? Wow!"

"Dad went to the public library to look up old issues of *Fortune*—to see what he could read about her. She's one of the richest women in this country. She runs a huge company—Dad says they have over two thousand employees. She represents everything I detest!"

"You don't know that," Wendy rejected. "And she has this terrific estate that you'll share in one day. Maybe it's crass to mention it—but you said she's seventy-four years old. You're twenty-three. One day you could be rich."

"It's such a turn-off—" Emily lowered her voice, though it was late and her parents were probably asleep by now, "to know that I was born into that kind of family."

"You were raised well," Wendy shot back, then sighed. "What kills me is the way your folks and mine have changed through years." Her voice deepened in determination. "We won't let that happen to us. I think back to stories Mom and Dad have told me—and your folks have told you—about their lives when they were our age, and I can't believe how they've changed. Of course, Mom and Dad talk about their lives in the late sixties as though those were strangers."

"I know. They look back on those years with amazement. Almost disbelief. I don't want that to happen to us."

"My folks were active in the protests against the war in Vietnam. Dad went to Canada to escape the draft—not that he was afraid but it was against his principles. Mom went with him. They lived together in Montreal for two years before they got married. Now if I come home from a date after one a.m., they're nervous wrecks—sure I'm sleeping around."

"I've caught Mom reading chick-lit novels," Emily reported.

"She hides them when she sees me. She's trying to figure out what goes on in our 'young minds.'"

"Chick-lit novels—to women like us—are fairy tales." Amusement blended with derision in Wendy's voice. "We don't live in rent-stabilized apartments in some big-city urban area. We don't buy designer clothes and—"

"On our salaries?" Emily broke in and giggled. "I'm happy with Jones of New York and Liz Claiborne."

"These women have mothers who're always poking their noses into their love lives. Of course, in those fairy tales they work for gorgeous bosses in important jobs and fall desperately in love with them. Our moms are just hoping we find a nice guy and marry before we hit thirty." Wendy paused. "I go along with that."

"We don't hang out at Starbucks, we both hate expresso, we're not cynical, we're not anorexic. I guess we just don't live right," Emily drawled, for the moment removed from anxieties that plagued her.

"The real fairy tale is the one you've walked into," Wendy reflected. "And it has a happy ending," she insisted, fighting yawns.

"As Mom always says, 'From your lips to God's ear.' And I think it's time we both go to sleep." *How can I sleep when this will be my last night in this house for a year? All right, I'll come home for some weekends.*

"Yeah. Call me as soon as you get settled in," Wendy ordered. "I'll be dying to know what's happening."

Off the phone, Emily focused on falling asleep—but this seemed a futile attempt. She'd always said it was easy to fall asleep on rainy nights. Rain was like a soothing lullaby. But tonight too many questions darted across her mind. She suspected she'd toss and turn until dawn.

She would be moving into an atmosphere she loathed. Her grandmother was head of a major corporation. Big corporations were taking over the world. People were losing their jobs. The government was ceding its power to greedy CEOs. It was obscene that CEOs were taking home many millions each year in salaries and bonuses while children worked for ten cents an hour in third-world nations.

What do I want to do with my life? Wendy says that every-

day people like us have to help to lead the way to a better world. Corporations shouldn't be dictating our lives, our futures. But if I try to work in politics, I'll clash with Mom and Dad. They're so conservative. They'll be so unhappy. Being a good teacher is a contribution. Why don't I feel satisfied with that?

Now she remembered Wendy's favorite response to their feeling different from their families: "Hillary Clinton's parents were Republicans, and she became a Democrat. And look where she is!"

With grim determination she leaned back against the pillows and ordered herself to meditate. Most times that helped her to fall asleep. But instinct warned that—with tomorrow's departure from the only home she'd ever known—meditation might not work tonight.

Four

Andrea was relieved when the children decided to leave. "Mother, give some thought to what we've been discussing," Leon said as he rose to his feet. "You've earned the right to a leisurely lifestyle. Winters in Florida or Bermuda—maybe Caribbean cruises, summers in the Hamptons or a cozy house on the Cape. Why run yourself ragged in an economy like this?" *He's blocking out Emily's arrival in our lives. He's not ready to face it yet.*

"I'm not selling." Andrea forced herself to be casual. "Other women my age may enjoy Caribbean cruises, beach houses, the leisurely lifestyle. I enjoy running my business."

"I'll be leaving some time tomorrow morning for East Hampton," Celeste said, her face taut. *Meaning, before Emily arrives. Did I expect anything else?* "September is still a good month out there. I have no taste for staring at my past." *So she's running away with her toy boy.*

"Mother, make sure this—this girl isn't just using you," Carol fretted. *The children and the in-laws are anxious to leave. To discuss the horrors of Emily's presence in their lives? Carol is distraught that scandal could touch her precious name. Celeste is furious at being unveiled as the mother of a grown daughter. Leon is unhappy that the Winston empire must be shared with another heir.* "We'll be worrying about you—" Carol's hands fluttered with a blend of alarm and bewilderment.

"Worry about more urgent things." Andrea's smile was dry. *Next they'll be suggesting I give up the house and move into a retirement community.* "I'll be fine."

She walked the others to the door, ignored the air of impending woe as they prepared to leave.

"Oh, it's raining," Carol complained. "Couldn't it have waited till we got home?"

David used to complain that all three kids were like his parents—devoid of responsibility, self-absorbed—though he admitted Leon had his grandmother's charm. More than the girls, Leon could at times manipulate her. But that famous charm had not been in evidence tonight.

Andrea's first impulse was to go to Hannah's room and talk with her about Emily's arrival in the morning. But no sliver of light showed beneath her bedroom door. Andrea's face reflected her deep affection for Hannah. She'd put in a long day—let her sleep.

Andrea tiptoed away from Hannah's bedroom. Hannah was a very light sleeper, she reminded herself. When—in those early years—Celeste or Carol or Leon woke up in the middle of the night with a stuffy nose or sore throat, Hannah was the first to hear.

In her bedroom Andrea prepared for bed—suspecting she'd lie awake far into the night. *David would approve of what I'm doing. He'd be proud of this grandchild.*

Tonight the suspense novel on her bedside table remained untouched. She was content to lie back against the pillows and visualize Emily's arrival tomorrow. The earlier drizzle became a downpour that lulled her into a heavy slumber.

Much later she was abruptly awakened. *Somebody's screaming! It's Hannah! What's happening?*

For an instant she froze in shock, then tossed aside the sheet and leapt from her bed. Her instinct to rush downstairs to Hannah's bedroom. But now she was conscious of a deadly silence below. Was the intruder climbing the stairs now?

Her heart pounding, she reached for the phone, dialed the police precinct.

"Something terrible is happening in my house," she whispered. "This is Andrea Winston. I—"

"Please talk louder," the voice at the other end said briskly. "Where's the trouble?"

"Andrea Winston," she repeated. Her voice terse with fear. Everybody in town knew where she lived—no need for further information. "Come quickly."

She put down the phone. *What's happened to Hannah? I can't just sit here and wait for the police. She may be badly hurt—she needs me!*

She reached for the robe at the foot of her bed, hurried from her bedroom to the head of the stairs. She hesitated for an instant—craning for sounds below. Only silence greeted her. Then she heard a door slam. The kitchen door, she recognized, and sped down the stairs.

Still, only silence greeted her. She sped to Hannah's bedroom—terrified of what had happened. The door to Hannah's room was half-open.

"Hannah!" she called as she approached the door. "Hannah?"

She thrust the door wide. "Hannah?" The bed was in disarray. "Hannah?" she tried yet again.

Only now did she realize that Hannah was sprawled on the floor—half-obscured by the door.

"Oh my God!" A mass of blood was seeping from beneath Hannah's body. A carving knife lay beside her. Her eyes stared lifeless at the ceiling. "Oh my God!"

It's happening again. Murder in this house. But Hannah wasn't the object. I was meant to be murdered. Who hated David enough to want him dead—and now hates me?

She stifled an impulse to cradle Hannah in her arms. The police wouldn't want the body touched. Nothing must be touched, she warned herself. What had happened thirty-seven years ago was happening again. *Somebody who knew Hannah was normally away from the house on Tuesday night came here to murder me.*

Minutes later she heard police sirens in the distance. Then the police cars were turning into the driveway, pulling up before the house. Andrea rushed to admit them.

"You okay, Mrs. Winston?" Bill Jackson, the older of the four detectives, demanded solicitously. His son had worked for the company for almost eight years—since high-school graduation. His sister was a supervisor in the Shipping Department.

"It's Hannah—" Everybody knew Hannah. "She's been murdered."

An hour later—struggling for poise while members of the police force searched about the house for clues—Andrea sat in a living-room chair and responded to Detective Jackson's questions. All the while striving to brush from her mind the image of Hannah's body lying on the floor in a pool of blood.

Once again, her whole world had been turned upside down.

The detectives were convinced Hannah had interrupted a burglary. The screen had been cut in a kitchen window—the point of entry. The killer had taken a carving knife from a kitchen rack.

"We'd like a list of items missing," Bill Jackson pursued. "Hannah heard noises—she went out to investigate. She saw him taking your best silver from the dining-room breakfront." *He left it scattered about the dining-room floor to make it seem a robbery.* "Terrified, Hannah ran back to her room. He followed, stabbed her to death."

Andrea's face was ashen. She fought to keep her voice even. Hannah's murder must not go unresolved.

"It wasn't Hannah who was meant to die," Andrea reiterated with an air of frustration. *They don't believe me. They think I've gone off my rocker. They were kids or not yet born when David was murdered. They think I'm a crazy old lady.* "Whoever killed Hannah meant to kill me."

"Why would anybody want to kill you?" Jackson chided gently.

"Why did somebody kill my husband?" she countered. "My every instinct tells me I was the intended victim. Not Hannah."

"Mrs. Winston, you should let me call your son—or daughters," he tried again.

"No." She shook her head—exasperated by Jackson's solicitude. What could Leon or Carol or Celeste accomplish by coming here in the middle of the night? She doubted that even they believed their father had been murdered. "Just do your job here. I'll be fine." *How can I be fine when Hannah lies dead in her bedroom?*

"I'll have one of the guys make coffee for you," Jackson said gently. "This has been an awful shock to you." He hesitated. "Shall I notify Hannah's family—or would you rather do that?"

"They're away—on Cape Cod. I'll track down the address in the morning and notify them." Hannah's sister would be devastated. In some odd fashion she felt guilty that Hannah had taken a hit meant for her.

Why? Why—thirty-seven years after David was murdered— is someone stalking me?

31

Five

Emily sat at the dining table and tried to conceal the anxieties that flooded her. She gazed about the charming breakfast nook as though to etch on her mind the memory of the sunlight-yellow and blue-flowered wallpaper she and her mother had hung just a few months ago. Dad had argued, she remembered, that Mom should call in a paperhanger—but Mom was nervous about spending money when business at the store was so bad in this rotten economy.

"Remember, call us collect—any time you like," her mother urged as she brought the first batch of waffles—heaped high with hothouse blueberries—to Emily. *At this time of year Mom must have paid a fortune for blueberries, but she knows how I love them with waffles.* "Not that Mrs. Winston—your grandmother—" She tried for a casual tone— "would resent your calling home."

"Look on this as an adventure." Her father repeated what had become her mother's mantra. His smile was bright but belied by the somberness of his eyes. *He was hurt—like Mom—by having to reveal that I was adopted. Surely they know it doesn't change my love for them. They are my parents.*

"I have to be honest. It's like a weird business deal to me." Her eyes swept from her father to her mother, at the waffle iron again. "I have no feelings about my—my natural family." *That's not true—I want to know what they're like. I want to know who I am. My roots.* "But there's the part about my sharing in the inheritance." *I sound so mercenary—but Mom and Dad understand.* "You two have been so good to me. I'd love to be able to do things for you."

She saw the tears that welled in her mother's eyes. "Darling, you've brought such joy into our lives. We just want you to be happy."

"Hey, you fed our daughter. What about the father?" he demanded with mock gruffness. "Am I supposed to sit here and starve?"

"I've got you both up so early," Emily apologized. "You could have slept another hour."

"We want you to be on the road well before eight a.m.," her father reminded. "You know how heavy the weekday traffic can be on the highway."

"We should turn on the radio or TV and get a weather report," her mother fretted and Emily laughed.

"Mom, look out the window. The rain's over—the sun is gorgeous."

"Turn on the radio or TV in the morning and all you get is bad news," her father grumbled.

At seven forty-five a.m.—fighting tears—Emily kissed her mother and father good-bye, promised to call later in the day, and hurried out to the white Toyota suburban that had been her mother's transportation. For a poignant moment she hesitated behind the wheel, then blew a kiss to the only parents she'd ever known. *It's silly to feel so torn apart—I'll be less than three hours away.*

Already traffic was heavy. She swung off the highway to take the back road to Woodhaven. Each mile seemed to build her anguish. *I feel as though I'm living two lives. I don't want to leave the old life—that's real.*

Halfway to Woodhaven she made a sudden decision to stop for coffee. She'd slept badly last night. When she was at college and driving home for some holiday, Dad had always warned her about stopping for coffee if she was sleepy: "All it takes is one second of dozing and you're plowing into a tree."

She watched for a pleasant diner, swung off the road as one appeared. Her heart was pounding now. Was this trip a terrible mistake? Should she forget this whole scene, put it aside as a grisly nightmare?

But an insistent inner voice hammered at her. Who was she? Everything she'd thought about herself was false. That she resembled her "maternal grandmother" rather than Mom or Dad. That her slightly curved right pinkie had been inherited from her paternal grandmother. Somehow, it missed me, Dad had said.

They hadn't been lying—they'd just been building up a family background for her. She'd never known their parents—they had died young. There had been no doting grandparents. They wanted to give her a semblance of family.

She drew to a stop in the parking area, well populated at this hour. Mostly trucks, a good omen. Truck drivers knew the best diners.

For an instant she hesitated—again beset by doubts. But if she was ever to discover who she truly was, she must meet this family she'd never known. Her grandmother had talked about an uncle and an aunt. Would her birth mother be there, too? *I don't want to meet her. How could she give up her own child? It wasn't as though she had to do this.*

Still caught up in an air of unreality, Emily left the car, walked to the entrance to the diner. In an hour and a half she'd be meeting the woman who was her grandmother. Somebody whom she hadn't known existed until a week ago.

She was to drive to the house, Emily remembered instructions. Would anybody else be there? Her heart began to pound again. She couldn't face a whole battalion of strangers!

She fought an urge to hurry back to the car, turn around and go home, to forget this insanity had ever occurred. Her father's words darted across her mind: "Mrs. Winston has waited a lot of years for this meeting. It's terribly important to her. You've been in her mind since the day you were born." How like Dad to feel compassion for her.

Last night's rain had given way to such a pleasant day, she thought gratefully. It would have been awful—prophetic?—to have arrived there in the rain. At the entrance to the diner, she reached for the door, pulled it wide.

She flinched at the rush of cold air. The air-conditioning was designed for men in business suits, she thought in fleeting annoyance. Most of the patrons male, as she'd expected.

She headed for the nearest empty table.

"Good-morning—" A vivacious young waitress came charging to her table, handed her a menu. "The breakfast special is—"

"Just an English muffin and coffee," Emily hastened to order. She wasn't hungry—she just needed to dispel this threatening drowsiness.

It felt so strange that school was opening and she wasn't in her classroom. Would her life ever be the same again? She was moving into a world of strangers. Why did this craziness have to happen?

The others—her grandmother's children and grandchildren—must resent her sudden appearance in their lives. They must know the condition of her arrival. That her grandmother's estate would be divided into yet another parcel. *Will they hate me?*

So her birth mother had been only seventeen when she'd realized she was pregnant. How could she be so callous as to turn her baby over to strangers! Thank God, she had been. Mom and Dad had been the best of parents.

She lingered briefly over the English muffin and coffee. Girding herself for the encounter ahead. Did her grandmother actually believe she would be so beguiled by the company that she'd wish to be part of it? Why weren't her children interested?

I'm going to spend a whole year in a strange house with a woman who is a total stranger to me—plus I'm supposed to work in the company. What will I do there?

Will I hate living with her? Will I hate working at the company? It sounds so boring. I wasn't bored teaching.

Her natural candor—forced into retreat in troubled moments—came to the surface now. She wasn't bored teaching—she loved kids. But she was always conscious of a restlessness, a need for something more in her life. She and Wendy had truly come alive those few chaotic days in Genoa. She'd yearned to go to Evian, France for the 2003 G8 summit at the end of May. To protest peacefully.

The loud conversation between a pair of new arrivals in the diner and a man behind the counter intruded on her introspection.

"We heard on the car radio—some woman down in Woodhaven was murdered last night," one of the pair reported excitedly. "Cops figure it was a robbery gone wrong, according to the news."

"Not much of anything ever happens down there," the counterman commented. "Quiet little town. Once in a while some addict goes on a tear and beats up his old lady."

"You talking about Woodhaven?" A woman at the table behind Emily's joined in the conversation. "That's a real hotbed of politics," she scoffed. "There's a bunch of locals fighting to oust the Mayor since he first got elected four years ago. They say he's always got his hand in the cookie jar. But who got murdered?"

"A woman named Hannah Burton," one of the newcomers reported. "Folks in Woodhaven will be lockin' their doors these nights."

Emily finished off her English muffin, swigged down her coffee. Woodhaven—where a woman had just been murdered and where there was, presumably, dirty politics—hardly seemed an inviting place to live for a year.

"More coffee?" Her waitress crossed to her table with a carafe in hand.

"Thanks, no." Emily smiled. Impatient to be out of here.

Behind the wheel again, she realized her drowsiness had evaporated. All at once Woodhaven seemed a fearful place. A town that had just experienced a murder, was deep in political battle. Hardly the serene little town that Dad had described.

In little over an hour Emily was driving into Woodhaven. On the surface it appeared a pretty little town, she conceded. Main Street had not succumbed to a mall, as back home in Evanston. Here Main Street was well maintained. Benches at intervals. Urns of fresh flowers. The shops were attractive, well kept. No buildings over three stories. An impressive red-brick building housed a local school.

She glanced at the directions she'd placed on the seat beside her. Make a left at Main Street and Hampton Road, follow Hampton Road for half a mile. Here was Hampton Road. She turned off Main Street. Her heart beginning to race. She drove past neat, modest houses similar to her own back in Evanston. Then the houses sat on larger plots, were more impressive.

The Winston house was a white brick colonial on the right, Emily reminded herself. The mail box at the edge of the road would display the family name. There was a pond on the opposite side of the road.

Last evening's rain had brought out the lushness of the greenery. Late-summer flowers bloomed in abundance. Emily felt a tightness in her throat as she watched for the house.

Then she saw an elegant, white brick colonial on the right, its grounds exquisitely landscaped. A pond across the road.

She leaned forward to read the name on the mail box. Yes! It read "Winston." *This is the house.* But now apprehension welled in her. The long circular driveway was lined with police cars. The three-car garage was open. A pair of men moved about inside, as though in serious search. The yellow tape that indicates a crime scene encircled the house. *Did the murder in Woodhaven—of a woman named Hannah Burton—happen here?*

Mom's words echoed in her mind: "When I talked to her, she told me about her husband. Your grandfather. The police were sure he'd committed suicide. She never believed that. She's convinced he was murdered—"

And now another murder? Who was Hannah Burton? A member of the family? Was there some strange curse on this house? No, Emily rejected. She didn't believe in curses.

But why has murder struck this house again?

Six

Shaken by the presence of the police cars, the telltale yellow tape, Emily threw open the car door, stepped out into the driveway. Instantly a police officer strode towards her.

"You can't park here, miss," he called out brusquely. "You'll have to—"

"It's all right, officer," a commanding feminine voice called from the doorway. Emily stood immobile as a slender, white-haired woman—her face pale and drawn—came into view. *She's Andrea Winston—my grandmother!* "Emily is a member of the family. She lives here."

"Okay, Mrs. Winston." His tone deferential.

"Emily—" Her grandmother walked towards her. *This is my grandmother—why don't I feel something for her?* Andrea's face incandescent, her smile exuding love. "I've waited so long for this day." Yet Emily sensed her determination not to be overwhelming. "I'm so happy to see you at last."

"I've arrived at a bad time—" *What a stupid remark—but what should I say?*

"This would be the most wonderful day in my life, except for this—" Andrea gestured towards the police cars. "In the middle of last night Hannah—my housekeeper since before you were born—was murdered."

"I'm so sorry—" *Why was her housekeeper murdered? First her husband, now the housekeeper.*

"You've had a long drive—" Andrea hesitated, seeming on the point of reaching for Emily's arm, then rejected this. *She's smart—she doesn't want to rush me.* "Come into the house—we'll have tea. We'll take care of your luggage later—" She glanced about, lifted a hand as though to signal a man emerging from the house. "Detective Jackson," she called.

"Yes, Mrs. Winston?" The detective came towards them.

"Could one of your men help us with my granddaughter's luggage?" *He looks surprised—he wasn't aware of a grown-up granddaughter. My arrival will start talk.*

"I can manage," Emily said hastily.

"No, no." A certain imperiousness in Andrea's voice—unintentional, Emily suspected. "I expected Jonah—my part-time gardener—to be here this morning to handle Emily's luggage. He was so upset about—about Hannah that I sent him home. Emily, give Detective Jackson your car keys."

Feeling awkward—abashed—Emily reached into her purse for her car keys, handed them over to Jackson. "Thank you," she told him with a shaky smile.

"Let's go into the house," Andrea repeated. "My daughter Carol—your Aunt Carol—is here. She'll put up tea. She came over as soon as I called to tell her the horrible news." Andrea flinched in pain. *She and Hannah were close. Did Hannah know about me? She was here all those years ago.*

"Hannah was so excited about your coming—" *It's as though she read my mind.* "She went out and bought new sheets and a bedspread for your room, badgered a wallpaper hanger to come on short notice and repaper. Oh, how she was fussing these last two days." Andrea's voice deepened in grief. "You would have loved Hannah. She was like a member of the family." Andrea struggled for poise. "Carol will put up tea for us."

She'd rather Carol wasn't here—that we could be alone together in this first meeting. What about her other daughter? Celeste. My birth mother. Is she here? I don't want to meet her!

Together they walked into the foyer. Emily suppressed an urge to run from the house. *I'm not ready for this.*

"This is all so new to me," she stammered. "It'll take a while—" For a moment the tears she saw in her grandmother's eyes unnerved her. This was rough for her, too. *But don't be taken in by her charm. Big-business executives are known for their ruthlessness. That's how they become big-business tycoons.*

"I know what a shock this has been for you—" Andrea's face reflected compassion. *Mom had explained that she and Dad had never told me I was adopted.* "I want you to take your time in adjusting."

"Thank you—" *Another stupid remark! But I can't just walk into the house and feel this is my family. That she's my grandmother.*

"Carol," Andrea called, a vein hammering at one temple. *Did the others—her children—object to her bringing me here?* "Emily has arrived—"

Moments later a tall, pencil-thin woman who would have been almost beautiful except for her air of petulance walked down the hall.

"It's hardly a pleasant occasion," she greeted Emily. "The house feels like an episode of 'Law and Order.'"

"What a cold way to put it," Andrea scolded her daughter. "Emily, this is your Aunt Carol. Your Uncle Leon had to leave on some business obligation—you'll meet him at dinner." *What about Celeste? How does she feel about my being here?*

"I've got water up for tea," Carol said before they could exchange perfunctory greetings. "That's Mother's addiction." *She's upset that I'm here. What about the others? The brother—Leon—and Celeste? Are they all furious with their mother?*

"There're still some of those delicious muffins Hannah made yesterday. We'll have those, Carol. Oh, put them in the oven for a few minutes." A flicker of pain on Andrea's face. "Hannah always insisted on that."

"I'll have to leave soon for a couple of hours." A strange defiance in Carol's eyes. *Does she expect an argument?* "A luncheon with my garden club committee. Afterwards I'll stop by the employment agency to set up interviews for a new housekeeper. I suppose you'll insist on interviewing them yourself."

"Emily and I can manage on our own for a few days. Hold up on that." Andrea recoiled from Carol's callous approach. *Carol is an iceberg. It doesn't bother her that Hannah was murdered. It's just an inconvenience.* "There were years when I managed the household and worked with your father at the company. I'm not in my dotage." Her tone acerbic.

Carol's face tightened. "I'll see to the tea and the muffins."

Emily felt covert hostility between her grandmother and aunt. *Because of me. The others are affronted by my sudden*

40

appearance, the talk it's sure to cause in town. And then there's the money angle. They resent another heiress to share in the Winston fortune.

"Carol means to be helpful." Andrea contrived an apologetic smile that was suspect to Emily. "This—this awful happening is so upsetting. It's still unreal to me. I wish you could have arrived under more pleasant circumstances."

"I'm so sorry about Hannah—"

"Tell me about your summer camp project back in Evanston," Andrea coaxed. "I was so impressed."

Emily was startled. *She knows about that?* Haltingly she began to relate how the summer camp had come about, how she'd managed to set it up at no expense to the town.

"We have a day care center at the company—for working mothers who need this arrangement," Andrea said. "It's worked out very well."

While she and her grandmother discussed the need for such arrangements for working mothers, Emily found part of her mind absorbed in a silent debate. *She comes over warm and charming, but is it all an act? This is a woman who runs a huge corporation. She didn't get there by being sweet and compassionate.*

Carol returned with tea and muffins. "I should leave now," she told Andrea. *It's as though I'm not here.* "You should try to get some sleep, Mother. Why don't you—"

"I'll be all right," Andrea brushed this aside. "How can I sleep at a time like this?"

"Should I call and have lunch sent over a little later?"

"I think I can handle that, Carol." Andrea frowned. "Run on to your luncheon. Oh, you put the call through to the locksmith? All locks must be changed immediately."

"I made the call," Carol assured her mother. "A workman should be here within an hour."

Over tea and muffins Andrea talked about her husband's death, her frustration that his murderer was never found. That the police would never recognize that he'd been murdered.

"Two unsolved murders in this town," she wound up. "Your grandfather's murder and that of a friend of mine some years later—also never solved. I pray that Hannah's murder doesn't follow that pattern. She shouldn't have died." Andrea paused, took a deep, painful breath. "Whoever invaded this house meant to kill me."

Emily gaped in shock. "Who would want to kill you?"

"I don't know," Andrea admitted. "But I'm sure I was the intended victim. Whoever killed your grandfather all those years ago came back to kill me." She gestured as though to dismiss this thought. "Do you play chess, Emily?"

"Yes—"

"For years I played chess every Sunday evening with my friend Roger. The one who was murdered. Such a kind man. He ran a local bookstore—did such fine things for this community. He was murdered almost twelve years ago." Andrea frowned in pain. " This has always been a quiet town. I recall only three murders in the past thirty-seven years. And all of them have touched me." *She sees a connection between them. She's frightened.* "But enough of this. We'll finish our tea and I'll show you up to your room. You'll want to unpack and settle in. We'll have lunch in a couple of hours." Her smile was ironic. "I'm still capable of preparing a meal."

If Mom and Dad have heard about the murder, they'll be so anxious. Is Andrea—my grandmother—right in thinking someone is trying to kill her? Will there be another attempt on her life? It's scary!

Seven

With the police still moving about the house, Emily and Andrea sat down to lunch in the small but charming breakfast area adjoining the super-modern kitchen—Hannah's happy domain. The three phone lines rang continuously. Andrea refused to pick up.

"Hannah was more than my housekeeper all these years. She was my very dear friend—" Andrea paused at the sound of activity in the foyer. "That's Paul," she told Emily. "He's heard about Hannah." She rose to her feet, crossed to the door that led to the hall. "Paul, in the kitchen," she called and turned to Emily. "Paul's the grandson of a very close friend—he's been with me almost two years now. He's a great asset to the company. You'll be working with him—he'll be your mentor."

Does he realize all the experience I have beyond school is a year of teaching? He'll hate having me on his hands.

"Andrea, we just heard—" A ruggedly handsome man in his late twenties strode into the room. His face reflected his anxiety. "I was worried when you didn't arrive at the office, but then I remembered you were expecting Emily—" He stopped short. *He knows about me. Who else in town knows?*

"This is Emily." Andrea confirmed his assumption, turned to Emily. "And this is Paul Cameron. I wished you two could have met under more pleasant circumstances."

"Hello, Emily—" His smile strained. *He looks so guarded. He figures Andrea has lost her mind in bringing me here.*

"Hi—" Emily managed a polite smile.

Paul turned back to Andrea. "Andrea, how awful for you! What can I do to help?"

"Sit down and have coffee with us." She poured coffee for him, brought it to the table. "Just keep things rolling at the

43

company," she said briskly. "I can't bring myself to come into the office until after Hannah's funeral. I gather it'll be a few days before the police release the body—" Andrea's voice cracked. "I can't believe she's gone. This is a nightmare—"

"Everything's under control," he assured Andrea. *Does everybody call her Andrea? I suppose I'm expected to call her "Grandmother"—but that seems so unreal.* Paul hesitated. "Do the police have any leads? But then it's still so early," he added hastily.

He knows about her husband's death—that she's convinced it was murder. He's anxious for her safety.

"The police haven't a clue. They suspect it was a robbery attempt that went wrong." Andrea's face tightened. "But I know better. I was meant to be the victim. And I'm not a nervous old bat," she said defiantly. "After all these years somebody has come back to kill me."

"I'll arrange for twenty-four-hour security at the house and at the company," Paul began. "I'll check with security people immediately. It's important that—"

"No," Andrea broke in. "I'll be careful."

"You can't be careful with a murderer on the loose," Paul rejected. "I'll set up twenty-four-hour coverage. That's important." *He's so intense. And I'll bet he's terribly bright.*

Andrea sighed. "As usual, you're right. But I'll loathe having strangers floating around the house."

Now Andrea and Paul discussed an immediate problem at the company, decided on proper action.

"I'll head back for the office," Paul wound up. "There should be security on duty within the next few hours. For now the police are on hand."

Seeming suddenly exhausted after Paul's departure, Andrea poured fresh coffee for Emily and herself, settled back in her comfortable captain's chair.

"Paul's very special. His grandmother—she has Alzheimer's now—was my closest friend since I was a little girl." Her face softened. "She had to be institutionalized last year. Paul's parents were killed in a plane crash—two years ago—he was all she had."

"That's so sad—"

"Paul was an only child. He came back home from New

York to see that she was properly cared for her. He's so good to her. He sees her regularly, though she seldom recognizes him. And when I offered him a job with the company, he accepted right away. He said he was fed up with the corporate rat race down in New York."

"These are rough times in the big corporations," Emily said, contempt creeping into her voice. "All the scandals that keep coming out into the open—" She paused, disconcerted. Winston Mail Order was a big corporation.

"I'm proud of the way I run my corporation." Andrea was all at once defensive. "We're what keeps this town functioning. We're the major employer in Woodhaven—and I make a point of taking good care of my people." She frowned, seemed to be fighting demons within. "There are elements in this town that are destructive. I won't allow them to take over. Your grandfather and I started this company forty-eight years ago— with nothing. And nobody—not even my own children—is going to tell me how to run it."

"I'm sorry," Emily stammered. "I didn't mean to infer—"

"I know you meant well," Andrea soothed. "But right now there are evil influences in this town that disturb me. Even my own children—" Her voice vibrated with rage. "Even my own children want me to sell out to those who'll destroy the company as David and I built it. But I won't have it, Emily. I'll win."

Emily was conscious of a soaring unease. What kind of internal battle lay ahead? Was murder the weapon that would be used to depose Andrea Winston? Some weird plot that dated back thirty-seven years, to when David Winston—her grandfather—had died?

Andrea—how can I call her "Grandmother"?—is convinced her husband's death and Hannah's are linked. Hannah killed because she got in the way. What about me? Will I be a victim because I'm in the way?

As Emily climbed the stairs to the upper floor, she heard Andrea in conversation with Detective Jackson in the foyer.

"I'd be grateful if you could have your men finish their investigation of the house before dinner time. This is hardly the welcome I'd planned for my granddaughter." *She's accus-*

45

tomed to giving orders—and having them respected. He must be terribly curious about this granddaughter who's suddenly appeared in town—but he wouldn't dare question the powerful Andrea Winston.

"We'll do our best, Mrs. Winston. We want to nail this murderer. We'll talk with Hannah's sister when she gets back into town. She may be able to give us a lead—some person with a grudge against Hannah. Somebody who—"

"Rubbish," Andrea broke in with a hint of anger. "Nobody meant to kill Hannah. I was the target. You know I have enemies in this town." *Why does she have enemies? Who hates her enough to try to kill her?*

With a sudden need to escape the horror of the past few hours, Emily hurried into her spacious bedroom, with tall, narrow windows on three sides. Part of an added wing, Emily surmised—when the family fortune soared. A glass slider led to a tiny balcony that looked out on the pond across the road. The rear windows looked out on the sprawling wooded area behind the house—providing a serene air of privacy. A small sanctuary for the moment.

She was conscious of an overwhelming tiredness. She'd slept little last night, then driven almost three hours. Lie down for a while, she ordered herself. No way that she would sleep, with her mind churning with questions.

She kicked off her shoes, stretched out on the queen-sized bed with its attractive brass headboard. Her eyes swept about the room. Andrea's words echoed in her mind: *"Hannah was so excited about your coming. She went out and bought new sheets and a bedspread for your room, badgered a wallpaper hanger to come on short notice and repaper. Oh, how she was fussing these last two days."*

Emily felt a surge of sadness that Hannah had met a violent death. She wished she could have known her. But moments later she drifted off into troubled slumber, to wake up with a start.

Feminine voices raised in anger floated up from the lower floor.

"Celeste, stop this tirade!" Emily recognized Andrea's voice. "I have a right to want to know my grandchild. You've never had a sense of responsibility. And you are not running an ad

46

in the *Enquirer* announcing that 'contrary to rumors I have no children.' I've never heard anything so insane in my life."

"Why are you doing this to me?" *That's Celeste—my birth mother.* "Why are you doing this to the family? The whole town will be talking of nothing else! Carol and Jane are distraught."

"I'm righting a wrong that happened twenty-three years ago. I've never had a day when I didn't feel sick about your giving your baby to strangers. My first grandchild."

"Derek and I are flying to East Hampton this afternoon. I'm closing up the house—I don't know when I'll be back. If I'll ever be back. Your precious granddaughter is tearing this family apart. I'll probably have to sell the house to survive—" Her voice exuded melodrama.

"You'll survive comfortably on the income from your trust fund," Andrea said drily. "Perhaps not in the style you and Derek would like."

Emily covered her ears with her hands. *I don't want to hear any more of this. Thank God, she's leaving town. I pray I never have to meet her.*

She heard the sound of a door being slammed shut. Exit Celeste. *I can sit down to dinner without facing her. Was she right, that Carol and Jane—my aunt and aunt-in-law—are distraught by my arrival?*

Eight

Sitting at the edge of her bed, Emily listened for sounds from downstairs. Celeste had left the house—she'd heard the slam of the front door. The police had left—at least, for the day. Just her grandmother and herself in the house. A wave of uncertainty swept over her. Was she supposed to remain here until somebody summoned her for dinner?

She glanced at the lovely, hand-painted porcelain clock that sat on the night table, was startled to realize she'd slept over two hours. *I haven't called home—Mom and Dad must be worried.* Fighting guilt, she reached for the phone, punched in the familiar number.

"Hello—" *Mom sounds breathless—she's been sitting by the phone, waiting for me to call.*

"Mom, it's me. I should have called earlier—but it's been kind of crazy here." She took a deep breath, launched into an account of Hannah's murder.

"Oh, my God!" Her mother was shaken. "Darling, I'm not sure you should stay there. Let me talk with Dad and—"

"It's okay," Emily soothed. "I'll be fine." *Will I?* "It's just that everything's in kind of an uproar. She—my grandmother—" Emily forced herself to this acknowledgment— "will have twenty-four-hour security guards around the house. The police are sure it was a robbery gone wrong." *What a convenient phrase.* "Probably a drifter going through town. It's going to be okay, Mom," she insisted with more conviction than she felt.

"Remember, darling—your grandmother truly loves you."

"I know." That was to comfort Mom.

Does Andrea Winston truly love me—or is she a woman desperately searching for someone with her own blood to carry on her empire? Does that give her a sense of immortality?

But what do I know about business? Who am I to try to learn to take over a huge corporation? I hate what they're doing to this world!

"Have you met the others yet?" Her mother's voice brought her back to the moment.

Emily answered her mother's questions about the family for another few moments. Clinging to this touch of home. Then her mother aborted the conversation.

"This isn't a local call—we really shouldn't talk so long. Next time let me call you back. But Emily, be careful." Anxiety deepened her mother's voice. "It scares me that you're living in a house where a murder has just been committed." And Andrea was convinced another murder had happened in this house thirty-seven years ago.

Off the phone, Emily tried to read for a while, abandoned this to pace about the room—debating about when she should go downstairs. She stiffened to attention at the sound of a car turning into the driveway, then moved to a front-facing window and gazed below.

As she'd expected, the police cars had all departed. A security-company car was parked down below. A security guard already on duty? Paul had worked fast. Did he believe that whoever killed Hannah would come back to try again? It was an unnerving possibility.

A small panel truck sat just before the house. She read its ID. Lamont Catering Service. Dinner was arriving. It was time to go downstairs. *Relax—you're not going to the guillotine.*

Walking down the stairs, she heard activity at the rear of the house. In the kitchen, she gathered. Uncertain of her destination, she paused in the downstairs hall, saw a woman setting the table in the dining room. The catering service waitress, here to serve dinner.

Feeling as though she was playing a role in a play, Emily walked into the elegantly furnished living room. She was conscious of a tightness between her shoulderblades. So tense, she scolded herself—just because she'd be meeting all those other family members in a very little while.

She glanced about the living room. Mom would love it, she thought. So elegant yet with an inviting air. She remembered the slipcovers Mom had wanted to order for their living room, but had refrained because of the drop in Dad's business. Dad said the Winston fortune ran into many millions. As one of the heirs, one day she could give Mom and Dad a house as beautiful as this.

Instantly she was suffused with guilt. *The others must think I'm here just to share one day in all that money. That's part of it, yes—but I want so much to know who I am. It's as though I've been living a lie all my life.*

Trying to gear herself for the encounter ahead, she reached for a suspense novel from a pile of books on the console table, sat in a lounge chair to read. *I won't panic. These are just people.*

She struggled to focus on the opening page of the novel, heard a car being parked outside, then voices. *Who's arriving? Carol—who clearly resents my presence here—and her family? Or Leon and his family? Not Celeste. Thank God for that.*

She heard a man's voice in the foyer now. Leon?

"Raymond, you behave yourself this evening. I don't want you upsetting your grandmother." *Raymond must be her grandson.* "Hello, Mother—" *Andrea is coming down the stairs.*

"Hello, Mother—" A feminine voice now. *Leon's wife, Jane.*

"Why is a security company car sitting at the foot of the driveway?" Leon demanded.

"Because Paul arranged for twenty-four-hour security for me." Andrea's tone was acerbic. "I'm not bucking for a third murder in this house."

"You heard the detectives—" Leon clucked in reproach. "Hannah was killed by a drifter trying to rob you. After all, this is the finest house in town—he expected to hit pay dirt. He's long gone by now."

"The police make mistakes," Andrea began. "They—"

"They found your best silver scattered about the dining-room floor. The burglar got scared when he heard Hannah moving about her room. He ran—"

"There was no robbery attempt—someone meant to kill me. He expected that I would be alone in the house—it was supposed to be Hannah's day off. It's not my first encounter with police bungling." *Her children don't believe their father was murdered. And she knows this.*

Emily heard another car arrive, then voices. Carol's, then two young girls. *Carol's twins, Elaine and Deirdre.*

"Can't you two ever stop fighting?" Carol complained. "Stop it this minute." The three were walking into the house, Emily gathered. "Girls, go kiss your grandmother," Carol ordered.

Emily rose to her feet. Her face tinged with color. *I'm not the enemy—I'm family.* Prodded by a sudden defiance, she strode across the living room and into the hall.

"Emily—" Andrea said tenderly. "I hope you had a restful nap."

"I did." Emily managed a tentative smile as she gazed at the gathering in the foyer. *They all look so hostile—even the kids.*

Andrea took swift steps to her, dropped an arm about her waist. "You've met your Aunt Carol," she began and frowned. "Carol, where's Tom?"

"He was tied up at the office—he'll be here shortly."

"This is your Uncle Leon—"

"You've had a rough welcome," he said gently, moving towards her. "Most of the time this is a very quiet town. And this is your Aunt Jane—" He reached to draw his wife closer. "Jane will be happy to show you around town, help you settle in."

"Thank you." *Jane didn't expect him to say that. Why does she seem so startled?*

Leon introduced the three grandchildren, who expressed only boredom.

"We'll go in to dinner now," Andrea announced at a signal from the dining room. "Tom will join us when he arrives."

"Mother, I can loan you Della until you hire a new house-keeper," Carol offered, breaking the strained silence as they strolled into the dining room.

"No need," Andrea dismissed this. "Emily and I will manage for the next few days on our own."

"I know you're upset, Mother—but do you really want security guards prowling around the grounds?" Leon grimaced as he considered this. "It's catering to a wave of fear in town."

"Paul suggested it," Carol pounced. "He has such a sense of melodrama."

"Carol, Hannah was murdered in this house last night."

Andrea struggled for poise. "That was not melodrama. Hannah lost her life." She gestured for silence as two members of the catering staff came into the dining room to serve the first course. "So, Raymond—and Elaine and Deirdre—are you happy to be back in school?"

The three youngest uttered their sullen complaints about their respective schools. Andrea was disappointed in these grandchildren, Emily interpreted. Smug, spoiled brats. Her first cousins.

"You kids are so spoiled," Leon interrupted them as the servers left the dining room. "Can't you find anything positive in your schools?"

Jane shot a reproving glance at Leon. "Lamont turns out fine meals. This mushroom sweet potato soup is delicious."

"Hot soup in summer?" Elaine grunted. "Yuck."

"This house is air-conditioned. We have hot soup in summer," Andrea rebuked. *She'd like to smack the bad-mannered little brat.*

"I hear Paul has been creating an uproar again with the Town Council," Carol told her mother. "He's dug up some old ruling that there must be a referendum before any major zoning change can be scheduled."

"That's the way it should be," Andrea said. "Paul and I have discussed it at great length. Nine people on the Town Council shouldn't have final say on any major subject."

"The Council is just trying to bring this town into the twenty-first century," Leon tried to placate his mother.

"We're still back in the nineteenth century," Carol jeered.

What kind of major zoning change? Something that would benefit a handful of people in town? Paul's so intense. He cares about people.

"Mother, you shouldn't have gone to the bother of having us all for dinner this evening." Carol shook her head in disapproval. "You should be resting."

"It was important for us to sit down together tonight as a family. Dinner was no trouble," Andrea insisted. "Just a phone call to the people at Lamont Catering. Raymond, you're gaining weight," she reproached. "All that junk food."

"Not much junk food in this town. We're still living in the Middle Ages." A sharp edge to Leon's voice.

"We don't need a mall in this town," Andrea said tersely. "To kill all the small businesses on Main Street?"

"But there's inadequate parking in town," Leon began.

"Let the town provide more parking." Andrea bristled. "There's that whole rundown area close to Main Street that should come down—it would provide all the parking needed. But of course"—She rushed ahead because Leon was about to attack this thinking—"the landlords want to keep on collecting rents for those hovels that aren't fit for human habitation."

All at once shouting somewhere close to the house destroyed the night silence. Male voices. One thunderous, the other sounding terrified. Those at the table exchanged fearful glances.

"I'll see what's going on!" Leon rose to his feet, strode from the room.

"Leon, be careful—" Jane called after him.

"The security man must have encountered an intruder," Emily said after a moment. "Shouldn't we call the police?"

"Call 911, Emily," Andrea ordered and pointed to a phone that sat on a table between two tall windows. "He may need back-up."

"It must be some lunatic on the loose—" Carol's voice was shrill. "The same one who murdered Hannah."

"Wow!" Raymond glowed, darting from his chair to a window. "This is like watching a TV program."

"Raymond, get away from that window!" Jane shrieked while loud voices ricocheted in the wooded area behind the house. "He may have a gun—"

"I hate this soup," Deirdre sulked. "What do we have next?"

"Deirdre, be quiet," Andrea said. But as a distraction she summoned the kitchen to clear the table and bring in the next course.

The two servers arrived instantly, seeming unaware of the fracas behind the house. They removed the soup course, returned to serve the main course. Grilled salmon, broccoli and baked potato.

"I hate fish," Elaine announced and turned to her mother. "Can I take mine home for Buffy?"

"We'll see." Carol was short. "But eat your broccoli and potato—it's good for you. Buffy's the twins' new kitten," she explained to her mother and Emily. "The girls adore her."

"What happened to the young Siamese?" Andrea asked as police sirens shrieked close by.

"Some bird-loving idiot put poison in her garden," Carol explained. "The Siamese died last week."

All eyes swung to the entrance as male voices were heard in the foyer. Leon strode into view.

"It appears Hannah's murder has been solved," he said with a reassuring smile. "You said, Mother, that it was someone who knew Hannah was always off on Tuesday nights. Except for last night."

"Frank, what is this all about?" Andrea demanded as two other men followed Leon. "This is Detective Harris," she told the others.

"Your security guard—" Harris identified the man to his left— "discovered a man lurking in the woods behind the house." He paused. "It was Dennis—" He seemed uncomfortable in this admission. "You know, the creepy guy."

"Sheila Lodge's son?" Andrea gaped in disbelief.

"Who's she?" Carol asked.

"You know her, Carol." Andrea was impatient. "She's the Wilson's housekeeper—her son Dennis has an IQ of about sixty-five. He's harmless, clumsy, a little afraid of almost everything. Hannah would give him treats when he wandered back of the house. He'd never kill her."

"He was asleep back there," Harris picked up. "Beside him we saw a sterling silver spoon—part of the set that was scattered about your dining-room floor the night Hannah Burton was murdered." He turned to Leon. "Your son identified it."

"That's right," Leon concurred. "He came in, meaning to steal the silver, was frightened when he heard sounds in the house. Hannah came out, he killed her—"

"I don't believe that!" Andrea scoffed. *Because she doesn't want to believe it?* "He cries if he sees a dead bird."

"We've taken him into custody," Harris said. "He'll go to the grand jury and then to trial." He flinched before Andrea's scathing glare. "He won't serve prison time—he'll probably be committed."

"He hasn't been convicted yet," Jane reminded timorously.

"He won't be," Andrea predicted. "You have no real evidence."

"He confessed," the security guard joined in now. "At first he denied it. He said, 'Hannah gave me cookies. She liked me.' Then he retracted his denial."

"Dennis would say anything to please someone questioning him," Andrea shot back. "Hannah's murderer is still on the loose."

Nine

At Leon's insistence the family had gathered again around the dining table. He was determined to maintain a flow of small talk as they resumed eating, though Andrea herself sat grimly silent—barely touched her food, Emily noted. It was a relief when dessert and coffee were served and the three youngest erupted into noisy argument.

"You got the biggest slice of cake," Elaine accused Raymond. "You told one of those dorks in the kitchen to do that!"

Andrea allowed the battle to continue for a couple of minutes. "That's enough," she ordered. "Why can't you teach your children manners?" Her eyes swept from Leon to Jane to Carol. *Carol's husband still isn't here. Is he just avoiding another unpleasant family dinner?*

"It's been a trying day, Mother," Leon soothed. "But you should feel better. You weren't the intended victim." *He's talking to her as though she was a difficult child.* "Dennis just thought he could steal the silver—and Hannah got in the way."

"Dennis is innocent. A trial will prove that." Andrea's eyes defied him. "We still have a murderer on the loose."

"Leon's right—you've had a trying day, Mother," Carol said. "Why don't we all clear out so you can get some rest?"

In a sudden burst of energy the others left. Andrea and Emily settled themselves in the living room. The catering people—perhaps feeling the undercurrent of unease in the house—departed in unexpected haste. An eerie silence engulfed the house.

Andrea rose from her chair, began to pace.

"I don't like this business of incarcerating Dennis. He's a twenty-nine-year-old with the mind of seven. He must be terrified."

"The police will take that into account," Emily comforted.

Andrea abandoned pacing. Her face tightened in resolve. "I'm not leaving him in the care of a legal aide. I know some are good attorneys—but I want the best for him." She crossed to the phone. "I'm calling Paul. He'll handle this for me." She punched in numbers, waited for a response. "Paul, I know it's late—but could you come over to the house? Something's come up—" She listened, took a deep breath. "Thanks, Paul."

"He's coming over?" *Why is my heart pounding this way?*

"Right away."

"I'll put up coffee—" Emily rose to her feet, all at once felt self-conscious. *Do I look as I'm taking over?*

"That'll be nice. And the catering people said there was leftover Black Forest cake in the refrigerator." She frowned in thought. "I know that my children are convinced I'm off the wall in believing somebody is out to kill me. But Hannah was murdered because the killer didn't expect her to be at the house on a Tuesday night. I'm always alone on Tuesday nights. The silver spoon found with Dennis," she pinpointed, "was planted there."

In the kitchen Emily brought out plates for the Black Forest cake, waited for the surge from the coffee-maker that said it was ready to pour. Now she heard a car pull up in the driveway.

Paul's here! Why do I feel so excited at the prospect of seeing him? Because he's so intense? Because he cares about people? Because he's so charismatic?

She heard the front door open. Andrea was greeting Paul. They were talking as they walked from the foyer into the living room. Struggling for poise, she prepared a tray, geared herself for the encounter with Paul. *What is the matter with me? I barely know him—and I'm behaving like a lovesick sixteen-year-old.*

She walked into the living room. Paul stopped in the middle of a sentence, hurried to take the tray from her.

"Hi. Emily." His smile was warm. His eyes quizzical.

"Paul, you understand the situation," Andrea said. "I want Dennis to have the best defense lawyer available—I don't give a damn what it costs."

"I'll make calls first thing in the morning," he promised,

depositing the tray on the huge mahogany and glass coffee table. He glanced at his watch. "Maybe I can get through tonight."

"Black Forest cake is my favorite," Andrea began, as though to ease the tension. "But I couldn't touch it earlier."

Andrea seems more relaxed with Paul here. I think part of him likes me—but another part distrusts me. He thinks I'm here to take advantage of Andrea.

"We're keeping the security on duty," Paul pressed. "Just because the police have Dennis behind bars is no reason to stop that." *He doesn't believe Dennis killed Hannah—or is he pretending to believe that to ingratiate himself with Andrea?*

"Security stays," Andrea said with conviction. "Indefinitely." She frowned. "The police will notify Dennis's mother. Sheila will be so upset."

"Has there been any word about when the police will release Hannah's body?" Paul asked. "Is there anything I can do to help with funeral arrangements?"

"They won't say just yet when they'll release Hannah's body," Andrea told him. "I don't know why there should be any hold-up on this. But I've spoken with Rhoda—Hannah's sister—and with her approval I've made all the arrangements." Andrea reached for her coffee, drained the cup. "One thing more. When you talk with an attorney about defending Dennis, tell him I'd like him to put a private investigator on the case. I want Dennis cleared."

Emily glanced at the clock on her night table with a flicker of guilt as she talked with Wendy. Andrea had encouraged her to use the phone for long-distance calls whenever she liked: "We have unlimited service." Andrea realized she was concerned about running up big bills.

"Tell me about this guy," Wendy brought her back to the moment. "Young, handsome, in an important job," she drawled. "You're living a chick-lit novel."

"He's probably dreading the thought of training me to do whatever Andrea expects me to do—"

"You call her Andrea?" Awe in Wendy's voice.

"I can't call her Grandma—not yet—" *Will I ever feel like that?*

58

"This business about the murder—" Wendy was serious now. "You tell your folks?"

"You know I did. They're so upset—but I told them I'd be fine."

"If it wasn't for Paul, I'd say you should run like hell for home," Wendy admitted. "But he sounds special."

"He's being nice to me for Andrea's sake. I don't think he trusts my motive for being here. He's probably sure I'm here for my prospective inheritance." *Why do I feel self-conscious at being one of her heirs?*

"That's a good reason. But don't let the other creeps in the family throw you," Wendy cautioned. "But face it, honey— sooner or later you'll meet your birth mother."

"The later the better." *She hates me. She wouldn't even allow her mother to adopt me. I feel nothing for her. Except disgust.*

"We'd both better get some sleep." Wendy smothered a yawn. "I have to be up by six-thirty tomorrow morning. My class is overcrowded again—and the town's still fighting about a raise in property taxes. The only way we'll ever get more teachers."

"I'm not to start at the office for another few days—but from what I hear, Andrea is there no later than eight a.m."

"And Paul?" Wendy teased.

"Now who's reading chick-lit?" Emily clucked. "On the job he'll probably be an ogre."

Leon emerged from showering, dressed. Sounds from the lower floor told him Jane was getting Raymond off to school. *Wait until the school bus picks him up, then go down for breakfast. Why can't Mother understand that this is the time to sell? The Clifford people are dying to take over Winston Mail Order. They'll make an offer she'll never see again. I'm bringing her the plum of her life, damn it. How much longer can she keep running the company?*

He heard Jane prodding Raymond to the front door. His posh private school had complained last semester about how Raymond kept the bus waiting. He was a teenager—they should expect rebellion.

"Leon—" Jane called from the foot of the stairs. "I'm putting up your breakfast."

"I'll be right down." Long ago he'd made Jane understand

their housekeeper/cook was to be on duty from after break-fast through dinner. He didn't want to deal with a stranger in the house before breakfast.

Walking down the stairs, he remembered his mother's insist-ence that Dennis wasn't guilty. She was becoming irrational of late. Did other people realize that? Like this craziness of bringing in that supposed granddaughter after all these years.

He opened the front door, picked up the morning's *Enquirer*, read the headline: "LOCAL WOMAN MURDERED. POLICE SUSPECT CLEARED."

Swearing under his breath as he read, he stalked down the hall to the kitchen.

"The cops are off their rocker," he told Jane as he contin-ued to read. "Some fancy lawyer showed up at the police precinct at two a.m., along with Dennis's mother. He got the creep released."

"How could his mother afford a fancy lawyer?" Jane was curious. "Maybe the Wilsons brought him in."

"I wouldn't put it past Mother—she was so upset when the cops took him in. Hell, the security guy found him hiding there in the woods. A piece of silver from the house lying right beside him. What more proof do they need that he killed Hannah?"

Jane glanced up from the griddle. "What else does it say?"

"Dennis's mother told the police that he periodically runs away for a couple days when he's been scolded for something. She said with his hands so bad he'd been told not to use the good glasses. What about his hands?" Leon demanded, then read on. "He has some condition where his fingers don't work properly. They decided no way could he have stabbed Hannah."

"What about fingerprints?" Jane pursued. "Wouldn't there be fingerprints on the knife?"

"They'd be blood-smeared," Leon guessed. "Unidentifiable. Damn, I thought we'd shown Mother that this wasn't an attempt on her life. Just a simple robbery. You know how touchy she gets every year at this time. The anniversary of my father's suicide." He squinted in thought. "If she's behind the lawyer that came in, you can bet Paul put her up to it."

"Isn't Paul a lawyer?"

"He has a law degree—or so he claims. Now he just wants to use it as a politician."

"Paul doesn't hold any political office." Jane slid pancakes onto a plate, poured coffee into an oversized mug. "Sit down and eat before your pancakes get cold."

"He's got political ideas. Why do you think he's trying to mess up that deal to bring a mall to town? I wouldn't be surprised to see him run for the Town Council next election." *She wouldn't admit it on her deathbed, but Jane is soft on Paul. She said once that he looks like a movie star.* "If he'll butt out, I can persuade Mother to talk to the Clifford people."

"Not just yet," Jane protested. "Give her time to get over Hannah's murder."

"If she keeps harping on this mania about somebody wanting to kill her, she'll discover people will see her as a candidate for a loony bin." He was thoughtful. "Maybe we should talk to a shrink about this obsession of hers. It's getting out of hand."

Ten

After a restless night Emily awoke with a sense of falling through space. She turned to the clock on her night table, was startled. It was almost nine a.m. With a feeling of guilt that she'd slept this late, she hurried to shower and dress. Conscious of the heavy silence of the house.

She debated about what to wear, settled on turquoise slacks and a matching top. Feeling at a loose end, unsure of what the day would bring, she opened the drapes of a front-facing window and gazed out at the new morning. Yesterday's glorious sunshine was not replicated today. Murky clouds floated across the sky, hinted at imminent storms. Not a leaf stirred on the towering trees that formed a barrier between the house and its neighbor to the left.

Andrea—her grandmother—was head of a major corporation, she considered. A category she loathed. But here was none of the opulence she'd feared she'd encounter. No huge staff of servants. Only a housekeeper and a cleaning woman who came in by the day. A gardener who came in as needed.

Leaving her room, Emily heard voices downstairs. Andrea and another woman.

"I just can't believe Hannah's gone," an unfamiliar feminine voice said. "When I tried to come in yesterday, the cops sent me away—"

"Doris, it's all right," Andrea soothed. "I understood."

"I know it's a bad time to ask, but could I take off today? My niece is coming home from the hospital with her new baby later this morning—and I want to clean up the house for her and see her and the baby settled in. Her husband's a long-distance trucker—he'll be on the road."

"Sure, Doris. No problem," Andrea said and smiled as Emily

approached. "Good-morning, Emily. This is Doris, who comes in by day to take care of the house—"

"Hello, Doris." *Mom is grateful to have a woman come in every two weeks.*

"This is my granddaughter, Emily," Andrea introduced her. *Doris is startled—she didn't know there was a third grand-daughter.* "She'll be living with me for a while."

"Now ain't that nice?" Doris turned to inspect Emily. "She's so pretty. And she looks just like you." *Do I?*

"Thank you." Andrea seemed pleased.

"I'd better get over to my niece's house. You're sure it'll be all right for me to take off today?"

"It's all right, Doris."

Doris sighed. "I can't believe somebody came into the house and murdered Hannah. It's like something you'd see on TV."

"Hannah will be deeply missed." Andrea's face tightened. "This never should have happened. I'm on my way over to see her sister Rhoda. She's devastated."

"Rhoda and her family go to my church. I'll be takin' time off for the funeral," Doris warned.

"A lot of this town will be there, Doris." Now Andrea gave Doris instructions about the blood-stained floor in Hannah's room. Awkwardly Emily stood in waiting. *What am I to do today? Wouldn't it be sensible for me to go in to the office? But what will I do there? So I'm computer-literate, as Dad said. How does that prepare me to work at Winston Mail Order?*

In a corner of her mind she knew the thought of going into the office was to see Paul. He was to be her mentor, Andrea had said.

"I shouldn't be leaving you alone this way." Andrea invaded her introspection. "But I know you understand. I must help Rhoda through this awful time."

"Of course—" *It's difficult to be distrustful of Andrea's motives. But am I being naively gullible? People don't get to the top without being tough, stepping on toes.*

"Why don't you drive into town? Play the tourist?" Andrea paused. "You might call Jane—her number's in the phone book on the desk in the den. She's very shy but she opens to anyone who's friendly. But you might prefer to be on your

own for a while. Have lunch at the Oasis. You can't miss it—
it's right on Main Street, at the corner of Clayton Avenue. I'll
be home well before dinner—which Lamont will send over.
Oh, but you haven't had breakfast—"

"I'll check out the fridge," Emily said quickly. "I'm sure
there'll be breakfast makings there."

"There's a carafe of coffee ready. And security is still on
duty—not that you should be afraid," Andrea reassured her.
"I'm the prime target—though nobody except Paul and me
appear to believe that."

Feeling herself an intruder in Hannah's kitchen, Emily reached
for a small, non-stick skillet suspended from a wrought-iron
fixture. *This kitchen is like something out of a fine magazine—
Mom would adore it.* From the top-of-the-line refrigerator she
brought out a container of egg whites, a slice of low-fat ched-
dar cheese. *Hannah was concerned about nutrition—like Mom
and Dad. I'm only about ninety-five miles from them—why do
I feel as though I was on another planet?*

She dropped two slices of wholewheat bread into the toaster,
crossed to the Garland range. Mom would be in heaven with
a range like this, she thought tenderly. She'd buy Mom a
Garland range! Not right away of course, but with the lavish
salary Andrea would be paying her—and no living expenses—
she'd be able to save up enough by Mom's birthday.

She prepared her cheese omelet, plucked her toast from the
toaster, poured a large mug of coffee, and sat down in the
breakfast area in an aura of unreality. A twenty-first century
Cinderella, she taunted herself.

Now she considered how she would spend this first full day
in Woodhaven. She wouldn't call Jane—she'd just wander
around on her own. Maybe shop some little gift for Mom and
Dad, visit the local library in the morning, have lunch at—
what was the place Andrea mentioned? The Oasis. But later
she'd talk to Andrea about starting work tomorrow morning.

*It's not that I'm eager to see Paul again. All right, maybe
I am. But he distrusts me—I see that in his eyes. The whole
family thinks I'm taking advantage of Andrea's offer because
of all the money involved. Can't they understand I need to
know who I am?*

What will Andrea tell people about me? She told that detective I was her granddaughter. Do they wonder who's my mother? How does she plan on dealing with that?

Breakfast swiftly eaten—because she realized with astonishment that she was hungry—she lingered over strong, fragrant coffee. One thing she must admit about Andrea. Despite her exalted position she was unpretentious, down-to-earth.

All at once she was aware she wasn't alone in the house. She heard footsteps in the hall. Heavy—male—footsteps, she pinpointed. Walking down the hall towards the kitchen. Her heart began to pound.

"Good-morning, Emily." Clutching a parcel, briefcase, and a large bouquet of mixed flowers—highlighted by exquisite red roses—Leon strolled into view. "Did I startle you?" He was solicitous.

"No," she said, her smile strained. "Well, a bit. I thought I was alone in the house." *Such a big house.*

"I gather my mother hasn't come down yet—and that's good. She needs the rest."

"She's out already. She's gone to be with Hannah's sister Rhoda."

"That's my mother," Leon said with affectionate indulgence. "Jane sent me over with this casserole she'd taken from the freezer—in the event you and Mother have a hankering for a late-night snack. Jane's good that way."

"How thoughtful of her—" Emily rose awkwardly from her chair, crossed to take the casserole from Leon. "I'll put it in the refrigerator."

"Jane insisted I put the flowers in Mother's bedroom—" He began to rummage in an upper cabinet, found a vase. "These are all from our garden," he reported while he put water in the vase, arranged the flowers. "Jane just creates miracles there."

"They're lovely." *Have I been misreading the family? He and Jane hardly seem to resent me. Maybe it's just Celeste and Carol.*

"I'll run up and leave the flowers on Mother's night table. She adores flowers—especially red roses." *Like me.* "Then I'll be on my way." He hesitated. "I know this whole situation must be very traumatic for you." He radiated sympathy. "But everything will work out in time."

"I'm sure it will." She felt an unexpected relief at this show of compassion.

With Leon headed upstairs, Emily carried the breakfast dishes to the sink, rinsed them, was about to place them in the dishwasher when an urgent voice—Leon's—stopped her short.

"Emily, get out of the house!" he yelled from the upper floor. "Get out fast—by the kitchen door! Emily, run!" His voice hoarse as he charged down the stairs.

Emily abandoned the dishes, sped to the kitchen door, hurried out into the humid, grey morning. *What's happening?*

"What's going on?" Gun in hand, the security guard on duty rushed to her side. "Are you okay, miss?"

"I'm all right," Emily gasped, just as Leon appeared— running from the front of the house.

"What the hell's the matter with you?" Leon demanded of the security guard. His breathing labored. "Who got past you and into the house? There's a bomb ticking away in the upstairs hallway!" He pulled a cellphone from a jacket pocket. "I'm calling the bomb squad!"

"Where is it located?" The security guard reached for his own cellphone.

"In the upstairs hallway, just outside the guest room," Leon spat out. *Outside my room!* "But don't go into the house unless you're trained for this," he warned, then focused on the cellphone. "This is the Winston house. We have a ticking bomb. Send the bomb squad!"

Cold with shock, Emily tried to understand what was happening. Somebody had sneaked into the house, placed a bomb in the upstairs hallway. Just outside the guest room.

Outside my bedroom! Am I meant to be the next victim?

Eleven

In minutes three police cars, a truck indicating it carried a bomb squad, and an ambulance swung into the driveway, pulled to a screeching stop. Occupants leapt out—equipment in tow.

"Where's the bomb?" a member of the bomb squad yelled, charging towards the house.

"At the door of a second-floor bedroom in the added wing," Leon reported. "To the right at the head of the stairs."

"You people—move back," he ordered. "Away from the house!"

He shouted orders to the crew. Lugging equipment, they charged into the house. Four who'd emerged from the police cars trailed them. A pair of detectives—unfamiliar to Emily—approached.

"Who found the bomb?" the older detective asked.

"I did," Leon told him. "I was carrying a vase of flowers up to my mother's bedroom—it's right across from the guest room. I didn't notice the ticking until I was almost at the top of the stairs. It came from a small, gift-wrapped box sitting on the floor outside the guest room. I shouted to Emily—" He nodded towards her. "I told her to get out fast—I didn't know when it would go off. I must have dropped the vase as I raced out of the house—"

The other detective focused on the security guard. "You're security?" The police knew about the arrangements.

"That's right," the guard confirmed, seeming uneasy.

"How did somebody get into the house?" the older detective challenged. "Where the hell were you?"

"I can't be everywhere at once." The security guard was defensive. Nervous. "This is a two-acre plot—"

"We'll beef up security." Leon was terse. He turned to Emily. "Paul's supposed to be taking care of that, isn't he?"

Emily nodded. "I believe so—" But Paul wasn't responsible for this invasion.

"It's not good enough." Leon reached for his cellphone. "Let's get him over here."

Leon called Paul at the company. With soaring apprehension, Emily focused on the house. Leon's voice was sharp as he spoke with someone at the company. Paul was unavailable.

"Page him. Tell him to come immediately to Mrs. Winston's house. This is urgent!" Leon slid the cellphone back into a jacket pocket.

"How did an intruder get in?" the younger detective probed. "Was the front door unlocked?"

"It was locked," Leon told him. "After what happened, I gave my mother explicit instructions to see that it was locked. I used my key to get into the house. The side door and the rear door were locked, also. I'm sure of that." He sighed. "Hannah's murder has us all on edge. Everybody in town is locking doors now."

"The house has CAC?" the other detective asked. Central air-conditioning. Leon nodded. "Then all the windows were closed," he assumed. "What about the garage doors?"

"They're secured," Leon said.

Conversation suddenly ceased. The bomb squad was emerging from the house. One member held a small parcel aloft.

"This is the sucker," he announced. "A homemade bomb—badly constructed. It was set to go off when the box was opened." Unexpectedly he chuckled. "I'm not sure it would have—a strictly amateur job. It gave us no trouble."

"Thank God, nobody was hurt." Leon whistled softly in relief, glanced at his watch. "I have to get going—I have an important business meeting. Emily, you'll explain to Mother what's happened. No need to alert her," he decided after a moment of thought. "Tell her when she comes home."

"I'll explain," Emily promised. *That bomb was meant for Andrea or me. It was in front of my door. By intent or accident? But why me?*

"You tell Paul he has to do something about security," Leon began and swore under his breath. An *Enquirer* car had turned into the driveway, followed by a car belonging to the local weekly. "The vultures are descending."

Leon rushed off to his car. The two detectives moved forward to deal with the press. Emily stood by with the security guard while reporters spouted questions and photographers shot photos of the house.

"I hope the newspapers don't make out it was my fault the perp got into the house," the security guard mumbled.

Emily stiffened in alarm. The reporters and photographers were gazing in the direction of her and the security guard. Then—in a surge of relief—Emily noted that the detectives were steering the reporters away.

"That's all we can tell you right now. No more discussion, no more photos." The older detective was brusque. "Check with downtown for further reports."

How awful if this is picked up by the newspapers back home. Mom and Dad will be horrified. They'll insist I leave immediately.

The bomb squad took off. The detectives—along with their own crew—remained for more explorations.

"We'll be here for a while," the younger detective said. "We're searching for fingerprints. Some lead to who came into the house to plant that bomb."

"It was a bad job," the other detective reminded, but he was somber. "We don't often see this kind of—incident—in Woodhaven."

The two detectives headed for the woods behind the house. Emily stood with the disgruntled security guard, who seemed uncertain about how to proceed. With the police here, it was unlikely there'd be any need for his services in the next few hours.

Paul would be arriving any moment, she suspected. Per Leon's instructions she would brief him on what had occurred. Leon was right—no point in bringing Andrea home just now. But she'd be shocked when she learned about this latest attempt at murder. *On whose life? Hers—or mine?*

"No way one man can keep watch of this big house," the security guard interrupted her introspection. "I don't have eyes in back of my head."

"I'm sure everybody realizes that," Emily soothed him.

We believed the presence of a security guard would scare predators away. It hasn't. Doesn't this prove Hannah wasn't murdered by a drifter intent on burglary?

Am I meant to be the next victim?

Twelve

Emily and the security guard waited in the sultry humidity of the overcast morning. Had Paul been reached? Was it ridiculous to stand out here and wait for him—as though he'd arrive at any moment?

"Who's that coming now?" The security guard stared down the driveway at the SUV that had just turned off the road.

"It's Paul Cameron." *Why is my heart pounding this way?* "He's handling security arrangements for the house," Emily reminded the security guard.

"I've been with the company almost eleven years." He seemed to be bracing for trouble. "We never had anything like this happen. Like I said, this is a big stretch of property for one man to watch—"

Paul left his car in front of the house, hurried to Emily and the security guard. His face etched with anxiety. "Is everybody all right?"

"We're all okay. Andrea wasn't here—she'd gone over to be with Hannah's sister. She doesn't even know yet," Emily told him.

"What's *happened*? Leon just said it was urgent I get over here."

Striving for calm, Emily explained, conscious of fresh alarm in Paul. "Leon feels the security needs beefing up."

"All right, I'll take care of that." He turned to the security guard. "This is no reflection on you. Just go and complete your shift. You'll have help on your next one."

"Okay—" The guard sounded relieved. "This is a nasty situation."

"The house is clear?" Paul sought reassurance.

"Absolutely," the security guard assured him. "The bomb squad had no trouble—it was an amateur job. There's just the police crew in the house now—searching for evidence."

"Good," Paul approved and turned to Emily. "Let's go inside—I'll put through some calls."

"Yes—" Emily managed a shaky smile.

In the house they settled themselves in the den. Paul called the security service, issued orders about increasing coverage.

"Immediately," he stressed.

"Would you like some coffee?" Emily asked when Paul was off the phone.

"Right now I want to arrange for floodlights to be installed—on every side of the house. And then," he said gently, "let's go out for an early lunch. It'll do you good to get away from here."

Tense, striving for calm, Emily sat in the den and pretended to read the *Enquirer*—delivered to the house each morning—while Paul made more phone calls. She was conscious of the steady hum of voices on the upper floor. The police investigators, searching for fingerprints—any small clue—that would lead them to the person who'd planted the bomb. A crude bomb, they'd emphasized. Would he—or she—have been sharp enough to have worn gloves?

Paul sat at the desk—phone in hand. Determined to set up immediate installation of floodlights about the house.

"No, next Monday will not be good enough," he rejected tersely. *This is the third firm he's called—he's determined to have those lights in place before nightfall. He's afraid somebody is out to kill Andrea—or me? Or both of us?* "I want a team out here within the next three hours. I want the floodlights to be operable this evening." He frowned, listening to the voice at the other end. "All right, get your team moving."

Emily discarded the *Enquirer*. "Mission accomplished?" She made an effort to sound cool.

"Done. Now let's get out of here and have lunch." Paul checked his watch. "An early lunch—but that means we'll be ahead of the mobs." His smile was reassuring. His eyes somber. *If Mom and Dad knew what was happening, they'd insist I come home. But if somebody is out for me, he—or she—could follow me to Evanston.* "I know this great place about three miles out of town. Quiet, tables far apart. I think you'll like it."

"Fine." *I don't want to leave Woodhaven. I'm staying. I've never felt this way about any man.* She hesitated. "Shouldn't we get in touch with Andrea?" All at once she felt uneasy about delay. "Tell her what's happened—"

"I'll drive over to Hannah's sister's house after lunch. Let Andrea have another couple hours without fresh anxiety. I told the police I'd brief her."

What is he thinking when he looks at me with such intensity? He distrusts me—that's it, isn't it? Why am I reacting this way? I barely know him.

A new—disturbing—thought darted across her mind. *Can Paul be behind all this insanity? If anything happened to Andrea, he'd take over at the company. No, that's absurd. And—unless the bomb was meant to be left at Andrea's door and leaving it at the guest room door was a mistake—I was the target.*

They left the house, walked to Paul's SUV. *Doesn't he know they're gas guzzlers? Why did I expect him to be respectful of the environment?*

"The car needs a washing," he apologized, pulling the passenger-side door open for her. "Somehow, there never seems time for routine things like that."

"You keep long hours at the company," she guessed.

He chuckled. "Andrea and I spend more time there than at home. Sometimes I'm convinced we're obsessed."

They sat in a strained silence while Paul swung out of the driveway onto the road. *What is he thinking? Is he regretting asking me out to lunch?*

"I'd like to start work Monday morning—if it's all right with you," Emily punctured the silence. "I don't know what I'll be able to do that—" She gestured a sense of futility.

"You'll sop up what you need to know," he predicted. "I guessed that right away." *He's staring at me that way again.*

"I'm computer-literate, of course—but I have no business experience." *Why am I chattering this way?* "Just a year of teaching."

"You'll do fine. Andrea told me about how you set up that summer camp back home. That took a lot of organizing—and convincing."

"It was so needed," she said in passionate recall. "Somebody had to do it."

72

"I'm glad Andrea persuaded you to come here—"

"I'm glad I came." For an instant his eyes left the road to meet hers. *This is happening too fast. It can't be real.* "But it's clear that Celeste and Carol don't share that feeling. Leon and Jane have been very pleasant," she conceded.

"Don't be thrown by those two witches." Paul's voice was laced with contempt. "How Andrea could have two daughters so different from herself is astonishing."

Then Paul was turning off the road before what appeared to be a small colonial house. The sign at the edge of the property identified it as the Colonial Inn.

"The house dates back to 1798," he told Emily. "It's been beautifully restored. For a while it was an inn. Then the son of the owner—a terrific chef—opened up the lower floor to expand restaurant facilities."

Walking into the Colonial Inn with Paul, Emily welcomed its air of serenity. For a little while, she thought, they could forget the horror that confronted them.

The hostess led them to an alcove table that was designed for privacy. *Does she think we're lovers?* Only one other table was occupied—by a party of what appeared to be four businessmen. Paul lifted a hand in polite greeting when the four turned to acknowledge their presence. *Why is Paul suddenly so tense?*

Not until a waiter had approached their table, taken their orders, did Paul explain.

"The four characters across the room—they're all members of the Town Council. They're champing at the bit to see a shopping mall installed at the edge of town." His face tightened. "They want to re-zone land my grandmother owns from farming to commercial—and offer that to the would-be mall developers." Now his face softened. "My grandmother loved knowing she was renting to organic farmers. The same family has rented since I was a baby. Now she's—not with it," he said painfully. "I go to see her every week, and she talks to me about her grandson, whom she loves. I'm her only grandchild. But those developers are not getting her farm."

"I suspect there're not many towns like this that don't have a shopping mall of sorts. Not many towns have managed to hang on to their downtown business sections." *Dad said he lost much of his business when the mall opened back in Evanston.*

"There've been sporadic efforts through the years, but we've been lucky here. So far—" All at once he seemed in deep thought. "Emily, I don't know what's behind Hannah's murder—and what happened this morning. But I believe—with Andrea—that Hannah wasn't meant to die. Andrea was to be the victim. This business with the bomb at your door—it was probably meant for Andrea." *Probably?*

Now Emily brought up the subject that had been haunting her. "Andrea seems convinced that Hannah's murder was connected with her husband's murder—" *My grandfather's murder. What was he like? I wish I could have known him.*

"And the murder of Roger Ainsworth. He was a longtime family friend. He and Andrea used to play chess every Sunday evening for years. Like her husband's murder, Ainsworth's murder was never solved."

"The police must realize now that Hannah wasn't murdered by some drifter passing through town." A sudden chill darted through Emily. "You believe there's a connection between the three murders?"

"I'm sure of it. But damn it, the police refuse to see this!"

"Should Andrea hire private investigators to pursue this? I mean, her life is in danger." *Why was Roger Ainsworth murdered? And that bomb this morning—it might have been meant for me.*

"I mean to urge her to do just that." Paul gestured for silence. Their waiter was approaching with their lunch.

When they were served and the waiter had left their table, Paul leaned forward with an air of urgency. "I'm suggesting she bring in private investigators from out of town. Let's break this weird cycle of murders. We can't allow Andrea to be the next victim—" He paused. "Nor you—"

Thirteen

Paul sat with Andrea in the tiny living room of the modest house occupied by Hannah's grief-stricken sister. Realizing Paul was here because of some new catastrophe, Rhoda had made a point of leaving him alone with Andrea.

"The police must realize now that Hannah wasn't killed by a drifter," Andrea pinpointed. *She's so cool about the bomb— but I know she's shaken. I see the tic in her eyelid that always surfaces under deep stress.* "But will this—this incident this morning lead them anywhere?"

"I doubt it." Paul was blunt. "This is going to require big-time tracking. Going back in time to your husband's murder, then that of Roger Ainsworth," he said gently. "I spoke briefly to Jim Reagan before I came over." The local District Attorney. "He's convinced we're off the wall in making a connection between the murders. I think you must bring in top-notch private investigators."

"Do it," Andrea ordered. Fire in her voice. "I don't care what it costs. I want the best investigation possible." She winced. "Before we suffer another murder."

"The creep has to be a longtime resident of this town," Paul stressed. "Somebody with an insane grudge against your family. Someone who began his vendetta with a determination to hurt someone close to you—to make you suffer. Then for some reason his rage turned against you personally. Only Hannah got in the way."

"Nothing must happen to my granddaughter. To Emily." For a moment Andrea closed her eyes in anguish. "That bomb this morning—was it meant for me or for Emily?"

"It was placed in front of her bedroom door," Paul acknowledged, "but that could have been in error." He squinted in thought. "I'll make phone calls to a contact down in New York.

We'll have investigators on the scene within twenty-four hours," he promised. "The police have little to go on—unless fingerprints surface on this morning's bomb—"

"And the investigators?" Andrea probed.

"They'll go back thirty-seven years—they'll try to solve three murders. Not just Hannah's murder." Now he re-routed the conversation. "Emily said she'd like to start work tomorrow—"

Andrea's smile was compassionate. "She's growing restless. She's not one to sit around idly—she's like her grandmother. And if she's at the office all day and home at night, the two of us can keep an eye on her." Andrea stared into space. "I know I should ship her back home—but I can't bring myself to do that. I've waited so long to have her with me."

"I was startled the first time I saw her. It was like turning the clock back and seeing you at her age. The resemblance is so strong. She's your granddaughter—nobody could ever dispute that."

"In time the children will come to accept her. Except Celeste." Andrea frowned in exasperation. "They're greedy— they don't want to share the Winston fortune with her. Though I suspect Leon is coming around to accepting her. That's because of Jane, of course. Jane can't bear to see hostility within the family."

"I should get back to the office—" Paul rose from the sofa he shared with Andrea. "But I'll get right on this business of hiring a team of investigators. Your safety—and Emily's— comes before anything else."

Am I misinterpreting signals from Emily? Does she reciprocate my feelings for her? I've been so tied up with the company I've had no time for a personal relationship. And then Emily walked into my life.

The police crew still moved about the house in search of some tiny clue. The security guard was on duty. Electricians worked at installing the battery of floodlights Paul had ordered.

Restless—uneasy—alone in the house, Emily decided in mid-afternoon to drive to the local library. Back issues of the *Enquirer* would surely be available on microfilm. She felt a compulsion to read up on the two earlier murders. That of her grandfather and of Roger Ainsworth, her grandmother's close friend. Perhaps in those reports was some minute item that had been overlooked then but offered a lead today.

She went to the garage, slid behind the wheel of her nine-year-old Toyota suburban, and drove out into the sunny afternoon. She paused to ask the security guard for directions to the library. He seemed startled that she was leaving the house. Was she expected to sit in the protected environs of the house, as though in terror of her life?

Sure, I'm scared. For Andrea—for myself. Someone out there means to kill one or both of us. That makes me fighting mad. We'll track down that maniac.

Driving away from the house, she heard in her mind the voice of Doris—the cleaning woman who came in by the day: "She's so pretty. And she looks just like you." Involuntarily her eyes sought the rear-view mirror for an instant.

Do I look like my grandmother? What about my father? Do I look at all like him? Who is he? Does he still live in this town? I could pass him in the street and not know him.

Does he know about me? All these years Celeste has refused to identify the man who made her pregnant. My father. Will I ever find him?

Following the security guard's directions, she drove up before the red-brick building that housed the library. Much larger, more impressive than she would have expected in a town as small as Woodhaven. She parked in the area beside the library and walked towards the entrance.

She paused there, read the inscription above the double doors: The David Winston Library. A small plaque indicated the library had been a gift to the community from Andrea Winston on the twentieth anniversary of his death.

Encased in a sense of coming in touch with her grandfather, she walked inside. Her heart pounding she stood before the oil painting that hung at one side of the reception area. Without reading the inscription she knew this was her grandfather's portrait.

She searched the face in the portrait. A kind, intelligent face, she decided. What sort of man had he been? He and Andrea had had a good marriage, she decided. Why could she think of this man as her grandfather, yet have so much difficulty thinking of Andrea as her grandmother? But moments later the explanation roared in her head. Her grandfather had run a small business. Andrea was the head of a major corporation. A breed of business people she had come to loathe as a scourge to mankind.

She walked into the library, up to the desk that was a replica of small-town library desks all over the country, asked for microfilm of copies of the Woodhaven *Enquirer* for the year of David Winston's death. Unsure just what was the actual date.

She settled herself at one of the microfilm projectors in the reference room to the right of the desk. A tension between her shoulderblades, a tightness in her throat, she began to search for an account of the murder. She sped through a series of reels before she reached her destination. August, thirty-seven years ago. Here it was: "PROMINENT BUSINESSMAN AND CIVIC LEADER MURDERED."

She read the account of the murder, the shocked reaction of the town. It was clear the business had been far smaller than today, but David Winston was regarded as a local success. She read on through successive reports. No suspect had surfaced. The case had never been closed, but after a few months it seemed to be relegated to the files.

She read about David Winston's younger sister—her great-aunt—who had died as a teenager. About the beloved grandmother who had raised him. But nowhere was there any indication of who had murdered David Winston, nor what the motive could have been.

She returned the rolls of film with a frustrating sense of missing out somewhere along the line. She waited for more reels of old issues of the *Enquirer*. Paul had said Roger Ainsworth had been murdered "a dozen years ago." She trusted that was an accurate time frame.

The librarian was returning to the desk. Emily was aware of the glint of curiosity in her eyes.

"I'm sorry to have taken so long," the librarian apologized. "One reel had been incorrectly filed—it took me a while to locate it."

"Thank you." *Somebody had recently looked at the back issues of that year. Why?*

Emily settled herself before a microfilm projector again. She sat motionless. Questions hurtling across her mind. Had somebody been checking into Roger Ainsworth's murder because he—or she—saw the link between that murder and Hannah's murder? Was it the murderer—gloating about his success?

The murderer has to be someone who's lived in this town at least thirty-eight years. Is it some former employee that David and Andrea had infuriated—and at intervals his rage soars to the point where he's determined for fresh revenge? But how does the Ainsworth murder fit into the pattern?

Impatient for answers, Emily threaded the film into place, began to race through the pages of the *Enquirer*, then stopped short. Here it was: "POPULAR BOOKSHOP OWNER MURDERED."

Eagerly she read the front-page account. Roger Ainsworth—fourth generation resident of Woodhaven—had been the sole remaining member of his family. The town had lost a valued citizen. He'd worked in collaboration with Andrea Winston, the article continued, to build literacy in the town: "Along with Andrea Winston, he chaired a committee to raise funds to establish our Senior Citizens Center."

So everyone in town knew, Emily pinpointed, that Roger Ainsworth and Andrea Winston were close. Could it be that Ainsworth had been murdered by someone who meant to inflict pain on Andrea?

Or was it jealousy? Some mentally disturbed suitor who had killed first Andrea's husband, then her close friend? Were they wrong in assuming Hannah was killed by mistake? Was Hannah killed because she was close to Andrea?

Talk to Paul—he knows Andrea's background. Is there a thwarted suitor behind these murders?

Fourteen

Emily left the library. She sat behind the wheel of her car and tried to dissect her hasty conclusions. Who was she to believe she could solve what had remained unsolved all these years? Still, doubts tugged at her. This area must be explored.

On impulse she reached for the cellphone her mother always kept in the car for emergencies. Paul would be at the company. *He'll think I'm out of my mind—and he'll be annoyed at being disturbed at work.* Yet compulsion forced her to call Information, request the number for Winston Mail Order, and then to call it.

"Good afternoon, Winston Mail Order," a pleasant voice responded.

"May I speak with Paul Cameron, please—" *I shouldn't be doing this.*

"Who's calling please?"

"Emily Mitchell—" *Will he know me by that name?*

A few moments later Paul's voice—almost harsh with anxiety—came to her. "Emily, you're all right?"

"I'm fine," she reassured him. "I know I shouldn't have called you at your office—" She was all at once apologetic. "But I—"

"Emily, it's all right," he broke in. "You wanted to ask me something," he said. "Or tell me something?" *About the murders—he understands.*

"I realize this is an issue that's probably been explored and discarded—" *I shouldn't have called him. I'm behaving like an idiot.*

"What issue, Emily?" he asked gently.

"Could there be an unbalanced suitor who's been wallowing in jealousy all these years. Some man who—"

"Oh, my God!"

"I didn't mean to be offensive," Emily apologized. "I—"

"I can't get away until about—about five. Meet me for coffee at the Oasis. It's—"

"I know where it is," Emily told him. *He's not angry at me. It's an angle that was never explored. And he knows something that should have been checked out years ago.* "I'll be at the Oasis at five."

Paul sat at his desk and stared into space. Feeling himself encased in ice. How was it that nobody had ever explored that angle before? Because it seemed so far out. Because nobody involved wanted to believe it could be so simple.

His mind shot back through the years. David Winston had been murdered before he was born—but he'd grown up hearing about it. He remembered Roger Ainsworth's murder, had been horrified. As a pre-schooler he'd gone to Roger's bookstore to attend story hours. When he'd become hooked on the Tolkien series at twelve—bought for him at Roger's bookstore by his grandmother—Mr. Ainsworth had pointed him in the direction of other writers he'd enjoy. *And now I see a possible link between his murder and David Winston's murder. And by some weird twist a sick motive for an attempt on Andrea's life. Or on Emily's life? Does he see Emily as his next victim?*

He sat immobile. His mind in chaos. Did he dare pursue this? But how could he not? All their attempts at protecting Andrea—the twenty-four-hour security guards he'd just put in place, the floodlights to surround the house at night—might not be enough. And with Emily's arrival, the whole sick plot might have changed. It could be Emily he'd meant to kill.

He struggled to clear his mind to cope with the current business crisis that had just arisen. Focus on that, he ordered himself. Put the coping mechanism into work. Out of here by five—to sit down to talk with Emily.

At a few minutes past five he drove out of the company parking area and headed for town. He was annoyed with himself for delaying the switch from SUV to a small car. The SUV had been bought as a company car, to be used for emergency deliveries to FedEx. When a drunken driver had smashed up his own small car three weeks ago, he'd taken on the SUV until his own could be repaired. Just last week he'd been told to forget ever using it again.

Forget about the SUV, he chastised himself. The urgent problem was to foil another murder. Why was this possibility never explored before? He felt himself breaking into a sweat. Thank God, Grandma would never understand what might be happening. Mom and Dad were gone. But he mustn't run from the truth.

How can I not follow this up? If he's guilty, then he must be put away before he can kill again. The town knows only a fragment of the truth. All that Grandma would allow to be acknowledged.

Emily sat in a rear booth at the sparsely populated Oasis. Over and over she probed the brief exchange with Paul. What had she said that so unnerved him? She'd been sitting here almost half an hour, she realized with a self-conscious glance at the waitress who'd served her coffee, then a refill: "I'm a little early—I'm meeting a friend."

She smiled with relief as she saw Paul stride through the door, held up a hand. He hurried to her booth.

"I'm a little late," he apologized.

"Just a minute or two—" *Why do I feel this way each time I see him?*

Their waitress came forward with a welcoming smile. She knew Paul, Emily realized as the other two exchanged light banter for a moment.

"Bring us your cherry cheesecake," he ordered, as though this was just a casual encounter. "You can't come to the Oasis without having their cherry cheesecake," he told Emily.

"And decaf for you," the waitress chirped. A glint in her eyes. *She suspects there's something special between Paul and me.*

Paul was silent until their waitress was beyond hearing.

"I don't want to believe what my mind tells me," Paul said quietly. "You've hit on a motive that I should have seen when Hannah was killed. Anyone who becomes close to Andrea is a victim in this man's eyes." His eyes were fearful.

The just revealed granddaughter? Me?

"Who is he?"

"Avery—" Paul's voice was choked. "The town weirdo. My grandfather."

"But you're not sure?" How awful for Paul—if what he suspected was true.

"No," he conceded. "But it's something that should have been explored when David Winston was murdered. At that time nobody knew the facts—except Andrea and my grandmother. And they never suspected Avery. It should have been explored when Roger Ainsworth was murdered—perhaps because he meant so much to Andrea. The whole town was aware that Roger was gay—there was nothing romantic between him and Andrea. Just a very warm friendship."

"What happened that your grandfather—" Emily abandoned conversation as their waitress approached.

"Two cherry cheesecakes coming up," their waitress drawled. "I'm hoping you're having a late dinner." Her smile suggested she thought they might be having dinner together, also.

"My grandmother and Andrea were friends from kindergarten. My grandfather was in love with Andrea." Paul squinted in thought. "Obsessed would be a better word. Andrea married David. My grandmother married Avery. Months after my father was born, Avery—my grandfather—told Grandma she'd been second choice. He'd always be in love with Andrea. Then thirty-seven years ago—not long after David's murder— he walked out on Grandma. Ever since he's lived in a little fishing shack he built not long after he married. He walks around with a long gray beard and a gray ponytail. He's out of his mind, survives on odd jobs he's picked up through the years. Now he's on social security, I imagine."

"How awful for your family," Emily whispered.

"I doubt that many people in town even realize that he's Grandma's husband. My grandfather. Only the old-timers. He's just Avery—the town character." Paul took a deep, painful breath. "And perhaps a triple murderer."

"He could be innocent," Emily reminded.

"I want to believe that," Paul admitted. "But if he's guilty, he must be brought to trial. He must be stopped before he kills again."

"Would he be capable of making a bomb?" *Paul will be devastated if his grandfather is guilty.*

Paul sighed. "As I understand, he was almost a genius at working with chemicals—before he went off the wall. Everybody thought he had a brilliant future."

"Are you going to the District Attorney?" she asked after a moment.

"I can't do that without some actual proof. The investigator I hired will be in town on Saturday. I'll talk to him, explain what we know. Let him try to check out Avery. I don't want him to be guilty," Paul admitted, "but if he is guilty and taken into custody, then we'll know this is the end of the line. No more murders."

"Shall I tell Andrea about your suspicions?"

Paul deliberated a moment. "No. Not yet. Not unless we have something to go on. She has enough on her plate. And we don't take this to the District Attorney unless the investigator comes up with something substantial."

"But in the meantime—" Emily hesitated, "shouldn't he be kept under surveillance?"

"I can put some local PI on that right away. Without letting on why we want to know about Avery's activities. I can say that there's been some pilfery in the Shipping Department— we want him checked out," Paul fabricated, glanced at his watch. "Damn. I have to get back to the company—I'll be tied up there for at least another two or three hours. But I'll come to the house later. The floodlights will be in operation by nightfall and a second security guard on duty."

"This is rough on you," Emily sympathized. "I mean, suspecting your grandfather—"

"If the investigator comes up with strong evidence, I'll have to turn him in. It'll be the hardest thing I've ever done in my life. I never really knew him—except to pass him on the street. There are times when he just walks up and down Main Street— sometimes for hours. He doesn't know me—he doesn't know anybody. Grandma never considered having him committed. She figured he'd be happier living as he does."

Returning to the house, Emily noted there was no police presence. Already a second security guard was on duty. Walking

84

into the foyer she heard the sound of music coming from the den. Instinctively she tensed.

It must be Andrea, she chided herself. Two security guards were marching about the grounds. How could a stranger have gained admittance? Brushing aside a surge of alarm, she walked down the hall to the den.

Andrea sat in a lounge chair. Eyes closed, hands clenched while the somber tones of a fine recording of Beethoven's "Moonlight Sonata" filtered into the room.

"Are you asleep?" she asked softly. The clenched hands said "no."

Andrea opened her eyes. "Just trying to relax. It's been a rough day. But I had one small success." A hint of relief in her voice. "The coroner has agreed to release Hannah's body tomorrow morning. We'll lay her to rest on Saturday morning. Thank God for that."

"How's her sister?" Emily fought back an urge to discuss her meeting with Paul. "This is a terrible time for her—"

"Rhoda's hanging in there. Her husband and three kids are very supportive. They were all close to Hannah. Her husband said it was a bad time to bring up the subject—but at the same time it might be helpful. He has a niece—Nora—who's been out of work for almost a year. She lives one town over, was laid off when her employer moved out to Arizona. Nora's not retarded," Andrea emphasized. "She's extremely shy. But she's a good housekeeper and cook. She'd be terrified if I was one to do heavy entertaining—but since I'm not, she'll be fine."

"That's one problem solved."

"I told him I'd talk to her after the funeral. Just a formality," Andrea said with a faint smile "I'll have her come into the house on Monday. My first day back at work." Andrea shook her head in disbelief. "I still can't believe Hannah won't be here to run the house for me."

Emily felt instant sympathy for Nora. She remembered a fight at school last year, when a guidance counselor had suggested moving one of her students—a very shy fourteen-year-old—into a "Special Ed" class. She hadn't been slow—or retarded. She'd been very shy. Emily hesitated for a moment. "Will she be upset at living in Hannah's room?"

"How observant of you to realize that," Andrea said softly.

"We'll put her up in one of the spare bedrooms upstairs." All at once her face tightened. "That is, if Nora is willing to take on the job. We haven't considered that."

"Why wouldn't she do that?" For a moment Emily was bewildered—but even before Andrea responded, she understood.

"Emily, how will she feel about living in this house where Hannah was murdered? Where there was a bomb placed in the house just this morning?"

Andrea and Emily both stiffened at the sound of a car drawing to a stop before the house.

"No bomb this time." Andrea strived for amusement at their reaction. "Dinner is on the way."

But how can we know if—when—the killer strikes again?

Fifteen

The Winston dining room was pleasantly air-conditioned, exuded a serenity refuted by the happenings of the past seventy-two hours. The unnatural outdoor spill of lights—creeping through the dining room—created an eerie atmosphere.

Emily sat at the table with Andrea and listened while Andrea reminisced about earlier days of Woodhaven. A safe subject of discussion in the presence of the Lamont Caterer's waitress.

I can't believe I've just been here since yesterday morning. It feels like a lifetime. Hannah's murder, Dennis's apprehension and quick clearance, the bomb outside my room barely ten hours ago. And Paul all at once so important in my life. But does he feel that way about me? Too fast—this is happening too fast!

"We've always been a town of independent citizens—" Andrea's voice brought her back to the moment. "Knowing what we wanted for our town. But in the past few years a greedy element has fought for control." *She doesn't talk like the corporate big wheels intent on controlling the government.* "We don't want a huge shopping mall that'll kill off our downtown, bring grief to our local businesses."

"That happened back in Evanston," Emily said with sudden intensity. "A huge mall opened, and Dad's business took an awful drop—" She faltered in dismay. Was it incorrect to talk about her other family? *Who is my birth father? Will I ever know?*

But Andrea was nodding in sympathy. "We've seen it happen endless times. But we're fighting it. And the next election for Mayor and Town Council members is just a year away." She frowned in anticipation. "That's going to be a vicious battle." *Another election to be bought?*

Andrea launched into an account of the township woes,

which were splitting the town right down in the middle. *She's head of this major mail order house that sells nationwide, that employs close to two thousand people—yet she seems so absorbed in the welfare of Woodhaven. Is it real—or is it a clever act?*

The waitress came back into the dining room to remove the main course, returned to serve chilled Strawberries Romanoff. Andrea lovingly touched the brandy snifter that held their dessert.

"Hannah always loved preparing this. She said it was beautiful to look at and healthful to eat." Andrea closed her eyes for a moment as though reliving happier days. "Hannah was like a member of this family."

"The only time I've had Strawberries Romanoff was two years ago—in Rome," Emily recalled. When she and Wendy had made their secret trip to Genoa. "We had dinner at a fabulous restaurant. Most of the time we were on a tight budget." *Why did I say that? What would Andrea Winston know about budgeting?*

But Andrea was nodding. A reminiscent glint in her eyes. Emily was startled. "When you and your friend went to join the protest at the G8 summit." *She knows about that? Mom and Dad don't know. And she isn't angry with me for being part of the protest?* "I was terrified when I heard you were there—but you were following your convictions." *We were protesting companies like hers.* "Emily, I want you to feel safe in this house. Nothing bad can happen here now. We have a pair of security guards on each shift, covering the grounds around the clock. The floodlights will be on from dusk to dawn."

"I'm not afraid—" Emily lifted her head in defiance. "I'm fighting mad." *But how can I not be afraid when some maniac is on the loose—and I could be his next intended victim?*

"We'll fight this through together. You and I and Paul. I know—only the three of us see any link between the three murders. The police are sure I'm off the wall in seeing a connection. Perhaps they'll come up with a lead on Hannah's murder—" She shrugged. "I'm afraid it'll follow the path of your grandfather's murder and Roger's murder. Unsolved, relegated to the files."

They left the dining room to settle themselves in the den to wait for Paul's arrival. They could hear the Lamont Catering waitress and her help clearing away the dinner dishes. This was the kind of luxury she'd always deplored because she felt the money to supply it was earned on the backs of the poor and exploited. How strange to be here, sharing in such luxury.

She sensed that what Andrea casually called "the den" was her favorite room in the house. It was beautiful—without being ostentatious. It radiated comfort and serenity.

"I've spent some happy hours in this room—" Andrea seemed to read her mind, she thought with a start. "David loved having cozy dinners here with me on summer evenings when Leon and Carol were away at camp and baby Celeste asleep for the night. Those were very special times for us. And later—when David was gone—I'd play chess here on Sundays with Roger."

And both were murdered. Her husband and a close friend. And now Hannah, who was "like a member of the family." But Andrea is convinced that Hannah was not the intended victim—that she was.

"Do you play chess, Emily?" Andrea brought her back to the moment.

"Yes. I'm not great at it," she added quickly.

"Let's play while we're waiting for Paul." Andrea rose from her chair and crossed to the wall of bookcases, reached into a cabinet that dissected one bookcase. She withdrew a leather-covered box with an air of reverence. "I haven't played chess since that last Sunday before Roger was murdered. He was so intense about it." Her smile was tender. "He was intense about so many things. His bookshop, town projects that he felt were important, his family history. He was the last of his family. That bothered him."

Lovingly, Andrea set up the chessboard on a table that flanked a wall looking out into the night. The pieces were exquisite ivory carvings. Emily remembered the inexpensive set that her father cherished. Dad had taught her on that set.

"All right, let's play—" For a moment Andrea's eyes sparkled. For a moment—

Both were too distracted to do themselves justice. Both conscious of the floodlights that poured down about the grounds—providing an eerie atmosphere. Both impatient to hear more about the investigation team Paul had hired.

Close to ten p.m.—when Emily and Andrea had abandoned their chess efforts—they heard a car pull up into the driveway, then male voices in conversation.

"That's Paul—" Andrea rose to her feet. "There should be coffee warming in the coffee-maker."

"I'll get it—" Emily headed for the kitchen. For Andrea coffee was a necessary ingredient of conferences.

When Emily returned to the den, Paul rushed to relieve her of the coffee tray. "Oh, I can use that—"

"It's decaf," Andrea warned. "The 'real thing' is served in this house only at breakfast time. Hannah's rule. But tell us— what's happening?"

"I stopped off at the police precinct." He grinned. "I have some friends on the force. But remember, it's very soon to expect action. They're closed-mouthed about possible leads."

"What about fingerprints?" Emily pushed.

"So far, nothing," Paul admitted. "And with present-day technology they check this out fast. But I've scheduled a meeting with this guy who's flying up from New York Saturday morning, when he's tied up the loose ends on a case. Jason Hollister. He's told me that if he feels it's necessary, he wants permission to bring in a second man."

"Let him bring in as many assistants as he wants—" Andrea gestured impatiently. "He's to spare no expenses. All I'm asking is that we get results. He understands he's to track three murders—not just Hannah's murder?" Andrea pinpointed.

"He'll go back to the day you opened Winston Mail Order," Paul began. "He'll—"

"He'll find a link! Paul, I'm convinced of that." A vein throbbed in Andrea's forehead. "Let him find it before that maniac strikes again."

Sixteen

The next two days dragged with painful slowness. Each morning Emily called home. Each time assuring her parents she was in no danger. She said nothing about the bomb placed before her bedroom door. She was relieved to discover the Evanston newspapers carried little about the case. Thus far.

On Saturday morning—in a dismal drizzle—Hannah was laid to rest. The entire Winston clan—except for Celeste—attended the church services and the burial in the cemetery. Again, Emily was relieved that Celeste was not present. She dreaded the inevitable encounter.

"Damn, Celeste should have been with us," Andrea complained when the family returned to the house for lunch. "She should have showed some respect for Hannah."

"Celeste is out in the Hamptons with her toy boy," Leon reminded in disdain. "When did she ever show a sense of responsibility?"

Over lunch—supplied by the caterer again—Carol brought up the subject of Hannah's replacement. Andrea was impatient with her.

"My God, Carol, we've just buried Hannah. But I'm hiring a replacement—a niece of Hannah's brother-in-law."

Carol seemed taken aback. "You haven't made a definite commitment?"

"I'm capable of that." Andrea was sharp.

"After all that's happened, whomever you hire should be carefully screened," Carol protested. "Leon, make Mother understand that—"

"I'm not senile," Andrea shot back. "I run a big business. I can hire a housekeeper."

"Hurry up, kids," Jane exhorted her son and twin nieces,

91

lingering over the remains of lunch—all three resentful at the lack of dessert. "You've got Little League practice, Raymond —and Elaine and Deirdre, I can drop you off for your ballet class at the same time."

"Yuck!" Elaine turned to Deirdre. "We don't want to go to ballet, do we?"

"You're going," Carol warned, "or you'll lose your allowance for two weeks."

"Why do we have to go if we don't want to?" Raymond whined. "That's nuts."

"You're going," Leon snapped. "Now."

Carol launched into a monologue of complaints about their lunch menu. Her husband Tom tried—futilely—to derail her. He never had much to say, Emily noted. Then only about his business.

He escaped from the family craziness into a private world of his own, she suspected.

They heard a car come to a stop before the house.

"More cops?" Carol lifted her eyebrows in disdain. "When are they going to get off their asses and clear up this thing?"

Andrea winced. "Hannah was murdered. It's not just a 'thing.'"

Emily's face lighted. "It's Paul—" He was talking with one of the security guards.

"Doesn't he have anything else to do?" Carol drawled and stared back at her husband, who was silently scolding her.

"Paul puts in sixty- and seventy-hour weeks at the company. He's bright, conscientious, and innovative. He's the best thing that ever happened to Winston Mail Order." Andrea was grim.

"He's a few years out of college." Leon's tone condescending. "You took him in because he was your best friend's grandson."

"Just before I hired Paul, I was desperate for top-level staff. I lost Jim Taylor and Bill Forrest within three months of each other. Both had been with me for over twenty-five years— they grew with the company. Their deaths were a terrible loss." Andrea paused, straining for calm. "If anything happens to me, Paul will run the company."

An ominous silence engulfed the room. As though, Emily thought, an undercurrent of war had become reality. It was

92

clear that Paul was not liked by Leon or Carol. Andrea's earlier observation darted across her mind: *"My children want me to retire—either go public or sell the business. They're all so greedy. They're afraid I'll run the business into the ground. But I treat my people like responsible human beings. I don't have strikes to battle. The company can survive despite the bad economy. I don't draw multi-million-dollar bonuses."* Did Andrea believe she was here out of greed? Emily asked herself. The money was part of it, yes—but the major incentive was to learn about herself. Who she was.

Leon rose abruptly from the table. "I have a business appointment—I have to get cracking."

"Tom and I are way behind on things—" Carol gestured vaguely. "This has been such an insane time." She turned to her husband. "Drop me off at the house. I have to check my appointment pad. I'm sure I have some meeting at three p.m."

Paul was at the tiny local airport to meet Jason Hollister, the private investigator being sent up from New York. The assignment was open-ended. Hollister was to remain on the job until dismissed. *It'll cost Andrea a fortune, but she'll have no peace until she has answers.*

Hollister's flight was announced as arriving. Paul rose from his seat and walked out to the gate. A handful of passengers were emerging. Right away he guessed that the tall, casually dressed man in his mid-thirties was Jason Hollister. He held up the sign bearing his name, saw Hollister focus on the sign and head towards him.

"You're right on schedule," Paul greeted him with outstretched hand. "Small passenger list."

Hollister grinned. "Woodhaven isn't exactly a prime destination."

"I suggest you register at the Holiday Inn—at the edge of town. You can arrange there for a car rental," Paul told him as they walked into the terminal to collect Hollister's luggage. "Once you're settled in, we can talk."

Hollister retrieved his luggage. Paul drove him to the motel, waited in the car while Hollister registered. When Hollister returned to the car, Paul suggested an early dinner at a restaurant at the edge of town.

"Not four-star," Paul conceded. "But the food is decent, and it'll be near deserted this early on a Saturday afternoon. We can talk in privacy."

As Paul had assumed, they were the sole patrons of the Waterside Restaurant except for a party of senior citizens on the opposite side of the sprawling room. They ordered leisurely, waited for their waiter to leave the table.

"All right, fill me in," Hollister instructed Paul. "I've just been given the basics."

Paul launched into a detailed report, pausing only when their waiter returned with food. He was blunt in acknowledging that the police were sure Andrea was off the wall in seeing a link between the three murders—and now the bomb threat.

"They could be right, you know—" Hollister was low-keyed, but Paul knew that his agency and its investigators were considered top of the line in the field. "These could be three isolated murders."

"We want you to work on the assumption that they are not." A faint sharpness in Paul's voice now. "Andrea Winston is a bright, no-nonsense woman. She—and I—are convinced these murders have been committed in order to give her deep pain." *Is Emily meant to be the next victim? That mustn't happen!*

"This bomb scare," Hollister pursued. "The efforts of a rank amateur, I understand."

"According to the police, it could have been made by anyone with some minor knowledge of bomb making." *No more stalling, tell him our suspicions of Avery.*

"Either someone very stupid—or the bomb was meant only to scare. Why?"

Paul hesitated. *I don't want to think of Emily as being in danger. I want her to be part of my life.* "We've spent a lot of hours trying to figure out the situation. We suspect the first two murders were meant to cause deep pain for Andrea Winston. And then—for some reason we don't know—he decided to kill her. He came to the house on a Tuesday night when the housekeeper would normally have been away. Expecting to murder Andrea. The housekeeper got in the way. And now her granddaughter has come to live with her. His sick mind can be operating in two ways. In one his plotting has switched again—to kill her granddaughter and inflict unfathomable pain. The other, he wants to frighten Emily—the granddaughter who's just come into her life after twenty-three years—into leaving, to give him free rein to murder Andrea." He took a breath. *Now. Tell him about Avery. How can I do this to my own grandfather?* "There's one other scenario to check out." Forcing himself to be candid, Paul gave Hollister a breakdown on the Avery situation. "We may be way off course, but I feel it needs follow-up."

"My first approach." Hollister seemed in deep concentration now. "But let's get moving on other angles. I'll need lists of names. I may need to bring in help to handle some of the 'donkey work'—"

"Bring in as many assistants as you need. And I'll talk with Andrea. You'll have your lists."

Now Hollister embarked on lengthy questioning, starting with the night David Winston had been murdered. Patrons arrived for dinner and departed while Hollister continued his probing. A fresh batch of diners arrived while Paul and Hollister talked over endless cups of coffee.

The sunny afternoon had moved into an overcast dusk by the time Paul and Hollister left the restaurant. Paul dropped off Hollister at his motel with a feeling that this investigation would unearth many hidden facts. Enough to nail the creep who had killed three times thus far—and plotted other mayhem?

Still, Paul was haunted by the possibility that he and Andrea were way off track in seeing a connection between the murders. Could they be coincidental? But there was nothing coincidental about Hannah's murder and the bomb incident. *They are linked. And if Hannah's murderer isn't caught, there'll be more killings.*

Twenty minutes after he'd left Jason Hollister at his motel, Paul was sitting in the den of the Winston house with Andrea and Emily.

"I had a three-hour dinner with Jason Hollister," he reported and turned to Andrea. "He wants a couple of lists of names right away—"

"We'll make the lists tonight," Andrea agreed. "We'll do it together."

"He said you must understand that this won't be an easy assignment—"

"Paul, I know that." Andrea's earlier anxieties crept through. "But does he realize just how difficult—how complicated—this investigation will be?"

"He knows. He thinks it's best that he doesn't come to the house to meet with you. The less people in town who know what's happening the better. Ostensibly he's a businessman hoping to deal with Winston Mail Order. He checked into the Holiday Inn at the edge of town, gave a fictitious business address. He'll meet with us at the company tomorrow morning." Paul chuckled. "The staff and folks in town are aware that you often work on Sundays."

"Spread the word—in an offhand manner," Andrea stipulated, "that—what's his name?"

"Jason Hollister," Paul reminded her.

"Spread the word that Jason Hollister is here to persuade me to abandon some of our Asian markets for homegrown manufacturing." *Is she considering that?* "And that I'm very interested." *Oh, wow!*

"All right." But Paul seemed ambivalent.

"That'll mean more jobs. It'll speed up the economy in town," Andrea pointed out. "Give them lots to talk about. You know how jittery most people are about the economy. They'll lose interest in the proposed mall."

"But if you don't go ahead with it—" Paul frowned, trying to follow Andrea's thinking.

"I'm going ahead with it. A 'Made in the USA' line. In a small way," she acknowledged, her smile ironic. "And we won't fight when our property taxes are raised because of new construction."

"A shopping mall will cry for tax relief," Paul surmised. "I read somewhere that in this country these 'tax breaks' reach about $75 billion a year. How many school budgets are slashed so that companies like Spiegel and Wal-Mart can be relieved of paying property taxes?"

"Can this factory be built right on company property?" Emily asked.

Paul nodded. "That area to the north of the Shipping Department. It'll cut deeply into the year's profits, of course—"

"It's an investment, Paul—the company can afford it." Andrea dismissed any second thoughts. "We'll issue a special catalogue—to focus on our 'Made in the USA' line." She turned to Emily. Her eyes tender. "This has been in the back of my mind for two years—since you went to the G8 summit protest." *Why does Paul look so surprised? Does he disapprove?* "I realized we were feeding on the backs of Asian workers—some as young as eight—who worked long hours in dreadful conditions for a few cents an hour. I was afraid to face the truth. Everybody was buying from these sweatshop markets. How else could we compete?" Andrea flinched in thought. "But we were depriving Americans of jobs. Destroying their security. Our unemployment rolls are soaring because jobs are going overseas."

"We'll have to keep the operation small," Paul cautioned, but Emily sensed his mind was in high gear. "No way can we set up the manufacturing to fill a large initial response—but it can be a real start. We're sending an urgent message: 'Keep our jobs home.'"

"We'll begin with basic sportswear," Andrea plotted. "For men, women, and children. Design costs will be minor. We can have a line set up in a matter of—" She frowned in thought. "In two weeks," she predicted. "Workers at the sewing machines in four weeks—"

"It'll require a major advertising campaign—" All at once Paul seemed anxious. "A promotion person to get the line off the ground. It'll be costly."

"But isn't the climate right for that approach?" Emily challenged, churning with enthusiasm. "Every day the media announce that more Americans are being laid off. We've lost more than two million jobs since Bush took office. Families are losing their homes, forced to go on welfare to survive—" Her voice trailed away. *Am I being presumptuous?*

Andrea turned to Emily. Her eyes bright with affection. "I thought about you—many thousands of young people like you—fighting for what is right. I felt such guilt that companies like mine were exploiting helpless Asian labor—and depriving Americans of so many jobs. Oh Lord, the sleepless nights I've endured. But as Paul said, it'll be a start—"

Emily was dizzy with excitement. "It sounds wonderful—"

Andrea's sincere. She's not like most CEOs of huge corporations—manipulating the government to fit their needs, destroying democracy as we've known it for so many generations. She cares about people.

"Of course, we won't be able to abandon our regular suppliers at this point," Andrea conceded. "It'll take us years to expand our manufacturing facilities to do that. And we'll have to tighten our belts," she acknowledged. "It's a whole new scene for Winston Mail Order." Her smile was simultaneously tender and sad. "David would approve." She lifted her head in a gesture of triumph. "We'll do this. We can make a beginning. Our new catalogue of 'Made in the USA' clothing will be in the mail—and online—in sixty days. Ready for shipment in ninety days."

So fast? But Andrea sees this as an important challenge.

"Can we set up facilities that quickly?"

Paul's excited at the prospect, yet dubious that it can be accomplished.

"We'll set up temporary facilities," Andrea pursued. Exuding determination. "We'll hire—"

Andrea paused mid-sentence as the night quiet was destroyed by a thunderous explosion. The house thrown into sudden darkness. Floodlights that surrounded the house blacked out. Male voices swore in shock somewhere outside.

"We're all right," Paul said, deceptively calm. "Andrea, Emily—stay where you are. There'll be matches at the fireplace," he assumed and an instant later groaned as he collided with a piece of furniture. "We're all right—"

How can we be all right when a bomb just exploded in front of the house?

Seventeen

In moments the den was bathed in candlelight.

"Flashlights are stored in the cabinet there—" Andrea pointed. "For those occasional times when we lose power in an electrical storm."

"I'll get them—" Paul moved into action.

Already Emily was on the phone and summoning the police. Paul placed lighted flashlights at strategic places about the room.

"Are the security guards all right?" Andrea strained to hear sounds in the restored quiet. "I don't hear them." Her voice anxious now.

Emily put down the phone. Her hands clammy, her heart hammering wildly. *When will this nightmare be over?* "The police will be here in minutes—"

"Let's go out and see how much damage was done," Andrea said with stoic calm, belied by the rage in her eyes. "The house seems intact."

"Stay here until the police clear the area." Paul listened for outdoor sounds. Nothing. Only an ominous quiet. "I'll take a look from the front door."

"The security guards are probably chasing the car the bomb thrower was driving." Emily's gaze followed Paul as he strode from the room.

The bomb didn't hit the house. Was it a bad aim—or was it just meant to scare us? Can this be Avery again? Paul said he was almost a genius in dealing with chemicals. Does he have access to the makings of a bomb?

They heard the sound of police sirens in the distance.

"I can't sit here like this." Andrea rose to her feet, reached for a flashlight. "What's Paul doing at the front door?"

Paul turned from the opened door as Andrea and Emily

approached. The outdoors shrouded in darkness except for the small areas that were the focus of Paul's flashlight. "It's difficult to assess the damage by flashlight—but there's a crater on the right lawn—"

"The police are close—" Excitement deepened Emily's voice. She peered out into the darkness. "They're here!"

Headlights indicated two cars and a police van were turning into the driveway. Sirens droning to a stop now. Powerful searchlights roamed about the grounds as detectives headed for the house, focused now on a crater Paul had noted. About four feet in diameter, Emily judged.

"It was another clumsy, homemade effort," Paul surmised as a police crew gathered about the crater.

Two detectives strode towards the entrance.

"The house lights are out," Andrea called to them.

How cool she seems—but I know she's shaken inside.

"Don't go outside the door," Paul cautioned Andrea and Emily. "We don't know where there might be craters."

"Where are the security guards?" one detective asked as he and his partner joined the others in the foyer. "I understood they were on duty around the clock."

"We heard a car drive off," Emily jumped in. "We assume the two guards are in pursuit of whoever tossed the bomb."

"That must be them coming back now," the other detective said as headlights pierced the darkness.

A car was driving up, came to a sharp stop. The pair of security guards leapt from the car, rushed to the house.

"The guy got away," one reported, fighting for breath. "But we got a license number before we lost him. He was driving a dark-green car—"

"We called the license plate number in already," the other guard added. "We ought to see some action soon."

"We can talk in the den," Andrea said. "We have flashlights set up around the room."

With candlelight and flashlights providing an eerie, otherworld atmosphere the two detectives questioned Andrea—with Emily and Paul contributing at intervals. The two security guards stood by, alternately self-conscious and sheepish.

"Let's go outside and see what the crew's come up with," one detective suggested to the other.

"In a bit," he stalled. "This has to be related to the bomb left in the house on Thursday morning. The same amateur effort—"

Paul said Avery was almost a genius with chemicals. But that was probably forty years ago. What he knew then would be almost obsolete now. But how painful for Paul if Avery is the killer. How painful for Andrea.

"A scare tactic?" Paul suggested. "This one missed the house by thirty feet."

"That or he misjudged his throwing arm," the other detective surmised. "The best lead we have at the moment is the car's license number. We should have names before the night is over."

Within an hour—with police still searching for other clues—an emergency crew was on hand to work on restoring electricity. At Paul's suggestion Andrea and Emily settled themselves in the den for what appeared to be a long wait. Paul stationed himself at a window to watch the outdoor proceedings. Restless, Andrea paced about the room.

"Paul, shouldn't your investigator—this Hollister man—be told about this latest insanity?" Andrea probed.

"We don't want to advertise that he's on the job," Paul reminded. "Maybe I'm paranoid—but I wouldn't want to bring him over to the house. You know the deal—he's here to do business with you about the company." Paul hesitated, exchanged a loaded glance with Emily. "I know we may be reaching into space, but one of the angles I discussed with Hollister was the possibility that—that Avery could be involved."

Even in the low-keyed lighting of the flashlights, Emily was aware that Andrea's face had drained of color.

"How can Avery be responsible?" Andrea shook her head. "Paul, I can't believe that."

"We have to consider every angle," Paul said gently. "Hollister will be checking on Avery's activities first thing tomorrow morning. He's—off the wall mentally and emotionally."

"I don't want to think that he's been doing these awful things—" Andrea's voice was hushed. "All those years ago the four of us were so close. David and I, Sylvia and Avery.

Until he went berserk, Paul—walked out that way on your grandmother, lived like a pariah." She closed her eyes for a moment. "I've made a point through the years—though your grandmother never knew—to see that odd jobs were thrown his way. I had a car—with the proper license plates, renewed each year—left at his cabin years ago—with a sign that said 'Happy birthday, Avery.'"

All at once the atmosphere was super-charged. "He has a car, even today?" Paul asked.

"Yes." Andrea winced. "A dark-green Dodge Spirit." *The security guards said the person who threw the bomb was driving a dark-green car. Andrea realizes that.* "They were still making them then—"

Close to midnight—while the three in the den geared themselves for an all night vigil—a detective, cellphone and flashlight in hand, strode into the room.

"We've located the car! It was abandoned eleven miles down the road. We'll pick up the owner within hours. He has a lot of questions to answer!"

Eighteen

"What's the license number of the car?" Paul asked with feigned casualness. *Is it Avery's car?* "Or is that top secret?"

The detective flipped open his notebook. "No secret. I have it right here—"

Instinctively both Emily and Paul turned to Andrea as the detective read off the number. Andrea replied with a silent shrug.

The detective gazed from one to the other. "Does the license number ring bells to either of you?"

"No," Andrea replied for the three of them.

Why would Andrea know the license number of Avery's car? We'll have to wait until the owner is picked up. If it's Avery, then the nightmare is over.

The detective cleared his throat. "We'll have people checking the grounds for a while yet—and the security guards for the midnight to eight a.m. shift have just come on duty." *Meaning we're safe overnight. What about tomorrow—and all the days ahead?*

"The guys working on the electrical system will probably be here for hours—don't expect service until tomorrow," the other detective told them. "Why don't the three of you call it a night? We're not likely to know anything until morning. There's no point in the three of you staying awake."

The detective's partner strode into the den. "A call just came through," he told the other detective. "An hour ago the car was reported stolen." He turned to Andrea with an air of disbelief. "By your son, Leon Winston."

Andrea was stunned. "Someone stole Leon's car—to use it in bombing my house?"

"That's kind of sick, isn't it?" The detective shook his head. "But guys who do this sort of thing are sickos."

103

The others were silent until the detectives left the den.

"There's a warped mind at work here." Andrea's voice was barely audible. "Could it be Avery?" *She knows how upsetting this is for Paul. She doesn't believe that.*

"It seems far out." Paul appeared to be in an inner struggle now. "We have to remember his mental state. He could have been spying on Leon's house—"

"Why?" Andrea was suddenly anxious.

"He was spying on Leon's house," Paul pursued. "And something clicked in his mind. He decided to take the car and—"

"Then Leon and his family are in danger!" Andrea agonized by this possibility.

"He's not rational," Emily reminded. "Perhaps he saw a dark-green car—and for the moment thought it was his. He had the bomb in his cabin—and his mind told him to take the car and—"

"The bomb was meant for Leon?" Andrea flinched. "He meant to kill Leon, to hurt me again?"

"But in his messed up mind he came here instead," Emily speculated.

"We're taking wild guesses." Paul dismissed conjectures now. "We may be way off base. Let's wait and see what the police come up with."

"They'll search the car for fingerprints." Emily strived to be logical. "If it was Avery, they'll know—"

"We'll hear nothing until morning," Paul summed up. "Let's call it a night, try for some sleep." *How can we sleep at a time like this?* "Remember, Andrea, we have a meeting with Hollister at the company tomorrow morning at ten a.m. I'll pick you up about nine forty-five?"

"Yes." Andrea nodded. "Emily and I will be ready."

I'm to go with them to meet the private investigator? But that seems right—we're in this together.

Later, lying sleepless in bed, Emily explored her feelings. She was conscious of an acceptance by Leon and Jane—even by Tom, Carol's husband. But Carol loathed her. The children—her cousins—ignored her. And her birth mother was furious that she'd been brought into the family.

But Andrea is my grandmother. She wants the others to

104

accept that I'm part of the family. Doris—the cleaning woman—said I look just like her. She wasn't shocked that I went to the Genoa protest. I'm not being disloyal to Mom and Dad in feeling this way. Am I?

After a dream-haunted night Emily came awake slowly—from habit at seven a.m. A blanket of silence lay over the house. In a sudden need to confirm that minimum damage had been inflicted by last evening's bomb, she darted from her bed to gaze out of a front-facing window.

A heavy fog hung over the area, lending a foreboding atmosphere. It was as though the house was isolated from the rest of the world. Her eyes settled on the small crater created by the bomb—surrounded now by yellow tape. The police cars were gone. She saw one security guard patrolling the grounds. A second would be somewhere around.

The lights must be on, she surmised—the electrical workers' truck was heading down the driveway. She reached for the lamp on her night table. Yes, electricity had been restored. Why did she feel this surge of relief? It was a sense of returning to normalcy, she decided. But it was hardly normal to be living in fear of what horror some sick mind was conjuring up, perhaps this very moment.

Now she went about the routine of preparing for the day. Their appointment with Hollister wasn't until ten this morning. She could linger in the shower, try to unwind. She'd go downstairs, put up coffee. This morning she'd prepare breakfast for Andrea and herself. *Please, God, don't let the newspapers back home play up what's happening here. Mom and Dad would be so upset. They'd insist I come back home. But I want to stay here. I want to know what's happening. I want to be near Paul.*

She was conscious of a chill now. The air-conditioning must have come back on—hardly necessary this morning. She hesitated. Should she go to the thermostat, turn off the air-conditioning? Would that be assuming too much authority? But Andrea would awaken and be cold, she told herself. Turn off the air-conditioning.

With the air-conditioning switched off, she went into her bathroom to check the hot-water supply. Yes, the boiler had been working for a while. She'd allow herself the luxury of a long, hot shower. Maybe that would ease the tightness between her shoulderblades.

Emerging from the bathroom she debated about what to wear. Her one elegant pantsuit, she told herself—worn only on special occasions. A birthday present from Mom and Dad, she remembered tenderly. A teacher's salary didn't allow for such extravagance. There were college loans to be paid off.

While she dressed, she heard sounds in the bedroom across the hall. Andrea was up. Hurry downstairs to make breakfast this morning. There was a waffle iron in the kitchen, strawberries and blueberries left by the Lamont people last night. She'd make waffles heaped with fresh fruit, she plotted. She was conscious of an urgent need to please her grandmother. As though to apologize for her earlier conviction that Andrea Winston, CEO, was part of the corporate conspiracy to take over the government.

I don't want anything to happen to Andrea. Is she the real object of murder now—as she believes? I don't want that to happen.

I don't want her hurt.

Emily and Andrea were finishing up what Andrea labeled a sumptuous breakfast when they heard Paul calling from the foyer.

"Anybody awake?"

"We're in the breakfast area," Andrea called back. "It's early—come have a cup of coffee with us."

Emily's heart began to pound as Paul appeared. *This is happening too fast. A few days ago I didn't know he existed. But these last few days seem like months.*

"Pull up a chair," Andrea ordered. *She seems to relax in Paul's presence. He's closer to her than to her own children.* "Emily, bring a mug for Paul."

He's so protective of her. Does he still believe I'm here to share in her estate? Am I off the wall in thinking he's drawn to me? As I to him.

Emily brought another of the large mugs Andrea favored in the morning to the table. Andrea poured for Paul.

"Did you manage to get some sleep last night?" Andrea was solicitous.

Paul chuckled wryly. "The mind was racing too much. But I'll catch up tonight." He took a swig of coffee, settled back. "I stopped by the police precinct before I came over—"

Andrea straightened up. "They couldn't have checked out the fingerprints they found in the car this fast?"

"They did. The fingerprints in the car were not Avery's." He seemed ambivalent. "That's good news and bad—"

"I'm glad Avery's not involved," Andrea told him. "That would have broken our hearts."

"But it means we haven't a clue to the identity of Hannah's murderer and the creep behind the two bombings."

"The three murders," Andrea insisted. "David's, Roger's, and Hannah's. The same person killed all three. Nothing will convince me otherwise."

"We'll meet with Hollister—" Paul glanced at his watch— "in about thirty minutes. I'm betting on his coming up with answers. Not right away," he cautioned. "It'll take time—"

"I've waited all these years," Andrea said quietly. "I can wait for the truth to come out. For justice to be done."

Emily cleaned off the table, loaded the dishwasher while Andrea and Paul discussed Hollister's credentials. Then they left for the company in Paul's SUV.

"Go through town so I can pick up the Sunday papers," Andrea told Paul while she settled herself on the rear seat with Emily. "I know," she added and sighed. "I'll only read tormenting news." The newspapers, the TV and radio news were peppered with the happenings at the Winston house.

The town wore its usual Sunday dress. Families driving to the church of their choice. The smaller immigrant population—less affluent—walked in their modest, immaculate Sunday clothes. The bells tolled as they passed one church. These might have been streets back home in Evanston, Emily thought. It might have been streets in a thousand small towns across America.

Driving along these streets of pretty houses with their neat lawns, nobody would realize the trauma the town's undergoing. It's not just Andrea and I who're afraid of what horror will happen next. Everybody is fearful. They're unaware of

Andrea's suspicions—they know only that Hannah was brutally murdered—and wonder if one of them will be next.

They drove on to pleasant Main Street—few stores open on Sunday morning. Paul pulled to a stop before a newspaper stand.

"I'll get the papers—"

Emily started in alarm when a middle-aged man approached the car.

"It's all right," Andrea told her quickly. She leaned forward. "Good-morning, Al. How's the family?"

"Everybody's fine," he told her. "I just wanted to tell you the family will be praying for you at church this morning." He chuckled. "We go to the noon service. Ella likes to sleep late on Sunday mornings, then cook up a storm at breakfast."

Andrea and he exchanged small talk until Paul returned to the car. *People in town like Andrea. They respect her.*

Paul returned to the car, greeted the other man.

"You take good care of her," he exhorted Paul. "She's a fine lady." But his eyes were anxious. *He's worried about a killer being on the loose—and those two bomb threats at the house.*

Paul turned off Main Street on the road that led to Winston Mail Order. "This wagon becomes company property after tomorrow," Paul reported. "I've got lucky. I'm getting delivery of a hybrid." He grinned. "The electric/gas deal I've been after for months."

"That's great." Emily glowed, then self-consciously retreated into an impersonal mode. "It's so good for the environment."

"A shopping mall won't do much for the environment," Andrea grunted. "Paul, how's the 'Stop the Mall' movement going? These last few days I've been living in a vacuum."

"We're picking up more people every day. They're getting unnerved as they realize what the mall could do to this town. We're sure the Mayor's playing games with the would-be developers. He sees a chunk of cash for him if he can push the deal through." He shook his head in exasperation. "We have to get him out in the next election."

"What's happening with the Town Council? Are we getting the referendum on the zoning law?" Her expression said she meant to fight for this.

"There's another meeting Friday evening. I'll be there." Paul's jaw tightened. "They have no right to re-zone Grandma's land without a referendum. That referendum is written into the town charter. We can't let the Town Council override it. And without Grandma's land the mall deal is dead, no matter what re-zoning the Mayor and the Town Council might pull off."

"They couldn't settle on another locale?" Emily asked.

"There's no stretch of acreage that's right—but yes," Paul admitted. "They might compromise. That's why the referendum is so important. With the way the 'Stop the Mall' group is fighting, a referendum has a strong chance of stopping any re-zoning."

Andrea sighed. "I should be working with them—but so much is happening—" She gestured frustration. "Let this Hollister man come up with answers—and I'll be out there fighting with you."

Paul swung off the road into the spacious parking area of Winston Mail Order. Emily leaned forward to inspect the huge sprawl of white brick buildings, set on fifteen acres of pristine property.

"The building there," Andrea pointed, "was the first to go up. Then after three years we had to add a wing—and then more buildings." A hint of pride in her voice. "All built by local construction people. Even a local architect. David insisted on that."

Paul scanned the deserted parking area. "Hollister isn't here yet. But he should be along in five or ten minutes."

Can Jason Hollister track down Hannah's killer—and perhaps the killer of Andrea's husband and her friend—before he strikes again? Those two bombs were warnings. Will the third be an attempt to kill?

Nineteen

Emily was enthralled by the tour of the Winston Mail Order sprawling headquarters that Andrea and Paul were providing while they awaited the arrival of Jason Hollister. All buildings interconnected—a silent witness to the growth of the company.

Now Andrea was leading them into a multi-windowed one-story wing designed to bring the view of towering trees indoors.

"This is our day care center," Andrea explained. "For employees with children from two to five. Mothers—and fathers—can visit with their children during their lunch hour."

"How wonderful—" Emily inspected the array of small-child oriented rooms with awe. Andrea—or whoever designed this wing—understood that small children could be intimidated by large open spaces. "I've heard, of course, that some corporations are providing day care—but far more are needed."

"Absolutely." Andrea nodded in agreement. "Here we are, the finest country in the world in most ways—and so backward in others. France provides day care for every child from three months to three years, and then pre-schools from two and a half to five. England provides day care for working mothers. How can we be so backward?"

"Don't get Andrea started on our shortcomings," Paul joshed. "My grandmother—before her illness—used to call her 'my favorite bleeding-heart liberal.' But she said that with pride and respect—not reproach." He paused as they heard the honk of a car somewhere on the parking area. "That's Hollister. I'll bring him in to your office," he told Andrea.

A few minutes later the four of them were seated in Andrea's office. Almost immediately Emily decided that if anyone could unravel the three murders that haunted Andrea's life, this was the man to do it. A no-nonsense, bright man.

110

Although Hollister had been briefed in detail by Paul, he asked to hear the facts directly from Andrea.

"Paul was thorough," he said, "but sometimes a tiny, seemingly insignificant phrase is a tip-off. Please, let's do this chronologically—beginning with the death of your husband."

Hollister listened absorbedly, interrupted Andrea with occasional questions while she sought to recall every tiny item in the three murders.

"I realize you're convinced the murders are linked," he told her when she'd finished her report, "but we can't rule out the possibility that they are not."

"I understand that," Andrea said with strained politeness.

"Every angle must be explored," Hollister pursued. "Large corporations have ex-employees harboring grudges—some to the point of paranoia. The news media tell us regularly about ex-employees who go berserk. Search through your records for a period of five years. Give me names of any former employees you suspect may be resentful towards Winston Mail Order."

"That's rare in this company—" A hint of reproach in Andrea's eyes.

"Every company runs into this on occasion," Paul agreed with Hollister. "We'll look into it."

"We have a multi-faceted investigation here," Hollister summed up. "I'll need a list of every person who had a key to the house at any one day—every workman in the past year."

"You'll have it," Andrea promised. *But she doesn't believe Hannah was murdered by a disgruntled—psychotic—ex-employee, nor by a workman who did repairs about the house.*

"This will require a lot of patience on your part," Hollister warned Andrea, and she nodded in acceptance. "We can't guarantee to come up with all the answers—we're going back thirty-seven years—but we'll give it the best try possible."

"David's murder and Roger's were swept under the rug. I'm afraid the same will happen with Hannah's," Andrea said. "I need to know who killed my husband, my close friend, and my housekeeper—who was like a family member. I need to know who out there means to kill me—and, perhaps, my son— my granddaughter. I don't care how much it costs, how long it takes. Bring me answers, Mr. Hollister."

*   *   *

111

It was past three p.m. when Hollister returned his notebook to his briefcase and left the meeting. Andrea had promised to have the lists he requested by noon the following day. In the meanwhile, he'd assured them, he had sufficient facts to follow up.

"You're exhausted," Paul sympathized as Andrea leaned back in her chair and closed her eyes for a moment.

"That doesn't matter if Hollister comes up with results," she shrugged.

"Let me take you both to lunch," Paul coaxed. "This has been a grueling morning."

"Take Emily to lunch," Andrea told him. "Drop me off at Rhoda's house—I want to talk to Nora about her moving in tomorrow. And knowing Rhoda, she'll insist on feeding me. Somebody there will drive me home." She took a deep breath. "I've got to dig into household records this afternoon, come up with names for Hollister."

Twenty minutes later Emily and Paul were waiting to be seated at the Colonial Inn. Sunlight poured in from the tall, narrow windows. Damask tablecloths, vases of exquisite fresh flowers, elegant place settings on every table. Here for a little while, Emily told herself, she could forget the terror that engulfed her like a straitjacket night and day.

"I forgot. At Sunday lunch there's always a wait here. People come out of church and come here like homing pigeons." Paul's smile was wry. "But their food is worth the wait."

"Yes—" Emily remembered the earlier lunch here with Paul. The same hostess was on duty. *She has that same glint in her eyes today. She's a romanticist—she suspects that Paul and I are in love.*

The hostess came towards them—though they were not the next in line for a table.

"There'll be a nice alcove table available in just a few moments," she murmured.

"Great." Paul approved. "We're starving."

Every single woman in town must have pursued Paul. He's been too busy with the company to be serious with any of them. Why do I have this weird feeling that there can be something serious for us?

The two older women at the alcove table were leaving. The

hostess beckoned to Emily and Paul. He reached for Emily's elbow, prodded her to their table.

Am I just imagining he feels something special for me? He asked to take Andrea and me to lunch. I mustn't allow my imagination to go berserk.

They made a game of ordering. Paul advising as they considered each item on the gourmet menu. As though lunch was an important event.

"When I was a teenager, my grandmother used to bring me here on special occasions," he reminisced. His eyes rested on Emily with an arousing intensity. "She would have liked you so much—before this cloud destroyed her mind." *How does he mean that?* "For all she teased Andrea about her liberal thinking, she cared about people. She used to boast to her friends when I was at Columbia about how I worked with volunteers distributing government-surplus food to the needy."

"It must have been exciting to live in New York." *Andrea said he'd lived there until his parents had died and his grandmother needed care.*

"For college and law school it was fine." He grimaced. "But working for a New York law firm was—" He was searching for words. "It was brutal. A rat race. Seventy-hour work weeks, internal back-stabbing." He shuddered in recall. *But he doesn't mind seventy-hour weeks at the company.* "I went to law school because I wasn't sure what I wanted to do with life. And in the back of my mind I figured it would be a good background if I ever went into politics. In a small-town situation—"

"In a way you're doing that now. I mean, working with the 'Stop the Mall' group." *He's found his way at Winston Mail Order. His life has a direction.*

"What about you? Did you always want to teach?" *He's worried that Andrea's taking me away from my chosen path.*

"Not really," she confessed. "I was full of doubts when I started college."

He nodded in sympathetic comprehension. "I know. Suddenly you're an adult—you have to make decisions. We're not always ready for that."

"My parents—especially my mother—felt it offered security in a rough world. I love kids, of course—and it was a chance to do something useful." *Am I making sense?*

113

"And now?" he pursued.

"I've taught just one year," she admitted. "And I'm restless."

"You're searching for something more," he guessed.

Their waiter arrived to serve their first course. They chatted briefly—lightly—with him. As though, Emily thought, this was no more than a casual Sunday lunch. For a little while the people here would thrust from their minds the knowledge that a murderer was on the loose in their town. But they'd go home and lock their doors.

"So on Monday morning you become a working woman," he said when their waiter had left their table. His tone of banter betrayed by the somber glint in his eyes.

"I'll try not to disappoint you—and Andrea." She hesitated. "I keep wondering—how is Andrea explaining my presence in her life? I mean," she stammered, "I heard her telling her cleaning woman that I'm her granddaughter—"

"You are her granddaughter," Paul said gently. "And she'll be introducing you that way at the company and around town." He chuckled. "Nobody dares ask Andrea Winston personal questions."

"Isn't my presence awkward for her children?"

"Everybody will assume that you're Celeste's daughter. Celeste was the wild one."

"I feel nothing for her. How can I, when she wants no part of me?" Defiance in her voice now. "But what about my father?"

"Andrea says Celeste has never identified him," Paul reminded her.

"I want to know my father," Emily said in sudden determination.

"If Andrea knew who he was, she'd tell you. That's a secret Celeste will take to her grave. I wish I could be more optimistic. But let me tell you about the company—"

With part of her mind Emily listened to Paul's report on the company's phenomenal growth through the years, about Andrea's shrewdness in expanding to its present eminence despite a stream of hurdles to be surmounted. In a private corner of her mind she probed the route to unearthing the identity of her father.

114

Is my father aware of my birth? Does he know that I exist? Celeste was seventeen—a senior in high school when she got pregnant. She was having a fling with a fellow student—that makes sense, doesn't it? Let me search records. Jason Hollister has one objective. I have another. I must track down my father. I need to know who I am.

Twenty

Emily felt tension spiral in her as Paul swung into the driveway, came to a stop before the house. One of the security guards raised a hand in friendly greeting, continued his pacing. Her eyes focused on the crater from last evening's bomb— still encircled by the eloquent yellow tape that said it was still the subject of police investigation. *Don't think about that now. I'm here with Paul. Nobody—nothing—can hurt me.*

They'd been shameless in holding on to a table when there were others waiting in line for one, she scolded herself. But then the line had disappeared—and they still remained, dallying over coffee, absorbed in talk. It was as though they were trying to make up for all the years past, before they'd met.

"We'll put you to work in the morning," he said lightly while they lingered at the front door. "I promise not to be a slave-driver." *But his eyes are saying so much more.*

"I have no real experience," she told him yet again. Reluctant to relinquish this magic spell that enveloped them.

"You're bright—you'll do fine," he promised.

"Thanks for lunch." *What can I do in a mail order house? Andrea has this strange idea that I'll be intrigued by the business. That in years to come I'll be a clone of her.* "It was lovely."

"Let's do it again soon—"

"I'd like that." *If a security guard wasn't just a few feet away, he'd kiss me. I'd like that.* "See you in the morning."

Walking into the house, Emily was conscious of its funereal quiet. She roamed the lower floor in search of Andrea. She was alone in the house. With an odd wariness she headed up the stairs to her bedroom.

I won't find a bomb waiting at my door. That can't happen again. The security guards are on duty—no one can break into

116

the house. When will I stop feeling as though something devastating will happen any minute? When Hannah's killer is caught—then I'll feel safe.

With a need to hear a friendly voice in the silence of the house, she reached for the phone, called Wendy's private line. She wasn't running up a huge phone bill—Andrea had this unlimited deal on long-distance calls.

"Hello—" Wendy's effervescent voice was like a potent sedative.

"Hi—" Emily punched pillows together against the headboard of her bed, settled down for a comforting talk.

"You're okay?" Wendy was anxious.

"I'm fine, but there's been more—" Striving for calm, Emily reported on the current happenings—punctuated by gasps from Wendy. "You haven't seen anything about it in the Sunday papers?" she asked in sudden alarm. *I'll have to tell Mom and Dad before they hear about it on the radio or TV news or read it in the local papers. But I'm staying here—I'm not running away like a puppy with its tail between its legs.*

"Nothing so far. Just a story about the housekeeper's murder. But Andrea Winston is a big wheel—there's sure to be a follow-up."

"Wendy, she's a good person—" Emily was defensive. "I haven't forgotten how we feel about the way corporate giants are running this country—but she's fine to her employees. They like her."

"You'll know more after you start working in the company." Wendy was skeptical.

"That's tomorrow." Again she was conscious of a tightness between her shoulderblades. She'd be walking into a whole new world. It wouldn't be like going into her classroom for the first time.

"With Paul as your mentor," Wendy recalled. "Hey, that should be cool. The big shot, young, handsome executive and the glamorous young neophyte."

"Wendy, this is life—not a novel."

"Okay, you're in a scary situation—but it's fascinating. Maybe your mom's right," Wendy added, somber now. "Maybe you should cut out, come home—"

"I can't do that. And I know I've got to stop feeling this

way about Paul—it's unreal, part of the craziness here. That's not what's keeping me here," she added. "I feel nothing for my birth mother—but what about my father? What's he like? How does he feel about me? Does he even know I exist?"

"You expect to find him when your birth mother hasn't told anybody who he is?"

"I'll dig," Emily vowed. "I want to know my father."

"Honey, that'll be tough."

"Celeste was in high school when I was conceived. A hundred to one my father is someone in her class."

"Emily, there were thirty-one boys in our senior class!"

"I won't stop till I find him," Emily vowed. "I don't care how long it takes."

Sunday evening's dinner was Lamont Catering's final assignment. Nora—Rhoda's niece—would move in tomorrow morning and take over housekeeping chores. Andrea talked compulsively over dinner. The outdoor floodlights seeped into the dining room despite the drawn drapes—an incessant reminder that a killer lurked somewhere in the darkness.

"I wish so much that your grandfather could have known you." Andrea's voice was wistful, her eyes pained. "He would have adored you. He was a warm, loving father—determined to build a business that the children could carry on when we were gone." *But her children want no part of the business. Why does she believe that I'll feel differently?* "Our whole lives were built around the children—"

"Was he—was he active in the local community?" *Why did I ask that? It sounds almost hostile.*

Andrea's face was luminous in recall. "Oh, David was into everything that was important to the community—even though we were working such long hours to move the business ahead. He always found time to help." She abandoned eating to reflect. "That's why we spoiled Leon and the girls—we felt guilty that there were nights when either David or I wouldn't be home until their bedtime. But we always made sure that one of us spent a little time with them before they went to sleep. It wasn't for ourselves," she said defensively, though guilt lurked in her eyes. "We worked to build for their futures."

"You succeeded." Emily felt an urge to comfort Andrea.

Leon and his sisters wallowed in luxury—but were they happier for it?

"I must become more involved with this re-zoning problem. Paul was one of the founders of the 'Stop the Mall' group—and I contribute regularly. But I should be more active," she chastised herself. "It's not enough to write a check. These developers are unscrupulous—they'll do anything to have that re-zoning overturned. And they have the Mayor in their pockets. But Paul controls his grandmother's estate—and they'll never get that choice chunk of land they're after."

"On that first day I drove into town I noticed how active—how attractive—the downtown business section was. And the line-up of shops was not a replica of malls across the country. It hasn't been like that for years back home."

"We need to restore communities. Allow everyday people to run their small businesses. We need to bring jobs back home," Andrea said with soaring intensity. I know—" And again she was defensive. "I run a major corporation. But I try to provide a decent living for my employees. Who was it that said, 'Most people live lives of quiet desperation'? I want people in this town to find good in their lives."

"I'm proud of what you're setting up with the 'Made in the USA' catalogue," Emily said unsteadily. She'd never expected to feel this close to her grandmother.

"We'll do it together." Andrea's smile was brilliant, but Emily was startled by the glow of tears in her eyes. Now her smile wavered. "It breaks my heart to suggest this—but perhaps it would be wise for you to go back to Evanston until Hannah's killer is captured. I'm terrified that you might be the next victim."

"I want to stay—" Emily hesitated—on the point of adding "Grandma". *Why can't I say that? I know she wants to hear it.* "I need to stay," she amended. "I need to know who I am."

But later—lying sleepless in bed—she asked herself if she was behaving recklessly. Should she go home until the killer was behind bars? Would he—or she—ever be behind bars?

No. I won't run away. I can't run away. I need answers that I can find only here. Who is my father? I could walk past him on the street and not know. And there's Paul. Am I out of my mind to think there can be a life for us together?

119

Twenty-One

Emily awoke in the early-morning semi-darkness to the sound of voices somewhere in front of the house. In instant alarm she darted to a window to look below, sighed with relief. *When will I stop being terrified at any unexplained sound?*

A young woman in jeans and T-shirt was lugging two valises from a beat-up station wagon.

"Stop tryin' to show how strong you are." A scruffy teenager was removing a large carton. "Mom'll kill me if you come down with some nutty backache your first day on the job. Put down one of 'em—I'll bring it into the house."

Emily retreated. That would be Nora, moving into the house. Not in Hannah's room, she remembered. Andrea wouldn't put Nora through that. The large, airy sewing room—with its adjoining bathroom—was to be Nora's.

"We don't use that room since the children are grown up. Hannah used to take such pleasure in altering clothes for them. Every now and then she would make a special party dress for Carol or Celeste," Andrea had explained.

Emily turned to the clock on her night table. It was barely six thirty a.m. Paul had said, "Come in at nine." But she knew that both he and Andrea were usually at their desks by seven thirty or eight a.m. If she'd been teaching, she'd have been out of the house before eight o'clock. Fighting off anxiety about this first day on the job, she rushed to shower and dress.

Out of the shower, she hovered before the wall closet that contained both summer and fall wardrobe. She was aware of a glorious display of sunshine, yet there was a chill in the air. One of those perfect early-fall days—though, no doubt, they'd swelter before the summer dissipated.

Why am I making such a production of deciding what to wear? What would I wear if this was just another teaching day?

120

But it wasn't. Instinct told her she'd spend much time in Paul's company in the course of this first day. She'd be meeting hordes of new people. They wouldn't dare ask embarrassing questions—but curiosity about her would be rampant.

She chose her smart black pantsuit, played it down with a bright-blue T-shirt. Paul's voice trickled across her mind: "You have the same gorgeous blue eyes as Andrea. Anybody who knows her would guess that you're her granddaughter."

With a sense of urgency she left her bedroom, hurried downstairs. She found Andrea and Nora in the kitchen in a discussion about breakfast.

"Nora, just orange juice, scrambled eggs, toast and coffee," Andrea said gently. "We don't worry about fancy breakfasts. And I've already put up coffee." She turned to Emily with a warm smile. "You're up bright and early."

"It's a habit from my teaching days—" She smiled reassuringly at Nora. Andrea had said she was very shy, insecure.

"Oh, Nora, this is my granddaughter Emily. I told you she was living here with me now. Emily, this is Nora—Hannah's niece."

"Hello, Nora—" Andrea said she'd been fired from her last job because she couldn't cope with a dinner party for fourteen. A large dinner party wasn't apt to happen in this house.

"Hello, Miss Emily—" Nora was fidgeting now.

"Just Emily," she corrected, her smile warm. *It must be rough to know her aunt was killed in this house.*

"What will you be wantin' for breakfast—Emily?"

"Just what my grandmother's having," Emily told her. *I can't call her Andrea to strangers. That sounds unfeeling.*

Nora moved to the refrigerator. Andrea and Emily seated themselves at the breakfast table.

"Take your car to work," Andrea instructed. "I keep insane hours—no need for you to hang around waiting to drive home with me. I've told Nora—she's to serve dinner for you at seven p.m. With a little luck I might be able to join you for the next two or three days. If not, she'll just warm up things for me. Oh, and about lunch. Did I mention that we have a company cafeteria? Lunch is available for all employees without cost. That's not all philanthropic," she jeered at herself. "I like to know they're eating healthful, well-prepared food. That makes for better working conditions for the rest of the day."

Within thirty minutes Emily was in her suburban and trailing Andrea's Mercedes. Again, she was beset by a flood of insecurity. What did she have to offer on this job? Why were Andrea and Paul so intrigued with running Winston Mail Order?

What are the odds that I'll want to stay beyond the agreed upon year? But will I be content to go back to teaching? What do I want to do with my life? I'm not a wide-eyed teenager. I should know.

Andrea swung off the road and into the company parking area. Emily followed. The parking area was deserted except for a sprinkling of cars belonging to security workers, Emily assumed, and Paul's SUV. The two women left their cars, walked into the before-business-hours stillness of the main building, which housed the offices.

Andrea led the way down the hall to her private office, paused before the open door of Paul's office.

Paul glanced up from his computer with a welcoming smile. "I'm checking on the delivery due from Indonesia," he told Andrea. "They're running a week behind." Unexpectedly he chuckled. "That's all right—I calculated a week's delay in our scheduling."

Emily stood by—fighting self-consciousness, feeling a surge of inadequacy—while Andrea and Paul discussed various problems anticipated during the coming week.

"All right," Andrea wound up briskly. "Let me get to my office and settle down to work. Emily, don't you let Paul be a slave-driver. He mustn't expect you to understand our whole operation in one morning," she gently joshed. She listened to the sound of heels in the hallway. "That'll be Gina. She's almost as bad a workaholic as Paul and me." She gazed out into the hall. "Gina, come say hello to my granddaughter."

Gina paused at the door. A small, graying, fiftyish woman who radiated efficiency. Emily recalled Andrea's calling Gina at non-business hours during the past hectic days, explaining, "Gina's my rock—she's been with me for eighteen years."

"This is Emily." Andrea glowed with affection. "Emily, Gina—"

"Andrea, I don't believe it!" Gina gazed admiringly at Emily. "She's the image of you."

"Okay, let's get this show on the road." Andrea turned to Emily. "You're in Paul's hands now. There's nothing he doesn't know about Winston Mail Order—"

Paul was a good teacher, Emily thought in a corner of her mind while she tried to absorb every small detail that he thrust at her. Fearful of appearing stupid. The scope of the business, the list of foreign suppliers astonished her. But she clung to the knowledge that Andrea was serious about cutting back on purchases from foreign sweatshops. About saving American jobs.

"It's nine a.m.," Paul said, finishing up a monologue about the shipping procedures of the company. "The cafeteria is open. Let's go grab a cup of coffee."

The cafeteria was all but deserted at this hour. But a coffee urn was available for self-service along with a line-up of bagels, Danish, and muffins.

"This is set up for early-morning fixes and morning and afternoon breaks," Paul explained, pouring coffee for the two of them. He grinned at her glow of astonishment. "This is not the everyday workplace—but then Andrea isn't the everyday workplace boss."

"She's not at all what I expected," Emily confessed. *I don't want to lose her—now that I've found her. How could anyone want to kill her?*

Paul stared into space. "I won't feel a moment of peace until Hannah's murderer is behind bars. The house is under around-the-clock guard," he conceded. "And I've arranged for stepped-up security here at the company—but I worry." His eyes rested on Emily. "I suspect you're meant to be frightened away—so the killer will have easier access to Andrea. But we can't be sure that we have every angle covered. We can just keep our fingers crossed and pray."

Twenty-Two

Jason Hollister stifled a yawn as he straddled a stool at the fourth diner of the morning. He stared with a lack of enthusiasm at the array of donuts, bagels and assorted cakes housed on a glass-enclosed shelf on the wall facing him. A carbon copy of the three previous diners. Plastic-upholstered chairs, plastic table tops, pots of greenery at intervals to relieve the astringent atmosphere. An ATM strategically placed.

It was close to nine a.m.—the en-route-to-work crowd had dissipated. The mothers with babies and toddlers were beginning to stream into the diner along with a contingent of the elderly. Not a crowd likely to provide him with the information he sought.

He'd started the breakfast rounds at seven a.m., after running the dinner circuit last evening. In situations such as his current assignment he made a point of ferreting out the local reaction to the murder in question. So far his informal conversation had netted nothing of value.

"Coffee to start?" the counterman asked as Jason pretended to peruse the menu.

"Yeah. Decaf," he added.

He'd worked out a routine on such excursions as this. Order something light that could be stretched out in the eating. Dawdle over coffee. Make casual conversation with the counterman. Most times another stool-straddler would join in. In his current case the routine had earned him zilch.

The counter was unpopular with young mothers and seniors, but a pair of forty-ish men in beat-up jeans, T-shirts, and not-long-for-this-world sneakers sat a few stools down from him. Unemployed—or just off the midnight shift? Possible founts of information.

The counterman returned with a mug of decaf. Jason ordered poached eggs and wholewheat toast.

"Orange juice comes with it," the counterman told him. "Breakfast Special Number Three."

"I'll skip the orange juice—I'm allergic," Jason lied.

He'd toy with the eggs, ignore the toast. How much could one man consume as breakfast? This was his fourth go-round. He managed a covert inspection of the two men a few stools down.

"I hear you had a murder here in town," he remarked when one of the men turned to view him with curiosity. The business-suit types had deserted the diner by now. "They catch the guy yet?"

"The cops ain't breakin' their backs on this one," the other man jeered. "They ain't catchin' the guy what done it. He was too smart for them."

"Hank, the fuzz don't break their backs on anything," his companion added. "Lucky we don't have murders in this town often. When we do, it's some guy beatin' up on his old lady."

"This one seems to be getting a lot of newspaper space," Jason remarked. "I'm in town on business—" He shrugged. "I don't have much else to do between appointments except to read the newspaper and watch television."

"Yeah," the second man drawled, "the newspapers and the radio and TV are playin' this up big because the murdered broad worked for old lady Winston. She owns Winston Mail Order—she's one of the richest women in this country, some-body told me."

"It should have been the old bitch herself who got murdered," the one called Hank said, his eyes smoldering with rekindled rage. "The guy killed the wrong woman. What do you wanna bet it was a mistake?"

"Hey, let's get outta here," the other man said, slapping down money for his check. "We ain't earnin' no money sittin' here on our asses."

Jason waited until the two men left the restaurant, then asked the counterman if he knew their names.

"Yeah—" But the counterman was wary. "Why do you want to know?"

"An ad agency I'm associated with is about to film a

commercial here in town. Those two look like perfect casting for walk-ons."

"You're kiddin'? Somebody doing TV commercials here in town?"

"Just a couple of background shots—then they wrap it up down in their New York studios."

"Lemme write their names down for you." The counterman bustled about for paper and pen. "Hey, let me know when it comes out. I'm here every day except Sunday."

Back in his rented car, Jason reached for his cellphone, called Andrea Winston's private number. Hannah Bolton's killer might be nailed in record time. So often these days, it seemed, an angry ex-employee turned killer.

"Yes—" Her voice—crisp, laden with tension—came to him on the second ring.

"Jason Hollister," he identified himself. "Do you know two men named Hank Reagan and Frank Mattox?"

"I know one of them," Andrea recalled after a moment. "Hank Reagan." *That would be the one who had called her "an old bitch."* "He worked in the Shipping Department for several years. He got fired for being drunk on the job. Not once—but three times. He was given two warnings, then fired. That was about six years ago. I remember because he became so nasty we had to get a restraining order to keep him off the property."

So the police have a file on the bastard.

"I suggest you call the District Attorney's office," Jason said. "Tell them you just remembered this incident."

"As soon as we're off the phone."

"I'll follow through, of course—but police detectives should check him out." *Reagan could be Hannah Bolton's killer. This will destroy Winston's theory of a serial murderer. Reagan was a small child when her husband was murdered.*

"The police are convinced Hannah was meant to be the victim." Jason heard frustration in her voice. "They don't believe I was the prime target."

"You have enough power in this town to order them to investigate Hank Reagan. Do it, Mrs. Winston. If he's guilty, you want to see him behind bars."

126

Off the phone with Jason Hollister, Andrea sat immobile, going over in her mind what he had told her. *Of course I want Hannah's killer caught. But if it's Hank Reagan, then I still don't know who killed David and Roger.*

Twenty-Three

Making a mental note that he was to be at Andrea Winston's office at noon to pick up the lists he'd requested, Jason Hollister laid out his morning's itinerary. Figure out how Hank Reagan would be apt to spend his idle time. What tavern in town he would visit, what pool hall or bowling alley.

Winston said he'd worked for her company six years ago. But sometimes these psychotic resentments built up over a period of years. *If the Bolton murder is a snap, that still leaves two cases to be solved. Her husband was killed thirty-seven years ago—and her friend a lot of years back, too. Both will be a bitch to close.*

Hollister roamed about town, made notes. How the hell did this Reagan creep earn a living? He wouldn't be too worried about how he picked up bucks for survival. This could have been a murder for hire.

From what he'd been told, the perp here was not a shrewd operator. Entry to the house on the night of the murder was uncomplicated. So he'd made it appear the murder was a robbery gone wrong—that didn't require brains. It happened often on TV crime shows.

Paul said the cops had reported no identifying fingerprints to track down: "They're making noises about 'following leads'—but I suspect they see it going nowhere." All right, he ordered himself, start with this Reagan character's neighborhood. Ask questions.

By noon Emily felt as though she'd been on the job long hours. She was tense, tired, struggling to absorb what was being thrown at her. Paul was warm, friendly—but his attitude towards her now, she taunted herself, was teacher to student. Nothing else showed through.

128

Have I been wrong all along? No—I wasn't wrong. There's this special chemistry between us. He knows how to draw lines. I don't. Not yet.

Paul paused in mid-sentence when his cellphone rang. He picked up. Emily heard Andrea's voice respond to his brisk "Yes."

"Jason Hollister has just arrived. I'd like you and Emily to sit in on our conference."

"We'll be right there," Paul said.

Brushing past a stream of employees en route to the building's cafeteria, Paul and Emily headed back to the main wing.

"He's here to pick up lists," Paul pointed out, his voice low. To anyone who might encounter Hollister, he was presumably a businessman here to make a deal with Andrea. "We can't expect any results this fast."

They arrived at Andrea's office as Gina was placing a lunch tray on Andrea's desk. Hollister was nursing a mug of coffee while he studied the contents of a sheaf of papers in one hand.

"Would you like coffee?" Gina asked Emily and Paul. Both rejected this with a smile.

"No calls, Gina," Andrea told her. "And close the door, please."

Emily sensed tension in the air. What had Hollister discovered?

Andrea waited until her office door was closed, then turned to Emily and Paul. "We have to rule out Hank Reagan."

In a way she's relieved—her serial killer conviction still stands. One killer responsible for three murders.

"Jason tells me Reagan was incapacitated last Tuesday evening. He was in a fist fight with a next-door neighbor. He was in the hospital emergency from around eight p.m. Tuesday night until he was dismissed early the following morning."

"That was a long shot. We have a lot of leads to follow—" Jason indicated the lists Andrea had supplied. "But it's important to check out every one. A chore—but essential."

"If there's anything we can do to help," Paul told him, "just whistle."

Emily realized there was little she or Andrea or Paul could do but wait while Jason Hollister pursued whatever leads he could unearth. Andrea was outspoken: "Don't count on the police. They're sure Hannah was murdered by a burglar. They'll put up some show of trying to track him down. But their search will go nowhere."

Emily made a point of calling home every two or three days—to reassure her parents that she was all right.

"Mom, there's no need for you and Dad to worry about me," she reiterated on each call. "I'm fine. The security at the house and the company is great. The police are sure Hannah was murdered by a would-be robber—probably some drifter." Unlikely, she thought guiltily, but it was reassurance for Mom and Dad.

She called Wendy on Sunday evenings, knowing Wendy was avid for reports.

"It's like following a new TV series," Wendy said, giggling. "I'm dying to know what'll happen next."

Life revolved around the activities at the company. Solicitous about Andrea and Emily's unconventionally late dinner hours, Nora had taken it upon herself to transport steaming hot food, dishes and silverware to the night-deserted company cafeteria and serve them—at what she considered "decent eatin' hours"—with Paul joining them.

Ever conscious that a murderer continued on the loose, Emily struggled to convince herself security was sufficient to protect both Andrea and her. Each morning she drove to the office at the same time as Andrea. She spent endless hours in Paul's company. Each day was the same.

She hadn't expected so much of Paul's enthusiasm for the business to be reflected in her. Winston Mail Order employees amazed her with their air of involvement in the business. She kept waiting to see some disenchantment. Those who didn't fit into the mold were given warnings before being fired, Paul explained.

"Our employees know that despite the bad economy their jobs are secure. When profits drop, Andrea cuts at the top— beginning with herself. She hasn't drawn a cent of salary in the last seven months. Some of us have taken a thirty percent cut. Andrea knows we can sit out the bad times."

Only during their shared lunch hour did Paul dismiss the teacher–student attitude. He talked about his hopes for the company and the town—and her heart would pound because his eyes told her he expected her to be part of his life.

He's afraid to rush me. We've known each other such a little while. But doesn't he realize how I feel about him? Or has he sworn total commitment to the business and there's no room in his life for anything else?

She was enthralled that work was going full blast on Andrea's "Made in the USA" line and that she was part of it. At regular intervals she phoned Wendy to discuss the company's new venture: "I know it's just a small step—but it's exciting to be part of something that could become so important to the country. Everywhere you look—it's constantly reported by the media—American jobs are being exported. If a thousand towns across the country would follow Andrea's lead, do you realize how many jobs would be saved?"

Blueprints were being drawn for new permanent manufacturing facilities even while temporary facilities were scheduled. Despite her conviction that a job at Winston Mail Order would be a deadly bore, she was engrossed every minute of the long days she spent at the company. She understood Andrea's and Paul's devotion to the company.

"Andrea's going ahead with construction before mortgage rates start soaring upward," Paul reported over lunch today. "How're you doing with the trailer people?"

"I cried a little—they've promised delivery within the next three days." She was pleased at pulling this off. They'd talked about delivery in two weeks.

Paul nodded in approval. "I have equipment ready to be shipped to us the minute we have working areas set up. We'll be manufacturing by the end of next week. We'll have another meeting this evening with the designers."

"Right," Emily recalled. Astonished but delighted to be involved with the myriad meetings—not only for the "Made in the USA" line but for the company's regular lines as well. At first she'd felt abashed at sitting in at meetings with high-level employees twice her age, but they accepted her. Their respect for Paul was obvious—and she was recognized as Andrea's granddaughter who'd someday rise to the head of the firm.

"The catalogue staff is almost ready to send the first 'Made

131

in the USA' catalogue to the printer—" Paul punctured her introspection. "And you're working with Andrea on setting up the ad campaign with our agency down in New York. We're right on schedule."

But neither the police nor Jason Hollister are coming up with any leads on the murderer who's running loose in this town.

"It sounds exciting—" Emily forced herself back to the moment.

"It'll be very small at first," Paul warned yet again. "And it won't be easy to sell."

"But it's a beginning." she said earnestly. "Someone has to lead the way."

By the Friday of her third week at the company Emily was rebellious at the lack of progress in nailing Hannah's killer. Jason Hollister had brought in another investigator to help him sort out all possible suspects. He was methodically going down the lists, eliminating those that must be ruled out. He made nightly reports to Andrea, brought up innumerable questions. *But nothing is happening.*

In no way could she help to nail Hannah's killer—but she harbored a growing compulsion to try to identify her father. *I might walk past him in the street and not know it. He may not even know I exist.*

She felt only contempt for her mother—but she ached to know her father. To know that he was a decent human being. That something of him was reflected in her.

Evenings Emily remained at the company along with Andrea and Paul—working as part of the team, thrilled when a small suggestion of hers was approved. She was impatient to see the new line blossom—though she realized it was a small segment of the Winston Mail Order empire. *But I'm part of making it happen!*

On this Friday evening Andrea insisted Paul join Emily and her for a late dinner at the house. They'd just emerged from a lengthy meeting about the launch of the new line. At times, Emily marveled, they became so engrossed in this they forgot the danger that hovered over them.

"I told Nora not to bring dinner here tonight. That we'd be home no later than eight thirty. We need an early night."

"Half a day," Paul joshed. "But Nora won't be expecting me."

"She always prepares enough for five." A glint in Andrea's eyes now. "You'd better come. She loves having a handsome young man at the table."

"If she doesn't stop feeding me the way she does," Paul warned, grinning, "I'll be a tubby young man."

As usual dinner conversation revolved around the business. Again—it was a question that haunted her at errant moments—Emily asked herself if Paul would ever have time in his life for anything but Winston Mail Order. Yet at regular intervals his eyes told her he felt more for her than for just a new addition to the company.

After dinner—when Paul had left and Andrea and Emily prepared to retire for the night, Andrea urged Emily to sleep late in the morning.

"Take the weekend off," she encouraged. "You've been putting in long hours. Give yourself a break."

Not just a break from the office, Andrea means. We're both so uptight every minute we're awake. Sleeping badly. The security guards around the house twenty-four hours a day, the floodlights that seep into the house, special security at the company. Constant reminders that a killer is on the loose. And Andrea—or me—the intended victim.

"Just this weekend," Emily stipulated. But her mind was charging ahead. *If I don't go in to the office tomorrow, I can spend the whole day at the library—scratching for a clue to the boy who made Celeste pregnant. Searching for my father.*

She remained in bed on Saturday morning until she heard Andrea drive away. Now she rose and dressed hurriedly, went downstairs for breakfast. Nora would be upset if she skipped breakfast—fearful of some lapse on her part. And after breakfast, she'd drive to the public library. A phone call gave her the Saturday hours. The library would open at ten a.m..

Without any specific plan in her mind other than to unearth whatever she could about Celeste's senior year in high school, Emily headed for the library—arriving there moments after it opened.

She inquired about the availability of local high-school annuals. *Let me discover what boys—now mature men—were in Celeste's senior class. Maybe there'll be some tiny link between Celeste and one of them.*

"We have a whole section on our school activities from kindergarten through high school. The high-school annuals, school newspapers, all special events," the librarian told her. Curious, Emily suspected, about her interest in these. "All the material is in the far corner of the research room there to the right—"

She pointed in that direction.

Her heart pounding in anticipation Emily walked into the research room. *The librarian didn't say how far back their records go. Twenty-four years? Please God, let it be.*

She was grateful that the research room was empty except for her at this hour. With a sigh of relief she discovered that the records went back for thirty years. Almost immediately she pulled from a shelf the yearbook she sought. She sat down at one of the long tables provided for researchers, flipped open the Woodhaven High Senior Annual. Wendy's exhortation tickertaped across her mind: "Emily, there were thirty-one boys in our senior class."

Flipping through the pages—convinced that one male student on these pages was her father—Emily tried to cope with reality. How could she narrow this down? Maybe the school papers would provide a lead. Some line about whom Celeste was dating.

She pored over the yearbook, then returned to the librarian to request copies of the school newspapers in that period.

"We have the school newspapers on microfilm," the librarian explained. "What years would you like?"

Churning with anticipation Emily settled herself at a microfilm projector in the research room, threaded the tape into place.

Her heart began to pound as she read. Here were reports on the school sporting events, proms, dances. Celeste seemed to dart from boy to boy. All right, she exulted at last—she'd nailed it down to five. *But where do I go from here?*

Twenty-Four

Emily sat before the microfilm projector and searched her mind for direction. Her eyes traveled to the wall clock. It was almost three p.m. *Have I been here that long? All right, call it a day.*

Now she was conscious of a deep hunger. She hadn't bothered to go out for lunch—she'd been too engrossed in her research. What had seemed an almost impossible task now appeared within reach. Leave the car in the library parking area, walk over to Main Street and find a coffee shop, she ordered herself. The Oasis. Have a late lunch—dinner was hours away.

Walking out of the library, she was aware of a drop in temperature. The sky was overcast, a sharp chill in the air. She quickened her pace. Her mind still reeling from the realization that finding her father was more than a fanciful dream. One of the five boys Celeste had dated in those months before she became pregnant was her father.

She turned left on Main Street, paused, glanced about for the Oasis. She smiled at the sight of an elderly man—white hair falling about his shoulders, beard unkempt—who was searching with such absorption for an occasional weed in one of the huge urns of chrysanthemums that graced Main Street sidewalks. Like the gardener at some palatial estate intent on providing perfection.

As though feeling her gaze on him, he turned around to face her. He seemed frozen—first in shock, then transfixed in wonder. Clutching at a side of the urn he pulled himself to his feet.

"Andrea," he called to her. Ecstatic. "Andrea, you've come back. You've come back to me!"

She stood immobile for an instant while he made a laborious move to her.

135

"No," she whispered, cold with shock, moving away. "I'm not Andrea. I'm Emily—her granddaughter."

"You're my Andrea." He held his arms wide. "I knew you'd come back to me!"

"No," she whispered while passers-by gaped in curiosity, then darted away. *He's Paul's grandfather! Who else can he be?*

She strode down the street—knowing she'd left him behind, sighed with relief when she spied the Oasis just ahead. The coffee shop was lightly populated at this hour. The public phone at the rear was not in use. She fumbled in her purse for change. Call Paul. Tell him what just happened.

"Yes—" His crisp, business-like voice responded on the first ring.

"Paul, it's me—Emily." She strived for calm. "Something weird just happened—" Stumbling over the words in her rush, she reported on her encounter with the man she was convinced was his grandfather.

"That's Avery," Paul confirmed. *He's upset. I shouldn't have told him.* "Where are you?"

"At the Oasis. I was so hungry—I came in here for lunch. I know it's late, but—" Her voice ebbed away.

"Wait for me. I'll be there in ten minutes. But don't wait for lunch—" His voice gently teasing. "Starving yourself isn't on the list of approved activities."

She settled in a booth, studied the menu the waitress gave her.

Seeing only the startled face of the elderly man at the urn of chrysanthemums. He must be Paul's grandfather.

"Sliced turkey on wholewheat toast," she stammered because the waitress was waiting for her to order. "And coffee. Decaf."

She shouldn't have called Paul, she berated herself again. He had enough problems on his plate. He'd worry about his grandfather—so confused, so removed from reality. But there was nothing Paul could do to help. *I shouldn't have called him.*

From her booth in the Oasis Emily saw Paul wedge his new hybrid—the Toyota Prius that operated alternately on battery and gas—into an empty parking spot out front. She was assaulted by fresh guilt at having called him. He cherished the hours at the company when he was alone there: "Weekends

136

are when I get the most work done—when nobody's around with questions and there's this beautiful silence."

Paul hurried into the Oasis, waved to a waitress en route to her booth.

"Coffee and a toasted low-fat muffin for me, Betty—" He indicated his destination.

Everybody seemed to know Paul—because he was so concerned about the welfare of the town. How often he left the company well into the evening and then raced over to some urgent civic meeting.

"Hi—" She managed a casual smile as he slid into the booth.

"The old boy scared you," he sympathized.

"No," she denied. "I was startled. I thought you should know his—his reaction to me. He was shaken—"

"Tell me exactly what happened," Paul ordered, his eyes clinging to hers.

Haltingly Emily reported on her brief encounter with Avery.

"I'll call Dr. Franklin." Paul stared into space. His mind racing. "The shrink that looks in on him every now and then," he explained because Emily seemed bewildered. "Grandma arranged for that years ago. She felt responsible for him— even though they were separated." He gestured his incomprehension, yet Emily suspected he shared his grandmother's feelings.

"Is your grandfather on medication?" Emily struggled to understand the situation.

"When Dr. Franklin prescribed medication a long time ago, he grew violent, Grandma told me. For almost a year, she said, he wouldn't let Dr. Franklin near him. When Grandma began to lose touch with reality, I took over—but so little can be done without his cooperation."

"It was stupid of me to drag you away from work this way—"

"No. I should be aware of his state of mind. When Grandma was all right, she'd leave bags of groceries at his cabin or slip money under the door. He lives in some private little fenced-in world that keeps out everybody else. I'll explain the situation to Dr. Franklin. Seeing you—thinking you were Andrea—sent his mind charging back through the years." He paused as Betty approached the table with his coffee and muffin.

"The muffin's a banana-nut, the one you like best," Betty

chirped. Emily was aware of her covert glance in her direction. An approving glance, she interpreted.

"And how are you observing your first Saturday away from work?" Paul asked when they were alone again. He meant to move away from serious talk, Emily interpreted.

She hesitated. Wendy accused her of always saying what was on her mind. "I was at the public library for hours—I forgot about lunch. I know there's nothing I can do to help solve Hannah's murder—and the two earlier ones. I want so much to know who is my father—"

"Honey, nobody knows that except Celeste," he reminded her.

"I mean to change that. I don't know how just yet," she admitted, "but I need to know who I am—and until I find my father, I won't know."

"What were you doing at the library?" His eyes searched hers.

"I realize I'm just fishing—but I'm searching for some unexpected lead." Striving for calm she reported on her efforts at the library. "In her senior year—according to her high-school newspaper—Celeste dated five boys. I'll begin with that list."

"Do you have it with you?" he asked after a moment. Coffee and muffin forgotten.

"Yes." She fished in her purse for her notebook. *He doesn't think I'm a kook. He wants to help me!*

Paul studied the names she indicated.

"You can cut it down to four," he told her. "Jeff Donavan died in a car accident eleven years ago.

"And the others?" she pressed.

"Bill Cabrini's parents still live in town. He moved to California a couple of years ago. He has a job out there with IBM." Paul's eyes were compassionate. "This will be one hell of a search—your father may be none of these—"

"It's something I have to do. I know—I may be way off track. But I have to begin somewhere." She was aware of a growing tightness in her throat at the task that confronted her.

"I'll try to help," Paul said after a moment. *He's humoring me—he doesn't believe I can find my father.* "It won't be easy—"

"You think I'm spinning my wheels." Despair was making inroads on rebellious determination.

138

"I didn't say that," he protested. But his eyes were a dead giveaway.

"Perhaps I jumped too fast," she acknowledged. "It's just that—that I'm so desperate to know my father. So we check out these four boys from Celeste's last year in high school," she jeered at herself. "One of them is going to come out and say, 'I had a fling with Celeste'? She wasn't even there the whole school year. She was sent to boarding school when she realized she was pregnant."

"We might have better luck if we can track down some girl friend she ran with that year." *He said "we"—he meant it about helping me.* "I'd say the most practical step is to go back to the school newspapers—maybe to the society pages of the *Enquirer*. Something there just might point to a girl-friend."

Emily's face lighted. "I'll go back to the library microfilm, see what surfaces." *This isn't a dead-end. Paul's right on target. Dig up Celeste's high-school girl friend. Ask questions. She'll know who was seriously involved with Celeste.*

"Give me a list of the whole senior class," Paul instructed. "I'll go over it, check if there's anyone that I might just casually question."

"Right." Emily searched her mind for other angles. "What about class reunions?" Instantly she rejected this. "Celeste wouldn't be the kind to—"

"That's it!" Paul snapped his fingers. "Last year was the twenty-third anniversary of Celeste's graduating class. Neil Roberts had been class president, was active in arranging the reunion, got a load of publicity for it. I remember because he was running for Town Councilman last year, used that in his campaign." He grimaced. "He's one of the bad apples on the Town Council. I'll steer clear of him—he hates my guts."

"You suspect Celeste may have attended the reunion?"

"I doubt it," Paul said. "But somebody at the reunion—still living here in town—might be in a reminiscent mood. Just might remember whom Celeste teamed up with in high school."

"Her girl friend in her senior year will know what boys she dated—which one was special." Emily glowed. "Which one is my father."

139

Twenty-Five

In the coming week Emily fretted that she could find no free time to return to the library for further research. The "Made in the USA" line was taking shape—she had time for nothing else. Nor would Paul have time to track down someone at Celeste's twenty-third high-school reunion who might be in a talking mood. The search for her father was on hold.

Jason Hollister was on a "ruling out" path. The lists Andrea gave him were growing smaller: "I warned you this would be a slow process. And I'm working on your conviction that the same person is responsible for three murders. Therefore, the killer has to be of a certain age. He has to have been in Woodhaven on specific dates. I'm narrowing it down."

Paul was disturbed by the battle being fought within the Town Council over the re-zoning law. Word had leaked out about an emergency meeting being held this evening.

"Even if the rotten law gets pushed through," he pointed out to Emily as he prepared to take off for the meeting, "I control Grandma's property. It won't ever be sold to the mall syndicate."

"What about other acreage?"

Paul frowned. "That's becoming a major problem. I hear that Bob Reynolds—he's a local real-estate broker close to Mayor Davis—is pushing the syndicate to settle for another tract—far less desirable but available. And included in the proposed re-zoning area. One that just happens to be owned by Davis's sister," he pointed out. "Reynolds is hinting at terrific tax abatements, other goodies to put the deal through. That's why I want to get over to that meeting."

"Will you be allowed to speak?" Emily was puzzled. Wouldn't the meeting be closed?

Paul chuckled. "I send in messages asking to be allowed to speak. I know it won't happen—but before the evening's over, word leaks to me about what's happening behind those closed doors." He reached for his briefcase. "If anything worth reporting comes through, I'll buzz you at home."

Forty minutes later—close to ten p.m.—Emily and Andrea were saying good-night to the security guards and heading for Andrea's Mercedes.

"Drive carefully," a guard called after them as they reached the side door leading to the parking area. Emily knew he'd been coached by Paul to watch until they were safely inside the car, even though a pair of guards patrolled the grounds since Hannah's murder. "The roads are kind of slick already." Emily and Andrea exchanged a surprised glance. Neither had been aware of the rain.

"Should I run back for umbrellas?" Emily asked while they peered out at what appeared to be a steady rainfall.

"Let's make a run for it," Andrea told her.

When they were halfway to the house, the rain became a thunderstorm. Lightning zigzagged across the sky. Thunder rumbled like cannon fire. The temperature felt as though it had dropped ten degrees, Emily thought when they emerged from the car in the garage.

"What a rotten night." Andrea grunted in distaste. "Rough on the security guards."

"Nora's probably been feeding them coffee every hour," Emily surmised.

Inside the house they noted Nora had retired for the night. She was up by six a.m.—determined to be on duty if breakfast was to be served earlier than the usual seven a.m. They discovered the inevitable carafe of fresh-brewed decaf kept warm on the coffee-maker—a plate of Nora's superb low-fat muffins beside it. Andrea had declared three days after her arrival in the household that Nora was a treasure.

"Paul said he'd call," Emily told Andrea while she reached into the refrigerator for milk. "If there's any word from the Town Council meeting."

Andrea nodded. "He's always there demanding a hearing as a representative of a property-owner. Leave it to Paul to know every tiny technicality that can be utilized. His law school training comes in handy." She gazed speculatively into space. "One of these days—when the business settles down

141

to a less hectic mode—he'll be a power in this town. In this state. He'll promote good things."

Emily poured coffee into the exquisite Haviland cups Nora had set on a tray along with sugar bowl and creamer, and she and Andrea settled themselves at the breakfast table. Both stiffened to attention at the sound of a car pulling up before the house. *When will any unexpected sound not alarm us?* They heard voices outside.

"It's Paul." Emily hurried from the breakfast nook and down the hall to the foyer to greet him.

"The rain's let up a lot," Paul told Emily as he strode to the opened door. *What is he carrying in his arm that way?*

"I hope you don't mind an unexpected visitor," he said, his smile whimsical. "I couldn't leave this little guy meowing in the middle of the road in a thunderstorm."

"He's sweet—" Emily reached for the tiny ball of black and white fur.

"He may still be wet," Paul warned, "though I tried to dry him with paper toweling I keep in the car."

"I don't mind. Oh, he's trembling," Emily realized. "Half-scared to death."

"Nothing that a saucer of milk won't cure," Paul predicted. "I found him sitting there in the middle of the road just wailing his little heart out. It's a miracle I didn't hit him."

"He must have got out of a door without anybody knowing—" Emily surmised. "He's so little—he can't be more than a couple of months old."

"I suspect he was thrown out." Paul was grim. "He looks battered around the face. I'll try to find a home for him tomorrow. If I kept him, he'd be alone so much."

"Maybe we can keep him," Emily said impulsively. "Nora would be here with him—and she loves everything on four feet."

Andrea glanced up with a welcoming smile as they arrived at the breakfast-room entrance. "And what do you have there?"

"Paul found him all alone in the middle of the road," Emily said. "He's so scared. I thought—maybe we could keep him?"

"Of course we'll keep him," Andrea crooned. "Nora will spoil him to death—he'll be ecstatic here."

"He may be hungry," Emily guessed.

"He'd probably love some milk." Andrea pulled the saucer

142

from beneath her cup, reached for the creamer and poured. "Put him on the floor—" Paul took the saucer, filled almost to overflowing and set it down on the floor while Emily deposited the kitten beside it.

"Oh, he's interested!" Emily's face glowed.

The tiny red tongue lapped in ecstasy while the three watched in approval. Then all at once he froze, an instant later seemed to go into convulsions.

"He was too young for milk," Emily whispered in anguish. "What can we do for him?"

"Nothing," Paul said quietly as the kitten lay still, already stiffening in death.

"Emily and I were meant to drink that milk," Andrea said with deadly calm. "That precious kitten saved our lives."

"Let's don't jump too fast," Paul cautioned. "It could have been a sick little kitten. Let me get Jamie Abel over here to give us a professional diagnosis—" He reached for the cordless phone in a niche on the wall.

"Jamie Abel is a veterinarian?" Emily asked Andrea.

Andrea nodded. "The best. Ever since he opened his office about fifteen years ago, he's cared for my pets. The last— Heidi, a wonderful collie—had to be put down about a year ago. Jamie tried so hard to save her. When I lost her, I swore I'd never bring in another pup—" She paused now so that she and Emily could listen in to Paul's conversation with the vet.

"We may be all wrong in suspecting poison," Paul told Jamie Abel. "You know how on edge we are these days. Before we bring in the cops, I'd like you to have a look at this poor little guy. I know it's late but—" He paused, nodded in relief. "I'll tell the security guards to expect you."

In a matter of minutes Jamie Abel—wiry, tousled-haired, with an expressive face that exuded compassion—was in the breakfast nook and inspecting the kitten.

"He was so little, so sweet," Emily mourned.

"He drank milk from the creamer there?" Jamie asked.

"Yes—" Andrea shivered. "If he hadn't been here, Emily and I would have poured it in our coffee."

Jamie reached for the creamer, sniffed, then winced. "He was poisoned. Cyanide in the milk." *Poison that was meant for Andrea or me. Or both of us.* "Call the cops," Jamie told Paul. "Now."

143

Twenty-Six

Emily and Andrea sat close together on the living-room sofa—as though finding comfort in closeness. *We were minutes away from death. How can Andrea appear so calm? But I know she's as shaken as I am. That poor little kitten— he saved our lives. Who is the monster out to kill Andrea— and now me, as well?*

Jamie Abel was explaining the situation to the pair of detectives who'd responded to their call within minutes.

"We'll have the kitten and the milk checked in the police lab," Detective Hendricks told Abel, "though I'm sure it'll confirm your diagnosis." Now he turned to Andrea. "Who served the coffee, Mrs. Winston?"

"A carafe of coffee was left on the coffee-maker for us," Andrea explained. "My granddaughter and I arrived home around ten—my housekeeper had retired for the night."

"I brought the container of milk out of the refrigerator," Emily began. "I—"

"Had the container already been opened?" the second detective—who'd introduced himself as Detective O'Leary—broke in.

"Yes—" Emily tried to follow his thinking.

"By the housekeeper," O'Leary pinpointed, exchanging a glance with his partner.

"We'd like to talk to her," Hendricks told Andrea.

"She's asleep," Andrea protested uneasily.

"We need to talk to her," Hendricks persisted. "Please call her."

Reluctantly Andrea rose to her feet. "She's very shy—and she'll be terribly upset—" All at once Andrea seemed alarmed. Emily read her mind. *Did Nora take a glass of milk to her room to drink before she went to bed—the way she did some nights? Is Nora all right?*

"Shouldn't the supermarket where the milk was bought be alerted to take other containers off the shelf?" Emily gazed from one detective to the other. *Can they suspect Nora? That's absurd.* "Shouldn't the supplier be notified?" *Why am I saying this? Andrea and I were the intended victims. The police won't find contaminated milk containers anywhere else.*

"That'll be handled." Hendricks was terse. He turned to Andrea again. "Right now we need to talk to the housekeeper."

"I'll wake her." Andrea strode from the room in sudden haste. Fearful, Emily interpreted, of what she would find.

"How long has the housekeeper been employed here?" O'Leary was being offhand, but Emily followed his thinking. Hannah had been murdered roughly a month ago. Nora had to be new on the job. *But Nora didn't put cyanide in that container of milk.*

In moments Andrea returned with Nora—wrapped in a faded robe, frightened. *But she's all right—she didn't drink any of that milk. Thank God for that.*

"Nora, we just have a few questions." Hendricks was gentle in his approach. "Mrs. Winston has told you what happened?"

"Yes, sir—" Nora gazed from him to Andrea, as though seeking support.

"Where did you buy the container of milk that was used tonight?" he asked.

"At the Woodhaven Supermarket," Nora told him.

"You opened it in the course of the day—"

"Yes." Nora's eyes clung to his.

"You prepared other food with it?"

"I just used it for my coffee when I had supper—" Her voice barely above a whisper. *And nothing happened to Nora. The poison was slipped into the container later. How could anybody get into the house with the security guards on duty?* "The milk just sat there in the refrigerator after that—" Nora's voice trailed off.

"It was used for nothing else?" Hendricks persisted.

"No, sir." Nora clutched one hand with the other in her nervousness.

"You didn't notice any odd aroma?" Hendricks seemed skeptical. "A bitter-almond aroma?"

"No, sir." *I didn't notice it—neither did Andrea. But we're both so uptight.* Nora hesitated. "I have a stuffy nose—I wouldn'ta smelled anything that wasn't awful strong."

"Bring me the container," Hendricks ordered. "That's evidence."

Emily sensed that Andrea was disturbed that the detectives continued to interrogate Nora—asking the same simple questions in a variety of ways. After a while O'Leary left to go outside to talk with the security guards. Hendricks quizzed Nora about possible deliveries made to the house—after her supper hour.

"We didn't have no deliveries," Nora told him—stifling yawns. *She looks so scared. Why don't they leave her alone?*

"You had no visitors?" Hendricks pursued. Nora shook her head. "You're sure."

"Yes sir. Nobody came into the house—" *But somebody managed to slip inside and put cyanide in that milk container.*

Now Hendricks back-tracked, repeated the same questions again. Trying, Emily interpreted, to trip her up.

Hendricks and O'Leary suspect Nora of meaning to kill Andrea and me. They figure nobody could sneak into the house with two security guards on duty. But it could happen—they can't watch every inch of the property! What motive would Nora have to kill us?

It was past one a.m. when the two detectives abandoned questioning Nora.

"We may have more questions," O'Leary told her casually. "Don't leave town."

Nora gazed at him in bewilderment. "Where would I go?" But she seemed mesmerized by the evening's activities.

Now the two detectives rounded up their crew, prepared to leave.

"You're notifying the supermarket people and the supplier?" Paul asked pointedly. "The supermarket opens for business at seven a.m. every morning."

"That's already in work," Hendricks snapped. "No milk will be sold at Woodhaven Supermarket—or anywhere else in this town—until further notice. Coleman Milk Distributors will be closed for inspection." *But they don't believe the cyanide was added either at the supermarket or the supplier.*

146

"It's been a long night," Paul said wryly as cars were heard driving away from the house.

"I should be taking off, too." Jamie Abel glanced at his watch. "I open up my office in less than six hours. I schedule surgery early in the day."

"Anything good occur at the Town Council meeting tonight?" Andrea asked Paul. *She's trying to divert us from what almost happened.* "I know it wasn't likely they'd allow you to speak, but—"

"Astonishingly I got in." Paul pantomimed his astonishment.

"We do have a couple of allies on the Council," Jamie reminded. *So he's fighting the mall, too.* "What happened tonight?"

"I was allowed to speak because Bob Reynolds was making a case for his real-estate office," Paul explained. *He's the broker, Andrea said, for the possible alternate site for the shopping mall.* "You know the routine. Both sides of a case must be heard."

"What happened?" Andrea demanded impatiently.

"Not much of value." But Paul seemed uneasy. "Reynolds yapped about all the extra jobs the mall would bring into town if the re-zoning goes through. Oh, the mall people are talking about extending the figure from thirty to fifty stores—to draw from a radius of seventy-five miles—"

"Part-time jobs paying six or seven dollars an hour!" Emily blazed. "And no benefits. We see this happening in malls all over the country! These thousand-store chains that care only about the bottom line."

"What about the re-zoning deal?" Jamie pushed. "Without that happening, there can be no mall."

"I insisted—again—that the town charter provides for a referendum in such cases. I finally got the Council to agree to set up a committee to study the charter." Paul gestured his doubts about the results. "Right now I'm anxious about that poisoned milk."

"That's got to take priority," Jamie agreed. "The big question: Is some creep poisoning milk either at the supplier's end or in the supermarket—and we've seen cases like that," he acknowledged— "or did a would-be killer sneak into this house despite the security guards and contrive to add cyanide to that container of milk? I suspect that's the real scenario—"

"I know it's a way-out thought," Emily began, almost apologetic, "but could one of the security guards be involved somehow?"

"One of Jason Hollister's side investigations was to check on them," Andrea reported. "He sees no connection on their part."

"We've got a time frame," Paul picked up. "The cyanide was added after Nora had opened it at her supper time. How the hell did somebody get into the house between the time Nora finished her supper and when you two—" He nodded to Andrea and Emily— "arrived home?"

"It could happen," Emily insisted. "The security guards have a lot of ground to cover. Even with those floodlights on from dusk to daybreak, somebody might contrive to get into the house." *Despite locked windows and locked doors? How?*

"The District Attorney's office is going to zoom in on Nora as a suspect," Andrea predicted, troubled. "That came across loud and clear."

"No way would Nora have poisoned that milk!" Emily rejected. But her mind was on an alarming track. Hannah was Nora's aunt. Nora had loved her deeply. Did the police suspect she might blame Andrea for Hannah's murder?

"Nora will need a strong criminal lawyer," Andrea told Paul. "Have someone top-drawer stand by." She took a deep, anguished breath. "The District Attorney's office will dig up her medical history." She closed her eyes in anguish for a moment.

"What medical history?" Paul tensed in alarm.

"Four years ago Nora spent three months in a mental institution—after she was accused of the death of a toddler she was baby-sitting in a town sixty miles from here. She was cleared," Andrea added defensively, "but was an emotional wreck. The District Attorney's office will make much of it."

That's why she seemed so terrified. She sees herself going through that whole deal all over again.

"I'll have a legal team standing by," Paul promised. "And I'll schedule an early breakfast with Jason Hollister."

"Right," Andrea said with a flicker of impatience. "It's time he came up with something helpful."

"I'll brief him on what happened here this evening." *Paul's so uptight. He's frightened for Andrea and me. If he'd arrived a few minutes later Andrea and I would have been dead.* "The police will follow up on their suspicions about Nora. They may even link her to Hannah's death—"

"We mustn't let that happen," Andrea flared.

"Hollister must discover how somebody is infiltrating the house without being detected by the security guards. He—"

"Surveillance cameras!" Andrea cut him short. "We have them set up on every entrance and exit at the company."

"No," Paul rejected. "Cameras will tell us who has invaded the house—after it's happened." His eyes were eloquent.

"What about having those mats at every door—or those sensor deals that beep when anybody tries to enter?" Emily was breathless with excitement. "My father has a mat in front of his shop door—because sometimes he's alone in the evening and in a storage room—"

"Oh God, how stupid of me!" Paul chastised himself. "We'll do both—the surveillance cameras and the door buzzers. The buzzers will sound off each time anybody enters—and the security guards will rush into action."

"Can they be in place by nightfall?" Andrea pressed.

"They'll be in place by nightfall," Paul promised. "We'll discover who's behind this nightmare."

Twenty-Seven

After a brief, troubled sleep, Emily came awake slowly. Then all at once—hearing a multitude of voices below—she was fully awake. She glanced at the clock on her night table. It was minutes past six thirty a.m. The sun rising over the pond across the road. *What's happening down there?*

In a surge of alarm she darted across the room to a front-facing window, gazed down upon a disconcerting sight. The two security guards were trying to dismiss a flock of people clustered about the entrance to the house. All talking at once, firing questions at the guards.

Emily's eyes swept across the line-up of parked cars, read the IDs imprinted on doors. They were the property of newspaper reporters, photographers. TV and radio newspeople. She flinched at the sight of a car from a New York tabloid. All at once the murder in Woodhaven and the failed attempts had become a national interest.

Now Andrea's commanding voice drifted up to her: "Please, there is no danger to the people in this town as long as they follow police guidelines." *Morning news carried a warning about the milk—everybody's terrified.* "We don't know if this was the work of Hannah Bolton's killer or was an unrelated incident." Andrea ignored the flood of questions aimed at her. "I have nothing else to say. All milk is being removed from store shelves. The supplier will make no deliveries until further notice. That is what the police have told me. Now please leave."

Emily reached for the robe at the foot of her bed, slid her feet into slippers. The loud thud of a door closing told her Andrea was back in the house. She left her bedroom, rushed down the stairs.

The comforting aroma of fresh coffee filtered through the

house. Though Nora had been unnerved by the police grilling last night, she was in the kitchen preparing breakfast, Emily interpreted. As though this was any other morning. After what Nora had been through in that earlier case, she must realize that once again she was the prime suspect in the eyes of the police.

"Did that insane gathering outside awaken you?" Andrea greeted her at the foot of the stairs.

"I was awake," Emily fibbed. "I couldn't figure out what was happening at first—"

"Since two a.m. this morning local radio and television have been warning people not to drink milk that was bought here in town. It was the headline on this morning's *Enquirer*. It was picked up by media around the country." Andrea gestured in frustration. "I can't understand this milk hysteria. Nora made it clear she drank that container and nothing happened. It's clear that in some fashion the cyanide was added here in the house. Nobody else is in danger—just you and me." A strident note infiltrated her voice, despite her efforts to appear unperturbed.

"The police may consider Nora an unreliable witness," Emily pointed out. Her voice low as she and Andrea approached the kitchen area.

Andrea sighed. "I suppose they have to cover all bases."

Nora glanced up from the range with a shaky smile for Emily and Andrea.

"It's a kinda cool morning," she told them. "I made corn muffins—they just came out of the oven." *Poor baby. She looks as though she hasn't slept at all. She's remembering that earlier nightmare—and here it is again.* "And I figured you'd like some Canadian bacon with your eggs. Aunt Hannah always told me how there's just one gram of fat in a slice."

"That sounds great," Andrea approved and headed for the breakfast table. "Start us off with a mug of decaf and a muffin."

Striving to pretend that this was just another morning—though the memory of last night's brush with death hung over them—Emily and Andrea ate with a show of hunger meant to reassure Nora that they knew she had not poisoned the container of milk. As Emily expected of Andrea, they would go to work as usual.

Driving away from the house after breakfast, they saw a panel truck turn into the driveway.

"The company to set up the surveillance cameras," Emily gathered from the name on the panel truck. "And the buzzers." Especially the buzzers, she thought with relief.

Andrea nodded. "Paul must have awakened them in the middle of the night."

Away from the house Andrea reached to turn on the car radio, grimaced as the voice of a newscaster warned of poisoned milk that might be on refrigerator shelves.

"We don't need to hear any more of that." Andrea switched off the radio. "Half the town will be on the edge of hysteria."

The parking area was deserted except for the cars belonging to the security crew and Paul's new hybrid. They found Paul already in his office.

"I had an early breakfast with Hollister. He'll be here shortly. More questions."

Andrea lifted an eyebrow, dismissed this. "What's with the equipment on order?" Andrea settled herself in a chair at Paul's desk. "We were to have delivery before this week was out. This is Friday."

"Delivery scheduled this morning," Paul told her.

For a few minutes talk revolved about the "Made in the USA" operation. Then the click of heels in the hall told them Gina had arrived. She paused at the entrance to Paul's office.

"You're all right?" Gina gazed anxiously at Andrea. "I couldn't believe the seven a.m. news!"

"The three of us at the house are fine." Andrea was crisp. "The sweet little kitten died."

"My sister called as soon as she heard. With three kids her refrigerator was loaded with milk." Gina shuddered. "It all went out."

"There'll be a lot of black coffee served in the next day or two," Emily surmised with an effort at humor.

"We hear about this happening every now and then—but you never expect it to happen in your own town." Gina frowned in sudden thought. "The cafeteria staff has been warned?"

"They know," Paul said. "That was my first stop this morning."

"Gina, we expect Jason Hollister to arrive in a bit. Will you please have the cafeteria send in a pot of coffee to my office?"

152

By the time the three of them were settled in Andrea's office—making every effort to approach this as just another working day—they heard Hollister in conversation with Gina.

"I know it's not a good morning," Hollister greeted them. "But better times are coming."

"You know something?" Andrea prodded.

"No," he conceded. *He feels guilty that he hasn't come up with any answers. But then neither have the police.* "I have questions."

"All right. We can deal with that." But Andrea's eyes were skeptical.

She's losing patience with Hollister. But Paul says his firm is one of the best in the field.

"After what's happened last night, I want to talk about keys to the house—"

"All the locks were changed after Hannah's murder," Andrea shot back. "And I gave you a list of every one who might have had a key before that. Plumbers, electricians—" she gestured broadly. "All the workmen who'd been in the house for the past year."

"I realize that," Hollister said gently. "But who has the new keys?"

"Just myself, Emily, Nora, Doris—my cleaning woman."

"Anybody else?" Hollister pressed. "Family members?"

Andrea bristled. "No, Mr. Hollister—"

"Jason," he corrected with a smile. "It's difficult to be formal in situations like this."

"Jason," Andrea said, her voice acerbic, "you remember that I'm convinced we're facing a serial murderer? You're working on that premise? That was our arrangement—"

"Yes—" Jason nodded, seemed to be searching for words. "But there is the possibility that these recent incidents are unrelated. We must—"

"I don't accept that," Andrea cut him short. "And this question about my children having the new keys to the house—" She dismissed this with a contemptuous gesture. "They don't—but suppose they did? You can't suspect my own children of being part of this nightmare!"

"Please don't misunderstand me, Mrs. Winston—" Jason was startled by her reaction. "I—"

"My husband was murdered thirty-seven years ago. My children were small—asleep in their beds when it happened. And whoever killed my husband killed Roger and Hannah as well." She paused, fighting for calm. "And means to kill Emily and me."

"I didn't mean to infer that your children could be involved," Jason apologized. "But one of them could have lost a key chain, had a purse stolen—a key could have fallen into the wrong hands."

"Neither Leon nor Carol nor Celeste has a working key to the house," Andrea reiterated—a vein in her forehead pounding. "This investigation appears to be going nowhere. I'd hoped to have some answers by now. If nothing develops within the next two weeks, I'll have to make other arrangements."

Twenty-Eight

Emily sat with Paul in the cafeteria over a very late lunch. The cafeteria deserted except for themselves. Only a small area illuminated to accommodate their presence.

"I've never seen Andrea so unnerved." Paul was anxious. "But I'm sure Jason understands—"

"When she talked that way, I was afraid he'd walk off the assignment right then."

"He's determined to come up with answers. Each new case, he said, is a challenge. He doesn't like to admit defeat. And I gather that doesn't happen often."

"If Andrea fires him, will she bring in another investigator?"

"If Jason and his team come up with nothing, I doubt she'll have better luck with other people. But the buzzers—and the cameras—will be in place by dusk. If there's another attempt to break into the house, we should catch the culprit on film."

"I was thinking about not coming in to the office tomorrow," Emily began. "If that's okay—"

"Of course it's okay," he chided. "You need to get away from the grind." *He's so worried about Andrea and me. But what can we do that hasn't already been done?* "You've been through a rough time."

"I'd like to go back to the library, try to follow up what you said about locating a girl friend of Celeste's during their high-school years. I'll read the high-school papers for that year—maybe I missed something last time—"

"A bright thought." Paul reached across the table to cover her hand with his. His eyes tender. "I'll do some research about the class reunion as soon as the pressure lets up on the new line."

"The police are way off base in suspecting Nora—" *What is he thinking when he looks at me that way?*

155

"To them it's the only show in town. They can't pin down any intruder—and Nora was in the house. It doesn't look good for her."

Emily felt a fresh surge of frustration. "They're focusing on the records of that poor little toddler who was strangled. But Nora was cleared—"

"For lack of evidence," Paul pointed out. "The case is still unsolved." His eyes were searching hers now. On a different track, she thought. *Doesn't he know how I feel about him? It's as though I've been waiting all my life for him.* "I've contacted lawyers. If the police take Nora downtown for more questioning, they'll jump into the scene."

"That won't change the situation at the house." *Why doesn't he say something about us?* "Whoever means to—to kill Andrea and me is still out there."

Paul's hand tightened on hers. "We won't let it happen. The cameras are set up—the security guards on duty. Whoever he is, he'll be caught." Paul frowned in inner debate now. "Maybe it would be wise for you to go back home until this craziness is over—"

"No," she whispered. "I want to stay here—"

Am I being absurd? Paul's right—but I don't want to leave. I'd worry about Andrea. I need to know about my birth father. I keep feeling Paul is on the point of talking about us—our future. How can I leave?

"When this madness is over—" Paul groped for words. "When we're not living in constant fear, we'll talk about us. I can't visualize a life without you—"

"Yes—" Her face was luminous. "Oh yes, Paul."

"We'd better get back to the salt-mines." He brought her hand to his mouth for a moment. "We've got a new line to get moving."

As on each evening—unless Andrea gave her other instructions—Nora arrived at the company shortly before seven p.m. with dinner in an insulated bag. She and Andrea went to the empty cafeteria—ghost-like at this hour. Emily and Paul had been summoned from one of the new temporary units where they were checking out progress.

"Two more detectives came to the house," Nora reported to

156

Andrea while she brought food, plates, and silverware to the table that had become theirs at this hour.

Andrea was on instant alert. "What did they want?"

"Some more questions." Nora strived for calm, but her hands were unsteady. "They said somethin' about maybe searchin' my room. I said they couldn't do that without talkin' to you. Then they went away."

"They'd need a warrant to search in the house." *What do they expect to find?* "I'll have Paul talk to them." She glanced up with a smile as Emily and Paul walked into the cafeteria. *Am I wrong in suspecting they feel something special for each other? That would be lovely.*

"Everything smells so good," Paul told Nora. "All this service—I feel as though I've died and gone to heaven—" He stopped short. Death was not a subject to be discussed in the current situation.

"Coffee's black," Nora reminded, bringing out the thermos. Her face somber. "Nobody's sellin' milk today."

Over dinner Paul sent frequent glances at his watch. "There's a meeting of the 'Stop the Mall' group at eight tonight. I figure on leaving here around that time." His eyes asked a silent question of Andrea.

"I should go," Andrea conceded, "but I've scheduled an evening conference with the designers. You'll bring me up to date."

Paul turned to Emily. "Would you like to go to the meeting? We'll call this an early night." He grinned. "We'll make up for it tomorrow."

Emily's face lighted. "Yes, I'd like that."

Emily's pleased. This isn't a date—but it isn't business, either. Those two are meant to be together. Is Paul too engrossed in the company to see that?

"First thing tomorrow morning, Paul"—Andrea dispensed with introspection—"buzz the lawyers you've set up for Nora. She had visitors today. They said something about searching her room. They had no warrant, but I suspect that's coming."

"I'll clue them in," Paul said. "Oh, I spoke with Jason Hollister late this afternoon. He—"

"I was hard on him this morning," Andrea broke in. "I was upset—"

Paul dismissed this with a shrug. "He knows how you're feeling. He's consulted a profiler, who confirmed his own suspicions. The picture that emerges, he said, is some person— it could be a man or a woman—who has an obsessive need to be in your good graces. He—or she—was jealous of your late husband. He—or she—was jealous of your closeness to your friend Roger."

"A serial killer, as I've always maintained." Andrea pounded on the table with a fist. Dinner forgotten for the moment. "Why can't the police see that?"

"When you brought Emily here, he—or she—felt betrayed," Paul continued. "Turned on you in rage. And he—or she— has vowed to kill both you and Emily."

Andrea recoiled from his assessment. *How could I have exposed my precious granddaughter to murder?* "I've searched my brain thousands of nights," she said exhaustedly. "I come up with nobody."

"Could it be someone who was with the company from almost the beginning?" Emily probed. "An employee with a sick mind who harbored a special—secret—feeling for you through the years?"

"I gave Jason a list of the few employees with us from those very early days," Andrea told her. "All retired now—several have died. I'm sure his team must have checked them out by now."

"Be patient with Jason," Paul urged. "He has an army out there working for us. Nothing is too far-fetched for him to follow."

Andrea paused, in inner debate. "Tell him to forget my childish outburst. It was just that when he asked about my son and daughters having the new keys to the house—as though one of them might be responsible—I lost touch with reality."

"What Jason was trying to learn was if they could have inadvertently supplied the new keys to the killer," Paul explained. "He's not discarding your serial killer conviction— but in his mind he must discount the possibility that Hannah's murder and these other attempts are not part of the same thread."

"They're the same." Andrea was defiant. "In my heart I know that. I've never felt truly safe since David's murder—

and that feeling intensified when Roger was killed. Celeste was only three when we lost David. For a little while she asked for her daddy, then she stopped asking. For Carol and Leon—they were ten and twelve—it was traumatic. Not only because they'd lost their father—they were terrified that they would be murdered, too. Thank God for Hannah—she was wonderful with the children." Andrea stared into space, reliving those years. "I was away at the company such long hours—it bothered me through their growing-up years that I wasn't always there for them. But it was urgent to save the business. That was their security."

"You were a good mother," Emily said passionately. "You worked to provide for your children. Nobody can deny that."

"I'm grateful that this monster hasn't tried to vent his rage on them. At least, not yet—"

"I had a long talk with Leon this morning," Paul began with an air of apology. "I suggested that he and his family—and Carol and hers—take precautions. That it would be wise to—"

"Because the killer might go after them to hurt me!" Andrea interpreted his suspicions.

"It's a far-out possibility," Paul said quietly, "but it's best to look ahead. At Leon's house and at Carol's floodlights are being installed today, along with surveillance cameras and door buzzers. And security guards will be posted," he emphasized. "Celeste, I understand, is staying with friends in East Hampton—out of the danger zone."

"Is there no end to this?" Andrea shook her head in anguish. "All this time—and we still know nothing."

Twenty-Nine

Emily was conscious of Paul's arm about her waist as they walked to his car in the near-deserted parking area. The sky devoid of stars. Murky clouds concealing the moon.

"It feels strange—creepy—to leave Andrea alone in the office," she confessed. "We've always left together—since I've been here—"

"Andrea's not alone," Paul comforted. "She's never out of sight of a security guard."

Emily was startled. "I never realized that." Now her mind flashed back through the day. *Yes. Even when we were at dinner in the cafeteria I noticed someone in sight. I thought it was someone working overtime.*

"You're never alone, either," he told softly. "How could we take a chance with either of you?"

"Where's the meeting being held tonight?" she asked Paul. Aware of this tortuous urge to feel herself in his arms.

"There's a room at the public library that's at the disposal of local groups," he explained, opening the door on the passenger side for her. "There've been complaints that we shouldn't be allowed to use it for the 'Stop the Mall' group—but so far we've managed to hold on to it."

"Jamie Abel is active in the group, isn't he?" she asked when Paul joined her in the car. She'd liked the veterinarian on sight.

"Jamie was one of the founders." Paul reflected a deep affection for what he'd called the town's favorite vet. "I remember when I was about twelve and Jamie was new in town how impressed I was when our dalmatian was hit by a car and Jamie worked to save her. I was too old to cry," Paul said humorously. "At least in public. But I stayed there with Angie—our dalmatian—while Jamie worked for hours to pull her through."

160

"Did he?"

Paul chuckled. "Through that scrape and two others—until she died at almost fourteen."

"Do you think the mall will be stopped?" Emily asked after a moment.

"I pray that it will." Paul's hands tightened on the wheel. "I've seen too many towns drown in traffic while people flock to malls—and Main Street becomes a blighted area. Small businesses go out."

"It happened in Evanston." Emily was somber. "My father runs a hardware store. Mom's helped out ever since I was in school full-time. They'd built up a strong following through the years. Then the Evanston Shopping Mall opened—and stores on Main Street began to close. Dad's managed to hold on—but with a sharp drop in business. It's not fair!" *What's happened to customer loyalty and reliability and appreciation for service?*

"We're fighting to keep that from happening here. You hear about towns who've managed to keep out chain stores that pay seven or eight dollars a hour and hire only part-timers so as to avoid benefits. We mean for Woodhaven to be one of them."

"If Winston Mail Order ever pulled out, moved to another town—or overseas—Woodhaven would be a ghost town," Emily guessed.

"God, that's a nightmare scenario." In the darkness of the car Emily saw Paul's face tighten in frustration. "It's unbelievable the way manufacturers are pulling up stakes and leaving the country. We're threatened with the prospect of becoming a ghost country—with only minimum-wage jobs and obscenely overpaid top executives."

"What can we do to stop them?" Emily's mind shot back to the Genoa protest, 2001. *Did the protests help?*

"We've got to convince people to go to the polls and vote," Paul said with a calmness she suspected he didn't feel. "In small towns like this and in the huge cities. To vote for office-holders who care about people."

"Andrea said it's important to vote out Mayor Davis," Emily recalled.

"You bet it is." Paul was emphatic. "There's a group in town

161

that wants Jamie to run—but he insists he can't give enough time to the job without damaging his practice. It's a part-time job, actually—but at times like this, it can be demanding."

Paul turned off the road onto the library parking area. Judging from the number of cars, Emily thought, the meeting was being well attended. The lower level was brilliantly illuminated. Voices drifted out into the night.

"We're late—" Emily felt self-conscious about arriving when the meeting was in full swing.

Paul chuckled. "I'm expected to be late. The crowd there knows about my commitment to the company—and that's good for the people in Woodhaven. Remember, we're the major employer. If anything goes wrong at Winston Mail Order, a lot of people will hurt."

"The company's supplying more jobs now," Emily pointed out while she and Paul strode towards the lower entrance to the library. "Not a lot," she conceded, "but that number could grow." *Are we living in a dream world to think the company can put across this "Made in the USA" line?* "And Andrea said she's not worried about making a profit." *"I don't need a larger salary. I don't need a salary at all if it comes to that. I just want to see more jobs staying in this country."*

"In every period of recession through the years," Paul said reverently, "Andrea has taken herself off salary to keep the business afloat. And does that piss off her kids!"

Paul opened the door leading to the meeting room, prodded Emily inside. Jamie Abel was on his feet, talking passionately about the need to keep the shopping mall out of Woodhaven. A crowd of about forty people sat on folding chairs and listened with avid attention to what Jamie said. The crowd ranging from very young marrieds to what Andrea called "elderly without being old."

"And here's our legal eagle," he said with a flourish. "Paul, tell us the Town Council can't pass a re-zoning ruling without a referendum!"

Emily sat at the rear of the room. Conscious of friendly stares. Everybody in town must know by now that she was Andrea's granddaughter. But everyone was engrossed in Paul's argument that according to the town charter no re-zoning could be done without a referendum.

"Starting tomorrow morning," Paul announced, "we're collecting signatures demanding the referendum. Everybody, off your butts and collect signatures!"

"What about their trying for a stretch of acreage that isn't covered by zoning?" an anxious grandmotherly type asked. "Maybe outside town limits?"

"We've checked all that," Jamie soothed. "A shopping mall requires certain highway conditions. It requires accessibility from several outlying towns. Mrs. Cameron's acreage is the perfect location—and there's no way the mall crowd can buy it."

"What about the other tract Mayor Davis has been yapping about?" a belligerent-faced man of about thirty demanded. "He claims that's available and suitable. How do we cut that out?"

"It's zoned for farming," Jamie said. "Look, it comes down to this." He extended his hands in an eloquent gesture. "We insist on the referendum our town constitution demands. And then we bust our butts getting enough signatures to make re-zoning unacceptable."

All at once—while Jamie stood there with outstretched hands—Emily felt a surge of excitement. She never noticed it before—but Jamie Abel's right pinkie was slightly curved. Like hers. She remembered Mom's remark when she'd once complained about this aberration: *Oh, that's something you inherited—I think from your grandfather on Dad's side. It's the sort of thing that runs in families.*

Thirty

Emily sat with soaring impatience through the heated meeting, drew a deep breath of relief when it was adjourned. Jamie was gathering a few members of the group into an extension of the meeting over coffee.

"What about you two?" Jamie focused on Paul and Emily. "Burn the midnight oil with us?"

"Tomorrow's a work day for Emily and me," Paul said. "We keep early hours. What about dinner tomorrow?"

"Great. Buzz me when you think you'll be breaking for the day—let me see if I can get away." Jamie's glance included her, Emily interpreted.

Paul reached for Emily's hand, walked with her to the car. Part of her was enthralled that he was being so open about their closeness. But questions hurtled across her brain.

Am I jumping to conclusions about Jamie Abel? So he has a curved right pinkie like me. When Mom said that about such things being inherited, she was trying to make me feel that I had a family. I don't know that my curved right pinkie was inherited.

"Glad you came to the meeting?" Paul asked when they were settled in the car. "I know," he joshed, "it couldn't compare to the Genoa protest."

"Yes, I'm glad! I want to be part of stopping the mall." She hesitated. "You've known Jamie a long time, haven't you?"

"Since I was fifteen."

"How old is Jamie?" *Paul will be convinced I'm out of my mind if I tell what I suspect.*

"Somewhere in the early forties, I think." Paul seemed puzzled. "Hey, am I losing my girl to an older man?" he joshed. Jamie was a bachelor, though Andrea said women had been trying to catch him for years.

"Could Jamie have been in Celeste's high-school classes?"

"I suspect he was a year or two ahead of her," Paul said after a moment. "Emily, what are you thinking?"

"I know it's a little thing—it probably means nothing. But I have this crooked right pinkie—and so does Jamie. My mother used to say I'd inherited it from my grandfather on her side. She was trying to build up an image for me because I never knew her parents nor Dad's. Paul, could Jamie be my father?"

"I can't imagine his being involved with Celeste," Paul admitted. "Even back in those years. I don't know that the crooked pinkie is a family trait—" Emily felt the tension in him as he considered this. "Let me talk to Jamie—"

"When?" she asked involuntarily.

"I'll have dinner with him tomorrow. You'll be tied up with something else," he plotted. He took one hand from the wheel, reached for hers. "Honey, don't put too much faith in this."

"I know," she whispered. "I'm reaching—"

After a night of broken sleep, Emily came awake with an instant realization of what the day promised. She lay back against the pillows and considered this. With any luck at all she'd know after Paul had dinner with him if there was a possibility that Jamie Abel was her father.

Now she remembered that she'd told Andrea that she wouldn't be going in to the company today: "I need some time to shop a birthday present for Mom." She'd felt so guilty about lying. But how could she explain to Andrea that she'd spend the day at the public library—searching for the name of Celeste's high-school girl friend?

Even though Paul would be questioning Jamie this evening, I must do this. I may be off the wall in thinking Jamie is my father—and Saturdays are the only days I can take off from work. I must discover who is my father if I'm to know who I am.

Already she heard sounds downstairs. Andrea and Nora were talking about breakfast. By the time she'd emerged from the shower, she was aware of tantalizing breakfast aromas floating through the house. Nora, bless her, always baked for weekend breakfasts. Fresh bread to be converted to French toast, luscious low-fat muffins from recipes developed by Hannah in happier days, a delicious coffee ring.

She dressed quickly, hurried downstairs. Andrea was at the breakfast table. Nora was busy at the kitchen range. As though, Emily thought tenderly, she was terrified of being taken in as a suspect in the poisoning attempt night before last. But top lawyers were standing by if that happened, Emily comforted herself.

"You're up early," Andrea scolded when she walked into view. "You should have slept late."

"I remembered that the shops don't open until ten," Emily improvised. The public library didn't open until ten on Saturdays. "I thought I'd go in with you for a couple of hours. I might be able to help Paul." Endless—and demanding— small problems were arising with the "Made in the USA" line. And the three of them were determined to meet Andrea's deadline.

"I'm sure he'll be glad to see you." The twinkle in Andrea's eyes said she approved of anything that brought Emily and Paul together.

"I hope you're feelin' like apple pancakes this mornin'," Nora said with a wan smile as she hurried to the table with a mug of coffee for Emily. "It's still black coffee," she apologized. "No milk's to be had at the stores."

"Black coffee's fine," Emily assured her. Nora was trying so hard to conceal her anxieties. How could they behave as though they were living under normal conditions?

The three of them started, then froze at the sound of the beeping at the door.

"It's just me," Barney, one of the two midnight-to-eight-a.m. security guards called from the hallway. "Nora said I could come into the house for coffee when I went off duty."

"Come in, Barney. Coffee's waiting," Andrea called back.

"Black coffee," Nora warned apologetically as Barney sauntered into view."

"Me, I always drink it black." But Barney was self-conscious at invading a family breakfast.

"Pull up a chair and have breakfast with us. I'm sure Nora's made plenty."

"Thank you, ma'am." He seemed self-conscious, though Andrea was known around the company as being "one of the folks."

"I've been thinking, Barney," Andrea pursued. "Talk to your boss about those woods behind the house. Ask him if we should arrange to have some of the trees cut back. They're those pines that don't live much more than thirty-five years— and they're pushing that now."

"I'll talk to him." Barney was solemn.

Was there another CEO in the world as unpretentious as Andrea? Emily asked herself. How could she have been so wrong in her first assessment of her?

Emily worked with Paul until almost noon, then at his prodding took off for the public library. The stores remained open until six p.m. on Saturdays, Emily remembered. To keep up the pretense she'd shop a little gift for Mom and for Dad. She knew Andrea would be convinced she was pushing herself too hard to try to identify her father. *Don't add to Andrea's anxieties.*

Ignoring the curiosity of the librarian, Emily requested endless material relating to Celeste's senior year in high school. School newspapers, local papers, the high-school annuals of the year before and after Celeste's senior year. No reference to any student who might have been Celeste's girl friend in that last year.

Now she was winding up her day's research with the high-school annual of the year prior to Celeste's senior year. She turned the opening pages, scanned the printed material, then moved on to the photographs of the senior class. The students were listed alphabetically.

Her heart began to pound as she stared at the page before her. The photographs of seniors whose names began with "A." The smiling face of Jamie Abel stared back at her. He had been one year ahead of Celeste in high school.

Emily returned all the material she'd been studying, hurried from the library to her car. In the car she called Paul on his private line in his office.

"Yes?" An undercurrent of anxiety in his voice because only someone close would phone him on a Saturday afternoon.

"Paul, it's me—" Emily was breathless with excitement. "I've just come from the library. I was going through high-school yearbooks—before and after Celeste's senior year. Jamie Abel was one year ahead of Celeste!"

Thirty-One

Paul headed for a rear booth at the Celestial diner—lightly populated at six p.m. on a Saturday evening, which he'd anticipated. Open twenty-four hours a day, Celestial patrons thronged the diner for breakfast and lunch. Other hours patrons were sparse.

"Coffee to start?" the elderly waiter asked, handing Paul a menu. "It's black," he added before Paul could reply. "You know—" He gestured philosophically. "That nutty business about no milk being sold in town till the cops okay it."

"Black is fine," Paul agreed. Didn't the cops realize by now that the only milk container with cyanide was the one in Andrea's refrigerator? "I'm expecting a friend. I'll order when he arrives."

Jamie was coming here to talk about their next move in stopping the shopping mall. He wasn't expecting to be quizzed about a possible relationship with Celeste. It sounded way out, but for Emily's peace of mind he had to go through with this.

He glanced up with an approving smile as Jamie—in jeans, a red turtleneck and sneakers—strode into the diner.

Jamie slid into the booth across from Paul, grinned. "I'm hardly late at all."

"Congratulations." Paul signaled the waiter. "Let's get ordering out of the way."

For a few moments the two men focused on the menu. Finally they made their choices.

"The coffee's gonna be black," the waiter warned Jamie.

"No problems," Jamie told him. "That's the way I drink it."

"Hey, everybody to their own taste." The waiter shrugged, left their booth with their orders.

"That big brouhaha about the cyanide in the milk—" Jamie

was serious now. "The cops come up with any answers about how it got into the house?"

"Not yet." Paul was searching for a road to questioning Jamie.

"It's weird. No end to the troubles that fall on Andrea's head. Now she's worried that one of her children might be the next victim." *She thought that for a brief time after the bomb was thrown at the house.* "I persuaded Leon and Carol's husband to arrange for security at their houses. Celeste, of course, took off as soon as Emily arrived."

"Celeste is always taking off somewhere," Jamie shrugged.

"You and Celeste were in high school together, weren't you?" *Emily said Jamie graduated a year before Celeste's class.*

"She was a year behind me, I think," Jamie said with a show of disinterest.

"Even in high school, I hear, she was a hot tamale."

"Not my type," Jamie dismissed this.

"She was supposed to have chased after every good-looking kid in her class." Paul contrived a chuckle. "You fit the category."

"Hey, what's bugging you? Why this inquisition?"

"Be patient with me, Jamie." Paul searched his mind for words. "I may be way off base, but you could be in for a gigantic surprise—"

"Something to do with Celeste?" Jamie scoffed.

"So I'll be blunt." *Hell, how can I be diplomatic about this?* "Did you have a thing going with her during her last year in high school? That is, in the early part of that year?"

"Are you kidding?" Jamie grunted in distaste. Then all at once he froze. Paul sensed his mind was charging back through the years. "We had a one-night stand—when I was home from college for the Christmas break. I read her mind—she was dying to sleep with a college guy. I guess I drank more than I should have." He stared hard at Paul. "After all these years Celeste is yakking about what happened to us on the back seat of her mother's Lincoln Town Car?"

"Celeste got pregnant. Andrea told everybody Celeste was too high-spirited for the local high school—she sent her off to boarding school, presumably, for the rest of the school year. Celeste had a daughter. The baby was put up for adoption."

170

He's met Emily—he knows she's Andrea's granddaughter, just now surfacing. Hasn't he made the connection with Celeste—like almost everybody in town?

"You think I'm the father?" He stared at Paul in disbelief. "You're off your rocker! I slept with her once!"

"All it takes is one shot." Paul braced himself to continue. "Celeste—"

"Celeste was sleeping with half the senior class!"

"I know," Paul soothed. "But there's one odd coincidence—"

"Like what?" Jamie scoffed.

"You know that crooked little pinkie on your right hand?" Paul took a deep breath. "Celeste's daughter has it, too."

"So have thousands of others! And how do you know all this?"

"For God's sake, Jamie—we're talking about Emily," Paul said in exasperation. "Nobody on this earth except for Celeste knows who fathered Emily. Not even Andrea."

"With the way Celeste played around, it could be anybody—"

"Maybe Emily's jumping to conclusions," Paul conceded. "She saw your pinkie—and took that as a sign. I think the possibility should be checked out."

Jamie shook his head in amazement. "Emily's lovely—a fine, sweet young woman. Any man would be proud to know she was his daughter." *He's torn—he'd like to believe this—but he's doubtful.* "This is unreal." Jamie strived for a realistic approach. "The pinkie is just a coincidence. It happens—"

He's trying to deal with this. Part of him is awed that he may have a daughter.

"A DNA test would tell us," Paul pointed out. "Would you be willing take the test?" *But if it proves negative, Emily will be so disappointed—so hurt.*

"I would, yes—but Emily?"

"I'm sure she would. It's terribly important to her to know her father. And if it proves to be you, she'll be happy. She has such respect and admiration for you—"

Jamie managed a self-deprecating chuckle. "Sure, I'm a vet and she's an animal-lover—"

"I've had some minor experience with DNA testing," Paul began and grinned at Jamie's raised eyebrows. "As a lawyer. We can handle the testing ourselves. I know a reputable lab in Albany that provides legally accepted testing. It's simple—I'm sure you know the routine. Cost runs around two or three hundred dollars, I believe—"

"I'll pay it," Jamie said quickly, then hesitated. "Damn, this is going to be awkward—"

"I know," Paul sympathized, thought a moment. "Let me act as the go-between. This isn't a paternity case—where the lawyers are demanding the collection of fluid is performed in the presence of a neutral third-party witness. I'll make the arrangements for both of you."

"If the test proves positive, I'll be enthralled," Jamie confessed. His face radiant. "Part of me has always regretted not having a family. There just never seemed time to pursue a relationship. People in town know—if there's a sick animal, I'm on call twenty-four hours a day."

"I'll contact the lab Monday morning," Paul promised. "We'll get this show on the road." *How can I be so casual about something so important to Emily? But Jamie understands.*

"I'm not sure of the mechanics of the test." Jamie's eyes were questioning. "I know—we see cop shows on TV where they talk about getting a DNA sample from a strand of hair, but—" He pantomimed his incomprehension.

"It's simple," Paul said gently. "The lab will provide what's called a buccal swab. It's an applicator that looks like a over-sized Q-Tip. You put the swab—it has a sponge tip—inside your cheek and rub it a bit. That's all you have to do. I'll return the swabs to the lab. They'll run the test. Twice—to confirm the original plus or negative."

"How long before we have a report?"

"No more than seven days after I bring in the swabs," Paul told him.

"It'll be the longest seven days in my life." Jamie's voice was hushed. "And except for that kitten you found abandoned on a rainy night, I might have lost my daughter."

Thirty-Two

Emily listened attentively to Andrea's report on her dinner meeting with the designers of the "Made in the USA" line. All the while conscious of the way the outdoor floodlights managed to penetrate the lined draperies at the windows of the den—lending an atmosphere of imminent danger.

Should I tell Andrea about my suspicions that Jamie is my father? Shouldn't I have confided in her right away? But I was so shaken—my first thought was to go to Paul. He said he'd approach Jamie direct. When?

"I realize we're running about a week behind schedule," Andrea acknowledged, "but I'm pleased with our progress. They understand what we need. Nothing far-out. Tailored apparel that'll be timely this year and five years from now— with extra small touches that people will notice and appreciate. And they're incorporating your suggestions."

"I'm so glad—" Never had she expected to become so involved in working with the company, Emily thought with fresh astonishment. The job—being created along the road— was challenging.

"I'd like you to sit in on the next meeting—" Andrea paused as the phone rang.

"I'll get it." A hint of expectancy in her voice, Emily hurried to pick up. "Hello—"

"Emily, I've just had a long dinner with Jamie. We need to talk. May I come over now?"

"Of course." Her heart began to pound. "Andrea's here, too." She saw Andrea's eyes light up with questions. "Please come, Paul."

"What was that all about?" Andrea managed a calm exterior, but Emily sensed her inner anticipation. *She thinks Paul has had word from Jason Hollister.*

173

"This is nothing to do with Hollister," she hastened to report. Disappointing to Andrea. "It's that—that something weird happened at the 'Stop the Mall' meeting last evening—" Emily was groping for words. "I may have jumped to the wrong conclusions—"

"What conclusions?" Andrea prodded.

Haltingly, Emily explained the situation. "My feeling was that curved pinkies could be an inherited family abnormality. And Jamie and Celeste were just a year apart at school—it seemed a possibility. Paul was to discuss it with Jamie—"

"After all these years to know—" Andrea's voice dropped to a whisper. "A fine man like Jamie. Emily, if it's true, you can be so proud of your father."

"Yes—" Emily glowed. *It won't mean that I love Dad any less. But I'll begin to know who I am.* "If it's true—"

"Nora's off to some doing at her church," Andrea recalled. "Put up coffee, see what goodie Nora's stored in the breadbox."

Ten minutes later the warning beep at the front door told them Paul had arrived.

"We're in the den," Emily called, breathless with anticipation. *What has Paul learned?*

"Emily brought me up to date," Andrea told Paul as he strode into the den. "You've learned more—" It was a statement.

"Yes—but there's more to be learned," he cautioned.

"Sit down, Paul—don't fidget," Andrea ordered. Straining for patience, she turned to Emily. "Pour coffee for us, please."

"We're not sure of anything yet," Paul warned, "but we'll have answers very soon."

Paul accepted a mug of coffee and one of Nora's carrot muffins, began to explain what he'd learned at his meeting with Jamie.

"Jamie's willing—eager—to have the DNA test," he wound up. "Nothing would make Jamie happier than to have the test come out positive. He's hoping you're willing to take the test, too," he told Emily.

"Yes! Oh, yes—" Emily's face was luminescent. "How soon will we know?"

"I can't approach the lab until Monday," Paul reminded her gently, "but once the swabs are at the lab we should know within a week."

174

"How lucky Celeste would have been if she'd married Jamie." Andrea was wistful. "But I shouldn't wish that on Jamie," she discarded this. "He deserves far better than Celeste."

"I want the tests to be positive," Emily said passionately. "It would make me so happy to know that Jamie is my father."

"Let's not jump the gun," Andrea exhorted. "We won't know until we have the test results. The test could go either way—"

At Sunday breakfast Andrea decreed that she and Emily would go to early church services. It was taken for granted that Andrea would be going in to her office after services—as usual on Sundays.

"Let folks in town know my granddaughter," she said with pride. "They're not going to ask questions about your mother." An amused glint in her eyes. "They won't dare."

Despite her fear at this exposure, Emily found attending church services with Andrea was a pleasant experience. Most people they met seemed so friendly—though she was aware of some cold eyes.

"I'm known by some residents as having a big mouth and throwing my weight around," Andrea whispered and pointed to a cluster of churchgoers who were leaving just ahead of them. "That's the contingent in town who'd like to see me dead." She chuckled at Emily's grimace. "Loosely speaking. They're the ones—for greedy reasons—who want the shopping mall to be approved. The man in the jacket is the Mayor—he's livid with me for fighting along with Paul against the mall. I hear he's convinced Paul would sell his grandmother's acreage except for me."

"Does Jason Hollister know about him?" Emily asked, fresh suspicions taking root in her mind. *Jason said—at one point—that we must consider that Hannah's murder was not related to the other two. Could the Mayor and his group have hired a killer—who killed Hannah for getting in his way?*

"I'm sure Jason knows." Andrea was defensive. "But that rotten group had nothing to do with Hannah's murder—or the two bomb incidents or the poisoned milk. I can't believe that—even considering how much they loathe me."

* * *

175

Early Monday morning Paul called to say he was heading for the lab in Albany.

"I'll be there when it opens. I'll return with the swabs in the afternoon. By next week this time we'll have our answers."

"It'll be the longest week in my life," Emily declared.

"If the tests are negative, honey, it won't be the end of the world." He was troubled. "I hate to see you building yourself up to a terrible let-down."

"I have this inner conviction," she insisted, "that the tests will be positive. I just know it." *Paul is right—I won't know until the tests come through. Two tests, he said. To make sure there's no error.*

She knew, too, that the next week would seem endless despite the long hours at the company, her involvement in the new line. Each evening Nora arrived at Andrea's office with dinner—always prepared to accommodate Paul's joining them. At some point in each day Jason Hollister appeared for a brief conference.

On Thursday Jason appeared while the three of them argued business details over coffee.

"Nothing special to report," he apologized. "That is, not yet." *Why does he seem so wary?* "Suspicions aren't enough—I need back-up facts."

"Whom do you suspect?" Andrea pushed. The atmosphere electric. *Is he talking about Hannah's murder—or all three?*

"I can't say yet—just that the hackles on the back of my neck tell me I'm on the right track."

"What can we do to help?" A vein pounded at Andrea's forehead.

"At the moment nothing." Jason was guarded. "I'm superstitious about these things. The less said the better."

"Is that what you came to tell us?" Andrea was reproachful.

"No," Jason admitted. "I wanted to tell you that if my suspicions are correct, we'll know who murdered your late husband and your late friend as well as Hannah. We'll know who's trying to kill you and Emily."

So it is a serial murderer. If Jason is correct in his suspicions.

Thirty-Three

Emily awoke on Friday morning with an instant awareness that this would be a gloomy, chilly day. Today and what would seem an incredibly long weekend, she told herself— then she would know the results of the DNA test. No need to tell Mom and Dad about the test, she told herself yet again. Not yet.

Will they be upset? Will they fear this will be a wall between us? No! They're Mom and Dad, forever. Knowing my natural father won't change how I feel about them. They're the ones who raised me, loved me, cared for me.

In a sudden need for action she tossed aside the comforter, hurried into the shower, lingering briefly under the hot spray. There was much to do at the company today, she reminded herself. Thank God, she thought, for the need to be busy.

She was dressed and about to head downstairs for breakfast when she heard voices in the foyer. Andrea and Paul. Had something happened? she wondered in sudden alarm, and darted down the stairs.

"Paul, he's precious," Andrea crooned. "Emily will adore him."

Paul held a young pup in his arms. His breed was difficult to tell this far away—but he seemed a bundle of affection as he ecstatically kissed Paul's chin.

"Someone new in the family?" Emily asked. Another stray that Paul had picked up on the road? But a chill darted through her as she remembered Paul's last stray.

"Meet Lucky," Paul introduced. "A gift from Jamie—if you'll have him."

"Hello, Lucky—" Emily fondled his head.

"Very original name," Andrea teased.

"The most popular name for a dog, I read somewhere—

Max is second. Jamie chose Lucky because the little guy was dumped on his doorstep last night and will be damn lucky if you give him a home."

"He's adorable—" Emily turned to Andrea. "May we keep him?"

"Of course we'll keep him." *She's remembering that poor little kitten. But nothing must happen to Lucky.*

"What is he?" Emily reached to take him from Paul. Oh, he was cuddly. "Not that it matters."

"I think his collie mother had an affair with a golden retriever," Paul surmised. "Jamie said he found him tied to one of the posts at the entrance to his office. He was terrified at first, but kind words and food restored him."

"Nora will love him." Andrea squinted in thought. "I gather it's safe to say Nora is off the hook—at least, in Jason's investigation. Because Nora hadn't been born when David was murdered."

"If Jason's suspicions are right, he'll crack this case wide open for the cops. Along with the two unsolved cases," Paul said. "Oh, Jamie sent along a bag of puppy food for Lucky—" He pointed to the parcel at his feet. "Along with a dog bed."

"Honey, Nora will be feeding him what we'll be eating," Andrea predicted. "And Lucky will be another security guard."

"How old is he, do you suppose?" A hint of laughter in Emily's voice.

"Young for a security guard," Paul conceded. "Jamie said he's about three months old."

"Thank Jamie for sending him to us," Emily said. *I think Lucky's kind of a gift for me. Jamie's way of saying he hopes I'm his daughter.*

"Let's go introduce Lucky to Nora. And Paul, stay for breakfast," Andrea ordered.

After a hasty breakfast the three of them were about to leave the house when Nora summoned Andrea to the phone.

"It's Mr. Leon's wife Jane—for you, Miz Andrea."

Emily and Paul waited for Andrea to return from taking the phone call. Lucky was devoting himself to Nora, they gathered.

"Nora will spoil the hell out of him," Paul surmised. "But hey, he deserves it. Jamie said he'd been through some rough treatment." *First that darling little kitten and now Lucky? How could people be so awful?*

"Jane wants us to come over for dinner this evening," Andrea reported. "Along with Carol and Tom. She said Leon feels badly about our not having our usual once-a-month Friday-evening dinner. It never crossed my mind in all that's happening," Andrea admitted. "But she said Leon had an attack of conscience last night. He's forever worrying about me, she said."

"That's natural—to worry about his mother," Paul pointed out. *But Paul's aware that Leon loathes him. He thinks Paul takes advantage of Andrea.*

"Let's get to work," Andrea said briskly. "We're not accomplishing anything here."

Already Emily was dreading dinner this evening. To the rest of the family—at least, to Carol and Celeste—she was an intruder. But thank God, Celeste wouldn't be there.

At eight p.m. Andrea rounded up Emily for their dinner at Leon and Jane's house.

"Leon knew better than to try to schedule dinner at seven," Andrea said with a flicker of amusement. "He knows how we're racing to meet our deadline for the new line."

"We're just running a bit behind," Emily consoled. "You knew it was kind of unrealistic," she added gently. But it was exhilarating to see the "Made in the USA" line taking shape. A minuscule advance against the exporting of jobs. *How can the economy improve when people have less money to spend?*

"If we're eating this late, I suspect the children won't be at the table," Andrea assumed—not with an air of regret. "The three most spoiled kids in the country."

"I suspect it's easier to spoil than to discipline." Emily remembered the children in her class. When she'd been their age, she'd never have dared to behave as some of them did.

"I spoiled my kids—and I'm paying the price." A rare bitterness crept into Andrea's voice. "But thank God for sending my unspoiled granddaughter to me."

Arriving at Leon and Jane's house, Andrea noted that Carol and Tom's car sat in the driveway.

"Normally Celeste would be here," Andrea commented. "I

gather from Carol that she's still sulking in East Hampton." *For which I'm grateful. I never want to see her.*

Jane welcomed them at the door. "We'll sit down right away—" She was almost apologetic. "So Denise can go home."

At their arrival in the living room Carol and Tom rose to their feet—with an air of "let's get this show on the road," Emily thought. Carol kissed her mother with an air of covert reproach, was cool in her greeting to Emily. Tom always seemed to be off in another world—as though escaping Carol's hostilities.

"Mom, you look tired—" Leon was solicitous. "When are you going to forsake your dreadful working hours?" His eyes said, "When are you going to retire?"

"I enjoy my work." Andrea's usual response. "And if I look tired, it's because I've been sleeping badly."

"Leon is a poor sleeper, too," Jane sympathized. "Sometimes I wake up for a minute or two in the middle of the night and realize Leon isn't in bed. He's downstairs somewhere reading or trying to relax in his lab in the basement. And he refuses to take sleeping pills." She gazed at Leon with a blend of reproach and admiration.

"You don't need sleeping pills," Carol told her mother. "You need to face the calendar. Be realistic—learn it's time to slow down."

"Let's go in to the table," Jane said—in an uneasy effort to puncture the sudden tension in the atmosphere. *She always seems unsure of herself. As though she's in awe of being part of the family.*

It was clear Denise was an excellent cook. *Leon wouldn't tolerate anything else.* Still, Emily was barely aware of what she was eating. She listened to the bland conversation around her, made an occasional contribution because she sensed that Andrea expected this of her.

Not until Denise served her superb tiramisu did the table talk take a less bland turn.

"I had a long talk with the District Attorney this afternoon." Leon focused on his mother. "You're not going to like what I'm about to tell you," he warned.

Andrea stiffened, stared hard at Leon. "You're going to tell us Hannah committed suicide?" she challenged. "That we just imagined the two bomb scares and the poison in the milk?"

"They're closing in on Nora," Leon began.

"That's absurd!" Andrea blazed. "And I don't see detectives coming to take her in."

"The DA explained they're waiting to tie up loose ends. They want to be sure they'll have enough evidence to convict her before they bring her in for arraignment." Leon was choosing his words with care. "I know how you feel about her, but you're putting your life in danger by keeping her in the house. Mother, be realistic. You're harboring a murderer."

"I'll never believe that." Andrea's face was drained of color. "I'll—"

"Who else could have put that poison in the milk? And the DA told me in deepest confidence—" Leon paused for emphasis. "They've checked out her background. She has a medical history of emotional imbalance. Plus she can't account for the night that Hannah was murdered. She told the police she was home with her aunt—but the DA says Rhoda was visiting a sick niece ninety miles away that night. It's a matter of hours before Nora will be charged with Hannah's murder."

Thirty-Four

Emily's somber gaze roamed from Andrea to Paul as they sat, tense and anxious, in the den and dissected Leon's report of his meeting with the District Attorney.

"Paul, I know I shouldn't have called you this late, but Emily and I were both so shaken," Andrea apologized.

"You were right to call me," Paul insisted.

"What's this sudden concern about Nora's not being at Rhoda's house the night Hannah was murdered?" Andrea pursued.

"She became suspect because of the poisoned milk—and then they backtracked." Paul shrugged this away. "But I have a legal team standing by to defend Nora if it becomes necessary. I'll be in touch with them first thing in the morning, alert them on what's happening." *He's trying to be casual about this—but he's anxious.*

"You said Leon insisted Rhoda lied about Nora's whereabouts that night," Emily reminded him. "Why would she do that?"

"To provide Nora with an alibi." Paul was blunt. "When the police questioned Nora, she must have told them she was at Rhoda's house that night. It was just a routine question—then. If Nora wasn't there, where was she?"

"Nora wasn't even considered a suspect in Hannah's death—until the poisoned milk surfaced." Emily was exasperated. "Now they're trying to link her to Hannah's murder and—this latest insanity?"

"They're convinced this is a link." Paul stared into space. "But why was Leon talking with the District Attorney? I know—he's concerned about your safety," he added before Emily or Andrea could reply. "And it's better that Nora be forewarned that she might be questioned further."

"It would be outrageous for the police to take Nora into custody," Andrea declared. "How can they be so stupid?"

"You're saying we should talk to Nora—before any action is taken," Emily interpreted.

"Warn her—gently—that she may be questioned. But remind her she'll have lawyers on her side."

"Will Rhoda be in trouble for lying to the police?" Emily asked.

The police appeared convinced that she had lied.

"Let's don't jump," Paul scolded, thought a moment. "I'll talk to Jason about this development—"

Over Saturday-morning breakfast—while Lucky slept beneath the table—Andrea told Nora that the police detectives might have some questions to ask.

Nora's face was drained of color. "What kind of questions?"

"It's just routine," Emily soothed. "They like to be sure they have all the necessary facts." *She's terrified. Where was she that night?*

"Miz Andrea, you know I didn't put that poison in the milk!"

"That's not what they'll be asking you." Andrea hesitated. "It's about Hannah's murder."

Nora gaped in disbelief. "The police think I killed Aunt Hannah?"

"I'm sure you can explain the situation," Emily soothed, exchanged an anxious glance with Andrea. "They're trying to establish where everybody close to Hannah was that night. They—"

"They're rememberin' about that darling little boy who was strangled," Nora gasped in sudden comprehension. "But everybody knew it couldn'ta been me. I was cleared—"

"Nora," Emily began gently, "they know that you weren't at Rhoda's house the night Hannah was killed. They know Rhoda lied for you—"

"Oh no—" Nora began to cry. "I told Aunt Rhoda she shouldn'ta lied. But she didn't want folks to know I did somethin' bad."

"What did you do, Nora?" Andrea's voice was compassionate.

"I spent the night with—with Roscoe Ames," Nora whispered.

183

"We're hopin' to get married once his divorce is final. I know I shouldn'ta stayed with him—"

"It's okay," Emily comforted. "If his divorce is in work, then he's free to be seeing someone else. You just explain that to the detectives. You'll be in the clear."

Provided Roscoe Ames confirms that she was with him the night Hannah was murdered.

In their usual Saturday routine Emily and Andrea left for the office after breakfast. Emily impatient for the weekend to be past, to have the Albany lab's report on the DNA test. Paul promised to call first thing Monday morning. Emily had hoped wistfully that the report might arrive earlier.

"Paul isn't here yet," Andrea noted when they arrived in the company parking area.

"He has an appointment here at eleven a.m.," Emily recalled. "With the public relations woman who's coming up from New York."

"Right. He's trying to steer her away from including all the madness here at the house in conjunction with the story about the new line." Andrea winced as she considered this. "I know— any kind of publicity is useful."

"Paul said she'll set up some TV and radio appearances for you to discuss your feelings about the exportation of jobs— and how you've organized the new line to highlight this." *Wendy's awed by what we're doing—she says we're making an important statement.*

"You'll come with me on all interviews," Andrea began and paused at Emily's consternation. "Darling, it was your going to the Genoa protest that pushed me into this. That made me realize what was happening in this country. Remember," she coaxed, "it'll be for an important cause."

"I'll be terrified," Emily protested. *Mom and Dad don't know about Genoa. Wendy's parents don't know. But I'm a grown woman. It's time I learned to make my own decisions.*

"You'll be eloquent," Andrea predicted. "You'll sit in with me on the meetings with the PR person."

Early in the afternoon Paul sat with Jason Hollister in a rear booth at the lightly populated diner across from Jason's motel.

He listened with stunned fascination while Jason brought him up to date on his investigation into the three murders plus the three aborted attempts. Despite the air-conditioning—on high because a late heat wave had descended on the area—Paul was perspiring.

"We say nothing yet to Mrs. Winston," Jason cautioned. "Not until every small bit of information falls into place. And we're still missing conclusive proof," he admitted in exasperation. "We don't know when another attempt will be made on her life—and on Emily's."

He didn't say "if another attempt will be made on her life—and on Emily's." "You expect that to happen—"

"It's inevitable. It's part of the pattern." Jason's eyes were compassionate. "He's growing more frustrated at each failure. More dangerous—"

"But careless in his frustration?" Paul reached for hope. "What can we do to nail him?"

Jason took a deep breath, slowly exhaled. "We must be watchful, outguess him. I'd like to have this creep shadowed. Under our watch twenty-four hours a day."

"Do it," Paul ordered.

"I'm short one man. He came down with bronchitis—I shipped him back home. But a replacement will arrive sometime tomorrow. I'll set up a watch to begin at eight a.m. Monday morning," Jason summed up. "We'll know every move he makes."

"Damn it!" Paul exploded. "Why do we have to play these games? Why can't we just nab the creep right now and put a stop to any more violence?"

"We mean for the accusation to stick," Jason pointed out. "We must go to the District Attorney with irrefutable evidence. Make sure he has a solid case. All we can do, Paul, is be watchful—and wait."

Thirty-Five

Closing down her computer, Emily heard a car drawing to a stop in the parking area. She'd seen Paul for only a few minutes in the course of the day, she thought wistfully. He'd popped in her office when he arrived for his eleven a.m. appointment, and disappeared after the appointment. Probably he'd taken the public relations woman out for lunch. *It's ridiculous to miss him this way.*

A few minutes later she heard him in conversation with Andrea. They were discussing the proposed promotional campaign, she gathered. She reached for her purse, retouched her lipstick, ran a tiny brush over her hair.

"How would you feel about an early dinner?" Paul hovered in the doorway. "Andrea said she's exhausted—she's going home for a cup of tea and a nap. She's not sure she won't sleep straight through."

"I'd like that." Her smile was dazzling. *Why do I feel so warm and protected when I'm with Paul?*

"I've heard about a great new restaurant. It's about fifteen miles out of town, set right in the middle of the woods. Perfect for a hot night like this."

"It sounds wonderful."

"What sounds wonderful?" Andrea paused at the door.

"A new restaurant Paul's discovered. We're going there for dinner. If that's all right with you—" All at once she was uncertain.

"You don't have to ask me for permission," Andrea scolded, a hint of laughter blending with approval in her voice. "Nora was leaving a casserole for us—I'll probably dip into it before I head for bed. This has been a grueling week."

"Is Nora a nervous wreck?" Paul's wry smile radiated sympathy.

"She's not happy," Andrea admitted. "Anyhow, I told her to go to Rhoda's house and not be back until Monday-morning breakfast. It can't be pleasant for her to be living in the house where her aunt was murdered." She paused as a security guard strode down the weekend-empty corridor, chuckled. "They try so hard to pretend they're not shadowing me. So let's call it a night—give them a break."

Emily and Paul saw Andrea to her car, then headed for Paul's hybrid. His arm at her waist. Andrea sensed how close they'd become—in so little time—and was pleased, Emily told herself. But every minute of every day a cloud hung over them.

When would horror strike again? Instinct told her the fiend who sought to kill Andrea or her—or both—would try again. *Will there be a future for Paul and me?*

The restaurant was reached by way of a long road through a heavily wooded area. *Could we have been followed? Is this a bad place to be at a time such as this?*

Emily pretended to be enthralled with the charming, elegant restaurant that looked down upon a tiny waterfall that fell into a narrow brook. As she forced herself to relax, she became aware of an inner excitement in Paul.

They lingered over ordering, accepting advice from the genial waiter. When they were alone again, Paul reached across the table for her hand.

"Sundays I always go to visit my grandmother. Sometimes she recognizes me, is coherent. Sometimes she's escaped into another world. I'd like to take you to meet her. If she's well, I know she'll be so happy to know you."

"I'd love to go with you."

"Soon, I suspect, this nightmare will be over. We'll be able to make plans for the rest of our lives." A question in his eyes now. "You won't say 'no' to me?"

"Absolutely not," she promised and laughed at her impassioned reply. Now her eyes searched his. "Paul, you know something. You met with Jason—he had news!"

"We're hoping for a fast solution," Paul hedged. "I'm hoping within the next seventy-two hours. But we're getting there."

"Whom do you suspect?" Emily tingled with excitement now.

"Jason could be way off base. Let's just say I'm all at once superstitious. I'll jinx it if I talk too much—"

"Not Nora," she pushed. "It can't be Nora."

"No way," Paul conceded. "This would confirm Andrea's conviction that all three murders were committed by the same person. Her husband was murdered before Nora was born."

"I don't understand why you're so secretive." Emily gazed at him in rebellion. *It's not that he's superstitious.*

"By Monday morning," Paul began, seeming to reach for words, "the suspect will be under twenty-four-hour guard. He makes a move, we'll grab him. And he will make a move. His profile tells us that."

But will he make a move before Monday morning?

A slight drizzle began to fall as they approached the house. Darkness was a huge umbrella that provided a sense of isolation from the rest of the world. Emily was startled when Paul pulled to the side of the road.

"You're going to meet my grandmother tomorrow," he reminded her. "You know what that means?" He reached to pull her into his arms.

"What?" she questioned.

"We're officially engaged. Not ready to announce to the world," he granted, "but we have privileges."

"Yes," she whispered, welcoming his arms about her, his mouth on hers. "Oh yes—"

A few minutes later—with obvious reluctance—Paul reached for the ignition, turned into the driveway. As usual glaring floodlights surrounded the house.

"I'll walk you to the door," he said, and chuckled. "I know, you have two security guards pacing the grounds, and that damned alarm is going to screech like hell when you open the door. But if I walk you to the door, I can kiss you good-night."

"That's a good reason," she murmured. *I can't believe that in the midst of all this horror I can feel so happy.*

In the somber of the quiet of the house Emily climbed the stairs to her bedroom. She paused for an instant at Andrea's door. No sounds emerged. No sliver of light beneath the door. Andrea was asleep—exhausted from the fears and uncertainties inflicted in these past few weeks, Emily thought tenderly.

She opened her bedroom door. Lucky leapt from the foot of her bed to greet her with ecstatic barks. In loving welcome he rolled over onto his back, small legs beating the air.

She dropped to a crouch to caress his belly. "Oh, you're a wonderful baby," she crooned. "You're the greatest—" A bundle of love from the man she prayed was her father.

Lucky cavorted at her feet as she prepared for the night, paused at intervals to lap at his bowl of water—placed in the tiny dressing area between her bedroom and bath. Instinct told her that he'd ignore the dog bed Jamie had sent over for him—as he had last night.

Despite her conviction that she'd lie sleepless far into the night, she drifted off minutes after she settled under the light coverlet that the central air-conditioning made necessary. Lucky sprawled at her feet in instant slumber.

She came awake reluctantly. Lucky was barking—inches away from her ear. *What's the matter with him? It's the middle of the night.* "Sssh," she scolded. "Lucky, be quiet—" And then all at once she stiffened in alarm. *What's happening here?* "It's all right, Lucky. It's all right."

But it wasn't all right. Her throat was scratchy. She began to cough. *What's that strange smell? Something's happened to the air-conditioning system! We have to get out of the house!*

She bolted out of bed, reached for the robe at its foot, all the while murmuring reassurance to Lucky. Now she reached down to scoop him into her arms, darted from her bedroom across the hall to Andrea's bedroom.

She knocked. There was no response. Her heart pounding she opened the door, hurried to the bed. "Andrea, we have to get out of the house! Grandma," she pleaded, "wake up! Please, wake up!"

Thirty-Six

"Emily?" Andrea was groggy. *She's alive. Thank God!*

"We have to get out of the house—there're awful fumes coming from the air-conditioning registers." Emily began to cough again. "Andrea, please—"

"Oh, my God—" Andrea was on her feet, reached for her robe. "Let's move—"

They charged out into the hall, down the stairs, out into the sultry night. Coughing at moments, intent only on escaping into the night air. They heard the sounds now of approaching fire trucks.

"Where are the security guards?" Andrea demanded, pausing to pull on her robe.

"They're at the back of the house," Emily realized.

"Why?" Barefoot, ignoring the dampness of the grass beneath her feet, Andrea charged in the direction of the voices. Emily—clutching Lucky—at her side.

The pair of security guards were hosing down a segment of the woods behind the house.

"It's okay," one of them called out. "There was a slight brush fire, but we've got it under control. You didn't need to come out of the house."

"We needed." Andrea was grim. "We have more than a brush fire to contend with. Someone got into the house, did something toxic to the central air-conditioning. We—" Fire trucks were slowing down, preparing to swing into the driveway.

"We called the Fire Department," the guard explained. "Just in case we couldn't control the fire."

"What's this toxic deal?" The other guard exchanged a nervous glance with his co-worker. "The CAC malfunctioning?"

"Possible," Andrea conceded. "But with what's been happening in this house, I doubt it."

190

"The brush fire," Emily reasoned, "was a diversion to draw you both away from patrolling the grounds. Some foreign substance was injected into the heating and air-conditioning ducts to destroy the oxygen in the house. We were meant to die." She bent to kiss the top of Lucky's head. "Lucky saved us."

"What about Nora?" one of the guards asked in alarm. Nora was known to bring coffee out to the midnight to eight a.m. shift as soon as she awoke in the morning—somewhere between five and five thirty a.m. "Is she in the house?"

"Nora's off," Andrea told him. *Will this make Nora a suspect again?*

"Where's the fire?" A cluster of firemen were striding towards them.

"We think it's out," a guard reported, pointing towards the woods. Three firemen rushed in that direction. "We hosed it down quick," he called after them.

"Don't go into the house," Andrea warned the other firemen. "An asphyxiant has been injected into the CAC unit. Call for your Hazardous Materials team. We do have one?"

"Yes, ma'am—" Another fireman was darting back to the truck to summon the team. "We're proud that our community set it up four years ago."

"Maybe you two ladies should be checked out in the hospital—" Another fireman was solicitous. "To make sure you haven't—"

"We're all right," Andrea broke in. "But I'd like to borrow a cellphone for a few minutes."

"Paul's here!" Emily was astonished at the sight of his car making its way past the fire truck.

"Yes ma'am," one of the security guards said. "As soon as we spotted the fire, I called him. That was his orders—anything not right surfaces, he's to be called."

"The fire under control?" Paul called, charging up the driveway.

"It was just a small brush fire," Andrea called back, waited for him to reach them.

"You're both okay?" His eyes were anxious as they moved from Andrea to Emily.

"Thanks to Lucky—" Andrea told him and explained.

A shrill siren splintered the night quiet.

"The Hazardous Materials team are volunteers," Paul said. "They'll be here in minutes. But there's no point of you two standing out here at two a.m.," he told Emily and Andrea. "I have two unoccupied bedrooms at my house. I think you'll be comfortable there."

Knowing Emily and Andrea were too wired to sleep just yet, Paul settled them in his pleasant living room.

"They'll be a little large," he warned, "but I'll bring each of you a pair of slippers. Is the air-conditioning on too high?"

"It's fine," Emily answered for both of them and Paul headed out to the kitchen to put up coffee. Fluffy tail wagging, Lucky followed, anticipating a treat.

How strange—and lovely—to be sitting here in Paul's house. One day it'll be "our house." Should I tell Andrea about us? That he's taking me to meet his grandmother. But perhaps this isn't the time. Not yet.

"Decaf," Andrea called after Paul. She gazed about the room as though to reassure herself that no danger lurked here. "No problem with Paul's CAC," she said wryly, "but it'll be a long time before I encounter air-conditioning without remembering waking up that way in my bedroom." Her eyes grew tender. "You called me Grandma."

"You are my grandmother." Emily tried for lightness. "I think of you that way now." She radiated love and admiration. "I'm glad you brought me out of the closet—"

"I've waited so long for this time with you. I pray it won't be aborted by whatever maniac is out to kill me." She hesitated, frowning in pain. "Or both of us—"

"Could we be jumping the gun?" Emily forced herself to bring her ambivalence out into the open. "Air-conditioners, furnaces, refrigerators—they do malfunction on occasion. People die of asphyxiation."

"I'd like to believe this is one such instance." Andrea considered this for a moment. "Instinct tells me it isn't. That it's another instance of a growingly frustrated—growingly dangerous—psycho."

The phone rang. Paul called from the kitchen. "I'll pick up out here—"

Minutes later he returned to the living room with coffee tray in hand.

"That was Barney—one of the security guards," Paul said. "I asked him to call me as soon as there was any word. He said the Hazardous Materials team are in the house. He gathers there's no question but this was an attempt at asphyxiation. One of the team ridiculed it as 'a dumb amateur playing terrorist.'"

"Dumb amateur." Will this increase police suspicion of Nora—who was not in the house when another attempt to kill was made?

"I know it would be absurd to try to talk with Jason Hollister at this hour—" Emily reached for the mug of decaf that Paul extended.

"But let's meet with him first thing tomorrow morning. It's time he leveled with us. No more playing super-detective. You said Jason's convinced he knows who killed Hannah—and my grandfather and Grandma's close friend." The atmosphere was electric. "Give us a name!"

"I don't have a name—Jason won't give us that until he has positive proof." *Paul knows. Why is he lying?* "It's already Sunday morning. In another twenty-nine hours our suspect will be under guard. This person won't be able to attack again—clumsy as in this last attempt, or otherwise. Jason will nail him—or her—turn over the evidence to the District Attorney's office."

Andrea uttered a long, anguished sigh. "Enough for tonight. Let's try to get a few hours sleep. Tomorrow morning," she predicted, "the media will be spewing out the story of what was meant to happen in my house a few hours ago. We'll be assaulted again by a battery of reporters and photographers."

Paul grinned. "They won't know you're here. I hinted that you were in a suite at the Woodhaven Hotel."

Thirty-Seven

Emily slept in jagged bursts of exhaustion, awoke to morning sunlight filtering between the bedroom drapes. At the foot of the bed Lucky snored lightly—as though, she thought, all was right with the world. But it wasn't.

One question haunted her now. Why had Paul lied to Andrea? Was he afraid she'd be so furious she'd alert the suspect before he—or she—could be apprehended? *Is it someone in the company?*

She felt a surge of comprehension. That would be a terrible blow to Andrea. She was so convinced that every employee at the company was loyal to her. But there could be one sick mind among them. One of those few people who'd been with the company since the beginning. Paul said the killer was responsible for all three murders.

She listened for sounds in the house—not knowing the hour. But the morning sunlight told her it was still early. Time to face the new day.

When will we be able to return to the house? How bad is the contamination? What about our clothes? What are we to wear today? We ran only in nightgowns and robes.

In quiet movements so as not to disturb Lucky—who seemed now to be enjoying a happy puppy dream—she left the bed and crossed to the tiny adjoining bathroom. She felt a sudden need to shower, as though to wash away the ugliness of a few hours ago. Paul had supplied soap and towels, even a toothbrush and toothpaste, she noted lovingly. She stood under the hot spray with a sense of quiet pleasure. For a few minutes—in this house where Paul had spent most of his life—she felt safe, hopeful for tomorrow.

In nightgown and robe and Paul's slippers that flapped noisily with each step she hurried downstairs—Lucky at her feet, eager to greet the new day. The aromas of fresh-made coffee and rolls heating in the oven filtered through the house. For an instant she could believe this was her home now—and Paul had gone downstairs to prepare breakfast for them.

Andrea glanced up from the kitchen phone while she listened to a voice at the other end, smiled reassuringly. "I've told you, Leon. We're fine. Don't be so upset. But I expect you and Jane and Carol and Tom to be at church this morning. I want the town to see that Emily and I are not devastated by this insanity." She listened now for a moment. "Yes, Leon, you call Carol. We'll attend the ten a.m. services as a family."

"We're not exactly dressed for attending church." Emily's smile was wry.

She and Andrea laughed at Lucky's tiny barks of pleasure as he discovered the bowl of puppy food and water that Paul had left for him.

"Paul's over at the house with a policewoman. She's going into the house in protective gear. She'll bring out a valise with a change of clothes for each of us and—" Andrea paused as Lucky abandoned eating to charge towards the front of the house. A car was pulling up in the driveway.

"Paul's back," Emily guessed, her face lighting up. "Oh, can I help with breakfast?"

"I've got everything under control. Breakfast rolls defrosting in the oven. The coffee's ready," Andrea said at the faint shushing in the coffee-maker. "I'll scramble up eggs for the three of us. Go talk with Paul. See what the policewoman chose for us to wear today."

Lucky was barking at the door, impatient to welcome Paul. Emily pulled the door wide as he hurried up the flower-lined path to the house. He held aloft the weekender he'd supplied for this errand, bent to fondle Lucky.

"The situation is better than we anticipated," he greeted her, leaned forward for a light kiss. He grinned. "If the neighbors are watching, let them get used to this." His voice was a caress. "I love being met at the door by you in nightie and robe."

"You said the situation is better than we anticipated," she probed, one hand in Paul's while Lucky followed them up the hall towards the kitchen.

"The creep goofed in every way. This was a clumsy attempt—well beyond his capabilities. The house will be considered decontaminated in another three or four hours. You'll be able to sleep there tonight. My loss—" His eyes said he was impatient for the time she would share the house with him.

"Ah, now Emily and I will know what we'll wear to church this morning," Andrea greeted them in the kitchen. "Breakfast can wait while we see what you've brought us," she told Paul.

The two women checked the contents of the weekender, agreed that the policewoman had chosen well.

"She realized the heat wave had broken overnight," Emily approved. "My silk pantsuit is perfect."

"Will you be going with us to church services, Paul?" Andrea headed to the range to scramble eggs while Lucky focused again on breakfast. "And what about a meeting with Jason? We'll be at church services in the morning, but—"

"I'll be seeing him in the afternoon," Paul broke in uneasily. "He suggested a meeting at your office first thing Monday morning."

"Damn!" Andrea grunted in frustration. "I'm paying the bills. I should have some answers."

"You will—by nine a.m. tomorrow morning," Paul soothed.

"I'm not happy about that"—Andrea was tart—"but I'll live with it. And if you have something interesting to report after your meeting, Emily and I should be home by two o'clock. We're making a family appearance at church services, then I'll take everybody out to lunch. I want this town to know we're not consumed by fright."

The parking area beside the church was already filled by the time Emily and Andrea arrived.

"We'll have to park on the street," Andrea said, searching the parking area to see if the rest of the family had arrived. "As usual," she said drily, "they're late. But let's go inside and wait for them."

Emily was touched by the flow of people who came forward to express their sympathy and support. Though she read curiosity in their eyes about her, they asked no questions. *People in this town—most of them—love Grandma.*

196

Leon and Jane, with Raymond, and Carol and Tom, with the twins, arrived moments before the services were to begin. They settled down after quick greetings to Andrea and Emily.

"We're going out to lunch together," Andrea whispered. "I made reservations at the Colonial Inn."

Emily was impressed by the sermon. The minister talked about the tragedy the town had suffered and the ongoing violent attempts. And he asked that the townspeople pray that the perpetrator be discovered and imprisoned.

With the services over, the family members approached their respective cars for the drive to the restaurant.

"Jane seemed abnormally quiet," Andrea reflected. "I hope she's not coming down with something."

"She's upset about all the craziness," Emily surmised.

Andrea allowed herself a mischievous smile. "When I made the lunch reservations, I asked for two tables. One for the adults and a small one for the three children. The Colonial Inn has marvelous food. I mean to enjoy it."

When everyone gathered together on the parking lot at the Colonial Inn, Andrea held up a commanding hand, focused on the children.

"I want you kids to listen to me. You're having a table of your own—and you behave. If there's any squabbling among you, any kind of bad behavior, I'm telling you right now. You'll see no Christmas presents for you under the tree this year." Her eyes moved from one to the other. "Remember that."

They were greeted warmly by the hostess, led to two adjoining tables. Raymond and the twins were seated at the small table, the adults at the large table.

"They'll behave." Andrea was complacent. "They know I meant what I said. And I'm always very generous with presents."

Emily was conscious of a deliberate effort on the part of everyone at the table to keep the conversation on an impersonal basis. When Carol introduced the subject of the "Stop the Mall" group—no favorite of hers—Leon silenced her. And then, over dessert, Andrea dropped her bombshell.

"I've been very private about my own action in these insane weeks," she began. Instantly four pairs of eyes settled on her in alarm. "Of course, the police are supposed to be trying to track down Hannah's murderer—and the other insanity that's followed Hannah's death. But I talked with Paul about my hiring private investigators. Paul brought in a top-notch team— and I'm told that by this time tomorrow we'll probably know who's responsible."

Those at the table gaped at Andrea in astonishment. Emily's eyes darted from one to the other. Only Tom appeared unimpressed. Leon and Carol were shocked—reproachful—that their mother had not confided in them. Jane was suddenly ashen.

"Shouldn't these PIs take their evidence—if they truly have it—to the District Attorney?" Leon seemed skeptical about this new development.

"By eight a.m. tomorrow morning the suspect will be under a twenty-four-hour watch," Andrea reported. "The investigators are convinced there will be another attack. He—or she— will be captured. Emily and I will be able to live normal lives again. And yes, they'll hand over their evidence to the District Attorney's office."

Why does Jane look so distraught? When Paul talked about the suspect, he referred to "the person" or "he—or she". He knows who murdered Hannah—and who has been trying to kill Andrea and, possibly, me.

Can it be Jane? The last person in the world who'd be suspect!

Thirty-Eight

After lunch Emily and Andrea returned to the house. A pair from the Hazardous Materials Division was just about to depart.

"Everything's all clear," one reported cheerfully. "You'll need some heavy cleaning done," he acknowledged, "and I'd suggest leaving windows open for the next few hours—to eliminate any unpleasant odors that might linger. But the house is safe."

"Thanks for taking such good care of us," Andrea told him. "It's been a rough twelve hours."

A few moments of casual conversation now, and Andrea and Emily were alone in the house.

"I should run over to the office—" Andrea was pensive.

"Not today," Emily scolded as Andrea suppressed a yawn. "You got so little sleep last night. Settle for a nap," she coaxed.

"Maybe I will," Andrea capitulated and listened to sounds outside. Paul in conversation with a security guard. "Paul had a short conference with Jason Hollister," she gathered, her voice acerbic. Jason's silence was a sore irritant to her.

Emily hurried to open the door. Paul—with Lucky chasing ahead—strode up to the house.

"How was lunch?" he asked while Lucky clamored for attention.

"The Colonial Inn is a treasure." Emily reached to scratch Lucky behind the ears. "I brought a doggie bag home for you," she crooned. "Later."

"I would have felt better if I could have told my children that—while the police are coming up with nothing—my private investigators are coming up with answers," Andrea greeted Paul.

Paul was startled. "You told them about Jason?"

"You know how upset they've been. They were relieved to

199

know that the end is in sight." *Jane was devastated.* "But what else did Jason have to say?" Andrea pressed.

"Just that his research bears out his suspicions," Paul hedged. "He's convinced we're on the right track."

Andrea suppressed another yawn. "I'm giving in to my age," she said with a gesture of amusement. "I'm going up to my decontaminated bedroom and take a nap. Emily, why don't you and Paul take a loaf of bread from the kitchen and go across the road to the pond and feed the ducks? They've been so neglected these past few weeks."

"We'll leave Lucky to guard the house." Emily reached down to fondle him.

"Give him the doggie bag when you go out for the bread," Paul urged Emily. "Consolation for not taking him with us. But I don't think the ducks would appreciate his presence."

With bread in tow Emily and Paul left the house, walked across the road to the pond.

"What an idyllic day." Paul's smile was whimsical. "Standing here by the pond, we can almost believe nothing terrible has been happening."

Emily viewed the serene picture of the duck and six duck-lings in her wake with mixed feelings. So peaceful here. So good to be with Paul. But why was he so startled that the others knew about Jason? *Because Jane is the suspect?*

"You're very quiet—" Questions in Paul's eyes.

"I was thinking about the conversation at lunch—"

"Did Andrea come right out and say we're shadowing the suspect?" Paul was tense.

"She said, 'By eight a.m. tomorrow morning the suspect will be under a twenty-four-hour watch. The investigators are convinced there will be another attack. He—or she—will be captured.'" Emily's heart began to pound. "Paul—is Jane the suspect?"

"I can't say who is the suspect—" Paul shook his head in frustration.

"But this is crazy!"

"We have to go along with Jason's reasoning. I know it sounds insane. But I'm guessing another move will be made at any time. I've talked with the security guards. They're to ignore any distraction—like the brush fire last night. Anybody makes an effort to enter the house, they're to stop him—or her—at gun point. If the suspect persists, they're to shoot to kill."

"And if a stranger enters the house," Emily said with an effort at humor, "Lucky will bark his little head off."

"Nora will be back at the house this evening," Paul assumed.

"Not until early tomorrow morning," Emily told him. "She's going to a cousin's wedding this evening." All at once she stiffened. "Nora was not at the house last night—will that heap more suspicion on her? In the eyes of the District Attorney?"

"Don't worry about Nora," Paul insisted. *Because he knows who's the killer. Why can't he tell us?* "She'll soon be in the clear. Very soon."

Monday loomed as such an important day, Emily thought, frustrated by the questions that lay unanswered.

"Paul," she began while they tossed more crumbs to the eager duck and ducklings—as though ignoring the ugly threats hanging over her head and Andrea's, "we're sure to know the results from the DNA tests by tomorrow morning?"

"Right. I'll call first thing in the morning," he promised. "Jamie said he'll send a courier to Albany to pick up the papers as soon as the results are in. By tomorrow this time you and Jamie will know."

Emily suppressed a shudder. *If I survive the next twenty-four hours, I'll know.*

Emily sat at one corner of the sofa in the den and tried to lose herself in the Sunday newspapers. Exhausted from a run around the pond, Lucky lay at her feet, uttered tiny sounds of puppy dreams. But every moment—in the heavy silence that lay over the house—she was conscious of possible impending disaster.

Paul didn't come out and say that he expected another driven-by-frustration attack within the next twenty-four hours, but she sensed he was convinced of this. And not until eight a.m. tomorrow morning would the suspect be under surveillance.

How does he—or she—get into the house with the guards patrolling outside, the alarms on every door, floodlights bathing the grounds? Every window locked—and no sign of forced entries. How does he—or she—contrive to enter the house?

201

Thirty-Nine

"I can't believe I napped so long—" Andrea's voice snapped Emily to attention. *I must have dozed off for a few moments.*

"You needed it," Emily said lovingly and reached to gather together the Sunday papers strewn across the sofa—most still unread.

"Nora left a casserole in the fridge for tonight's dinner. I've put it in the oven. And there's bread pudding with bourbon sauce to be heated to go over it." Andrea settled herself at the other end of the sofa.

"Sounds luscious." *How can we make such casual talk when we don't know what attempt will be made on our lives at any moment? Paul is sure the killer is growing more desperate by the minute. But it'll all be over soon—we can handle this.*

Andrea glanced at the clock on the mantle. "We'll have dinner in about an hour. All right?"

"Fine." Emily exuded love. "I'll set the table and—"

"Let's have dinner here in the den, on the tray tables—and watch something mindless on television. Pretend for a little while that 'all's right with the world.'" Andrea reached out in an impulsive gesture to take Emily's hand in hers. "It's so wonderful to have you here with me. I wish David could have known you. Your grandfather would have adored you."

"I wish I could have known Granddad." Tears welled in Emily's eyes. "But I'm so glad I found you—" She hesitated a moment. "Grandma—"

"Coming from you, that's the most beautiful sound in the world." Andrea's face was luminescent. "You called me that when you came to me last night—"

The harsh ring of the phone seemed an obscene intrusion.

"I'll get it—" Emily hurried to pick up. "Hello—"

"I'm just checking in—" Paul was struggling to be casual.

"After all, we haven't spoken in almost three hours."

"Everything's fine here," Emily reported and Andrea nodded. "We'll be having dinner in about forty minutes. A fashionably late dinner." She made an effort to sound amused. "I'm not sure Nora would approve."

"Of course, Jason isn't familiar with the local scene—" A taut quality in Paul's voice now. "But I've checked around to see if I could scrounge up another pair of security guards for the late shift. So far no luck—but I'm still trying."

"We feel as though we're living in a fortress right now," Emily soothed. *What does he know that's making him so anxious? He said it'd be a bad move to ask the police for more protection—they'd think he and Jason Hollister are off the wall.*

"Tell Lucky I expect him to be on twenty-four-hour guard duty." Again, Paul was trying for a lighter mood.

"He'll be stationed right at the foot of my bed," Emily surmised. "Or closer."

"I'm jealous," Paul murmured. "So jealous."

Rain began to pelt the house while Emily and Andrea ate dinner before the TV set. Sunday evening television did little to divert their thoughts from the possibility of impending disaster.

"If Nora was here, she'd be running out with a pot of coffee for the security guards—and hefty portions of bread pudding," Andrea mused.

"I could do that," Emily offered.

"No!" The harshness in Andrea's voice startled her. "You could be a sitting duck for that maniac if he's lurking in the woods. We'll watch a little more television—more ghastly international news." She clucked in distaste. "And we'll go to bed early. We're both running short on sleep. Not even my nap made up for the lost hours last night."

Surprisingly early Andrea decreed they should head for bed. "You're yawning your head off," she joshed. "And tomorrow's a big day."

"Right." *Tomorrow we'll have the report from the lab in Albany. We'll know if Jamie is my father.*

While the rain beat a steady drone on the roof, Paul completed his last phone call. He'd finally arranged for a pair of security guards from the company—about to sign off on the four-p.m.-to-midnight shift—to agree to moonlight at the Winston house until eight a.m.

"We can be there in about twenty minutes after we sign out," one of the pair assured him. "Twelve twenty at the latest."

He felt slightly reassured. But he couldn't brush aside the conviction that another attempt on the lives of Andrea and Emily would be made before Jason's surveillance team went on duty.

He kicked off his shoes, stretched out on his bed—knowing he was too wired to sleep. Sure, he conceded, he and Jason could be all wrong in their suspicions. But everything added up. *The creep will make a move tonight.*

Hell, what am I doing hanging around here? Go over to the house, park in that wooded enclave a hundred feet before the driveway—which local couples claim for trysts. Watch for an approaching car. His car. He has to come that way.

He parked his car—his wife's car, in truth—in a clump of woods behind the pond, stepped out into the night. His face half-hidden by the hood of his slicker. The rain was letting up. That was good. He glanced up at the sky, wine-red with clouds. Not a sliver of moonlight, not a star on view, he noted smugly. He couldn't have asked for a better night.

He walked with cautious steps, though the wetness of the earth eliminated sounds. Staying in the shadows of the thick old trees. The narrow road was deserted at this hour. Across the road he saw the garish spill of light that surrounded the house—not reaching out to the road. No way he could be seen.

He knew the security guards' routine by now. Each would encircle one half of the house, meet the other in front of the house for a moment, then retrace his steps until each was back at the end of the property. Neither did more than glance at the back—because that would leave the front of the house wide open.

He chuckled in vicious pleasure. They didn't know he could get into that mausoleum of a house without setting off any alarms. All he needed was a couple of minutes to charge across the road—when each guard was headed away—and in another minute he'd be inside that evil house.

Now, he ordered himself. Now!

204

Forty

Emily tossed restlessly beneath the light coverlet required by the drop in temperature—caused by the arrival of the rain. She listened now. No more rain. The weathercaster had said the rain would stop by midnight. She inspected the clock on her night table. It was a minute past midnight.

As always since being installed, wisps of the outdoor flood-lights seeped through the drapes—a constant reminder that this was a house under siege. To Emily the eerie darkness—relieved only by those wisps of light—all at once seemed threatening. She reached to switch on her bedside lamp. *I'm behaving like a two-year-old—afraid of the dark!*

She abandoned bed, stood indecisively at its side. Chilly in the dank midnight air, she reached for her robe at the end of the bed—where Lucky sprawled in rapturous slumber. She reached to stroke his head in a surge of affection. Such a sweet baby. He'd adored his share of the dinner casserole.

Fighting a sense of claustrophobia, she crossed to the glass slider that led out to the tiny balcony, walked out into the cold night air. She stiffened at the sound of a male voice some-where below, then realized it was one of the security guards on his cellphone in the routine hourly check with his office.

It was reassuring to know the security guard was right below. *How can anyone steal into the house with the light spreading that way and the two guards constantly scanning the area? Every door leading into the house set with an alarm to go off at the touch. But somebody did creep into the house last night—*

Now the outdoor darkness was intimidating. She went back into her bedroom, closed the slider to the balcony. She hesi-tated a moment, then locked it.

Knowing sleep would elude her, she went to the small, hang-ing bookcase to choose a book to read. She winced at the titles of the suspense novels that filled the shelves. Not the subject matter of choice for tonight, she told herself with ironic humor.

She froze at the sound of a knob turning. The knob on her bedroom door. Fearfully, she turned around. Her blood turning to ice. Knowing it would be futile to scream . . .

In the king-size bed she shared with her husband, Jane came awake with a start, frowned. What had awakened her? She'd slept so badly these last weeks, she thought fretfully. Lack of sleep always made her a nervous wreck.

She stared into the darkness, struggling to pinpoint what had awakened her. Probably a car backfiring—or the town fire-alarm system summoning volunteers. Then all at once another suspicion tugged at her. She reached out to emptiness.

He's gone out again. One of his nightly walks? Or is he going over there?

She lay still, heart pounding. Her mind in chaos. Remembering those other times. Each time he'd come home and fallen into deep sleep. *But he hasn't come home. It hasn't happened yet. Whatever evil he's planned.*

The first time—while he slept—she'd discovered the gun he kept in a drawer of his night table still warm. The police had never found the weapon that had killed Hannah. And the other time he'd spent hours down in his silly lab—working on one of his so-called experiments.

I tried to make excuses for his wild outbursts against his mother—then Emily as well. I didn't want to face the truth. Dear God, how can I turn in my own husband? Give me the strength to stop him.

In a surge of determination she reached out to switch on her bedside lamp, leaned across the bed to his night table.

The gun is missing. I can't let it happen again!

She reached for the phone, punched in the number, waited for a response . . .

"Why?" Emily gasped. "Why, Leon?" How long could she stall him? "Why do you want to do this?" Lucky slept in blissful ignorance—but how could he help?

"You'll both die," he said with an air of triumph. "Like the others."

206

"Your father?" Emily's mind was in chaos. *I must keep him talking. But who'll know to come?* "Why did you want your father dead?" She fought for a semblance of calm. Lead him on to talk. "You were a child—twelve years old."

"My mother loved me the most—but he demanded all of her attention. There was nothing left for me!" His face was distorted in remembered rage. "For a few years then everything was fine. She loved me most. The girls meant nothing. Then *he* came along. That Roger." He exuded contempt. "But I got rid of him. Life was good again. Until she ignored my wishes. I was right—it was time for her to sell the business. And then she brought *you* here. All she thought about was you."

"But why Hannah?" Emily searched for a way to keep him talking.

"That was a mistake. Hannah was supposed to be away that night. I told my mother to listen to me—to put the business up for sale. But she was going to let everything go down the drain. My inheritance would be nothing."

"How did you get into the house?" *How much longer can I keep him talking?*

He chuckled with vicious satisfaction. "Simple. When we were teenagers, Carol and I used to sneak out of the house at night and do crazy things. There was an entrance from the storage room of the garage into the house—by way of the kitchen. My mother found out—she had it closed off. But she's always a stickler for safety—she wanted that exit open in case of a fire. I discovered how the panels slid open to provide admittance." He glowed in triumph. "I have a key to the storage room of the garage. Long ago I took on the responsibility of making sure the garden equipment is in order. Playing the man of the house—which gave me entrée whenever I liked."

Who's opening the door? Please God, don't let him hear.

"But enough of this—" He moved closer. *It's Grandma—a gun in her hand.* "You're going out onto the balcony. You're going to have a tragic accident—"

A shot rang out. Lucky awoke to bark furiously. Leon fell forward, blood surging from his chest.

"Jane called me. She warned me," Andrea gasped. "How could I have been so blind all these years?"

Trembling, Emily rushed into her arms. "I was so scared—"

"You're all right now. We're both all right—"

"If you'd been minutes later, I'd be dead," Emily whispered while they clung together in shock. *And Grandma would have been next.*

"It's wrong for a mother to kill her child—but I couldn't let him hurt you, my darling. That would have been wrong."

They heard the guards charging up the stairs, then a car screeching to a stop in the driveway.

"Mrs. Winston?" one guard yelled anxiously. "Mrs. Winston?"

"Emily and I are all right," she called back, but her voice was wracked by pain. *How can she be all right when her son lies at her feet in a pool of blood?*

"What's happening?" they heard Paul demand as he bolted up the stairs behind the guards. "Who the hell got into the house? Who's been shot?"

"Paul, it was Leon," Emily called back shakily. "The nightmare is over." But she knew that for Andrea the nightmare would never be truly over. She had killed her son.

"Nobody in here—" The two guards had reached the top of the stairs, were at Andrea's bedroom.

"They're in Emily's bedroom—" Breathless from exertion, Paul rushed to the door. His eyes surveyed the scene—Emily and Andrea locked in each other's arms. A few feet away Leon lay in a pool of blood. "Oh, my God—"

"It was awful," Emily gasped. "Grandma saved my life. Leon meant to shove me off the balcony—"

"Call the police," Paul ordered the guards, hovering in the doorway now. "And an ambulance—" He moved forward, bent over the bloodied body on the floor. "The coroner," he corrected. "No need for an ambulance."

"That's why you refused to tell us of your suspicions," Andrea gasped. "You knew I would never have believed it was my son."

"We'll go downstairs," Paul said gently, prodded Andrea and Emily from the room. "He was a sick man."

"Jane called to warn me," Andrea began, then flinched into silence.

Haltingly Emily brought Paul up to date while he walked with them from her bedroom.

"How did you guess?" Andrea asked when Paul had settled them in the den. Already they heard police cars pulling to a stop in the driveway. One guard remained on duty on the scene. The other guard was waiting at the door to brief the police crew.

"Jason Hollister followed your conviction that this was a serial killer," Paul explained. "He started with the current attempts, then worked backward through the years. He brought in a profiler. Bits of information began to fall into place. The profiler suspected Leon. But then you told the family that the suspect would be shadowed twenty-four hours a day beginning tomorrow at eight a.m. We knew Leon was frantic—"

"Paul, Jane's alone at her house with Raymond. Please," Andrea told him, "call her sister. Tell her what's happened. Jane will need her."

A pair of somber-faced detectives appeared at the doorway of the den.

"I'm sorry, Mrs. Winston. So sorry," one of them apologized. "But we do need to ask some questions—"

"Yes, I understand." Andrea reached for Emily's hand. "We're prepared for that."

Forty-One

Now at last—with morning sunlight pouring past opened drapes—Emily and Andrea sat alone in the living room. Both exhausted from the trauma of the past nine hours. The police had taken off. Leon's body removed. Paul had managed to disperse the crowd of media people who'd surfaced with astonishing speed.

Newly arrived at the house, Nora was shaken to learn the events of the night but moved about the kitchen now preparing breakfast as though this was just any other morning. In the den Tom—with Carol at his side—was handling private funeral arrangements for Leon, once the police released the body. Carol had explained that Deirdre and Elaine were with the housekeeper. There would be no school for them today.

"How will they face their classmates?" Carol had wailed. "How could Leon do this to the family?"

"Poor Jane—" Andrea closed her eyes in anguish for a moment. "What a hell of a marriage she must have endured all these years. How brave of her to warn me—"

"Jane—and Raymond—will be all right now," Emily comforted. "They'll move away," she predicted. "Begin a new life."

"I, too, must begin a new life," Andrea said softly. "I've lost a son, but I've gained a precious granddaughter. It's almost like being reborn." She lifted her head with an air of defiance. "I can handle this. I should be at the company—there's so much to be done—"

"Everything at the company is under control. You can be away for a few days." But Emily knew the torment that haunted Andrea. The nightmare was over—but her son was dead, at her hands. "Every department will carry on just as though you were there. Paul will be in and out today, back on a regular

210

basis in the morning. I'll go in tomorrow." *How can I mourn for an uncle who meant to kill me?* A wisp of a smile now. "I guess I inherited it from you—I'm anxious to make sure everything is rolling for the new line—"

"You're my granddaughter," Andrea said with pride. "What David and I felt for the business skipped the children, blossomed in you."

Nora appeared in the doorway. "I know how you feel, Miz Andrea, but you got to eat. You and Emily. I'm puttin' breakfast on the table right now. And I'm expectin' to take back empty plates," she said with a bravado evoked by the situation.

"We're coming to the table, Nora—" Andrea said gently.

Paul arrived while Andrea and Emily lingered over coffee. Nora immediately brought him coffee and fresh-from-the-oven biscuits.

"Everybody sends their sympathy," Paul reported. "Every department is running smoothly. Gina has canceled your two meetings scheduled for today until next week. She'll reschedule all your appointments for the rest of the week." He gazed from Andrea to Emily with an odd air of excitement. "Perhaps this is not the right moment to bring this up—"

"Bring what up?" Emily asked. And all at once she remembered. *This is Monday. The DNA results are supposed to be in.*

"I called the lab in Albany. The results are in, Emily. No doubt about it—Jamie is your father."

For an instant Emily felt encased in awe. She'd found her father—and he was a wonderful man!

"No mistakes?" Her eyes clung to Paul. Pleading for reassurance.

"No mistakes," he told her tenderly. "Jamie's on his way to Albany now. He was afraid you wouldn't believe it unless you saw the official report. He should be back here in about three hours."

"Is he pleased?"

"He's ecstatic."

From exhaustion Andrea drifted off to sleep on the living-room sofa. Emily forced herself to go upstairs—avoiding even a glance at her bedroom—to collect a light comforter. Downstairs again, she draped the comforter about Andrea and tiptoed from the living room and into the den.

Earlier she'd called home to reassure her parents that she was all right. No doubt in her mind that the sensational story of Leon's death would headline all TV and radio news reports this morning.

"Dad just turned on the news—I couldn't believe what I was hearing. Emily, you're all right? I'm still shaking—"

Over and over again she had to reassure first her mother, then her father that she was all right. She restrained herself from telling them that DNA tests proved that Jamie was her biological father. Later she would tell them.

Will Dad be upset? No, he knows I won't love him any less for having found my natural father. I'm lucky—I have two wonderful fathers!

Restless now for Jamie's return from Albany—with the DNA report in hand, Emily paced about the kitchen while Nora plotted a lunch menu for an indeterminate number of people. Carol and Tom had left the house—they wouldn't be back for lunch. Nora knew that Jamie—probably along with Paul—was expected shortly.

"Maybe I should take a lunch basket over to Miz Jane and her boy," Nora said tentatively. "And you said her sister would be comin' over there—"

"That would be nice," Emily confirmed.

Both were conscious of a car turning into the driveway.

"I can have lunch on the table in twenty minutes," Nora promised. "If Miz Andrea's awake by then—"

"I'm awake—" Andrea's voice drifted into the kitchen. "I heard a car pull up out front." Walking into view, she appeared calm and in control. *Oh, but she's hurting.*

"It's Paul or Jamie—" Emily moved swiftly into the hallway.

She heard their voices. Paul and Jamie. The front door was open. They walked inside.

"You made marvelous time," she told Jamie. Searching his face for confirmation of the report so important to both.

"It's a miracle I wasn't stopped for speeding—" Jamie's smile was electric. His eyes tender. "It's true. I have a daughter. Her name is Emily—"

"How wonderful!" Emily rushed into her father's arms. "I prayed for it to be true!"

"This is the most exciting day of my life." Jamie held her close, his face against hers. "I'm a father. One day," he said with elfin humor, gazing from Emily to Paul, "I'll be a grandfather."

Forty-Two

S unday sunlight poured into the dining room, rested lovingly on the crystal chandelier that hung over the table, helped to belie the fact that this was a family emerging from deep trauma. Two weeks ago today Leon had been laid to rest in private services that had brought Celeste home fleetingly.

There had been little exchange between Celeste and her daughter, but Emily had convinced herself she could deal with this. She'd found her grandmother and her biological father—and loved both.

The atmosphere in the dining room—the table resplendently laid for ten—reflected the relief of those gathered for the early afternoon Sunday dinner. Emily gazed about the table. Her grandmother at the head, Jamie at the foot. She sat between Mom and Dad, with Paul beside Mom. On the other side were Carol and Tom and the twins.

Even Carol and Tom seemed subdued, Emily observed—though not entirely comfortable with the extended family. The twins—Deirdre and Elaine—were on their best behavior. Unsure of themselves, realizing their world had changed.

Nora and the cousin brought in to help prepare and serve moved about the table with an air of quiet satisfaction. Nora so determined to carry this off without a hitch, Emily thought affectionately.

How thoughtful of Grandma to have brought Mom and Dad here for this family gathering. They were so happy to be here. And they liked Paul! She'd been sure they would. And almost immediately she'd sensed their admiration for Jamie.

"Nora's been cooking up a storm for the past two days," Andrea told Joan and Bob Mitchell. "She wanted everything to be perfect for your first visit here." *Mom and Dad know I'll be going home for frequent weekends—and they'll come here often.*

"Everything is just perfect," Joan assured her. *Mom's relaxing—I was afraid she'd be uptight. But she isn't. Grandma has this way of putting people at ease.* "Do I dare ask Nora for her recipe for chicken Marsala?"

"Oh, she'll be flattered to death," Andrea assured her. "I'll have her write it up for you."

"I have to tell you two—" Jamie turned to Joan and Bob with a warm smile—"I'm so grateful that you've been such wonderful parents to our daughter."

Tears welled in Joan's eyes, her smile tremulous. "She's a wonderful daughter."

All at once Lucky—rapturous at his escape from the kitchen—was darting past Nora with excited barks.

"Hey, fella, you trying to crash this party?" Paul rose to reach for him.

"Oh, let him stay," Andrea murmured and extended a slab of chicken Marsala—instantly gobbled up. "After all, he's a hero in this family."

The shrill ring of a phone infiltrated from the den. Moments later Nora appeared. "It's for you," she told Emily, almost apologetic at this interruption. "She just said to say, 'It's Wendy.' Shall I tell her to call back later?"

"Go take your call," Andrea said indulgently. "But make it a quick one. Nora's about to serve Hannah's famous bread pudding with bourbon sauce."

Emily hurried into the den, unaware of Paul's excusing himself at the table, that he was following her into the den.

"Hi, Wendy—"

"Am I calling at a bad time?"

"For you no time is bad," Emily chided.

"I just want to remind you. You can't get married without me as maid of honor. It won't be legal."

"I haven't been officially asked yet," Emily began.

"I'm asking," Paul whispered, reaching for her hand. With the other hand he extended a small but exquisite diamond ring. "It was my mother's. She said, 'Give it to the one you're asking to be your wife.' I realize we'll have to wait a while in deference to the circumstances—"

"It's beautiful—" Radiant, she allowed Paul to slide the ring onto her finger. "It's okay," she told Wendy. "I've just been asked."

215